BODICHON

by

Mary Upton

Copyright © Mary Upton 2024

ISBN 978-1-3999-8729-5

First published in 2024 in the UK by
Tradewinds Publishing,
St Leonards-on-Sea, East Sussex.

The moral right of Mary Upton to be identified as the author of this work has been asserted by her in accordance with the Copyright, Design and Patents Act 1988.

All Rights Reserved. No part of this publication may be reproduced or transmitted in any form or in any means electronic or mechanical, including for photocopy, recording or any information storage or retrieval system without permission in writing from the author.

This novel is a work of fiction. Although names and characters do belong to actual persons, now dead, any resemblance to living persons is entirely coincidental.

Design and layout by Amanda Helm
amandahelm@uwclub.net

Printed by Short Run Press Ltd
www.shortrunpress.co.uk
Exeter EX2 7LW

Cover image: *Rocklands* by Barbara Leigh Smith,
courtesy of Hasting Museum.

BODICHON

A novel based on the life of
Barbara Leigh Smith Bodichon,
*campaigner for women's rights,
professional artist and intrepid traveller.*

'I am one of the cracked people of the world, and I like to herd with the cracked, such as queer Americans, Democrats, Socialists, artists, poor devils or angels; and am never happy in English genteel family life. I try to do it like other people, but I long always to be off on some wild adventure, or long to lecture on a tub in St. Giles, or go to see the Mormons or ride off into the interior on horseback alone and leave the world for a month. I want to see what sort of world this God's world is.'

Barbara Leigh Smith
c. 1857

A Family

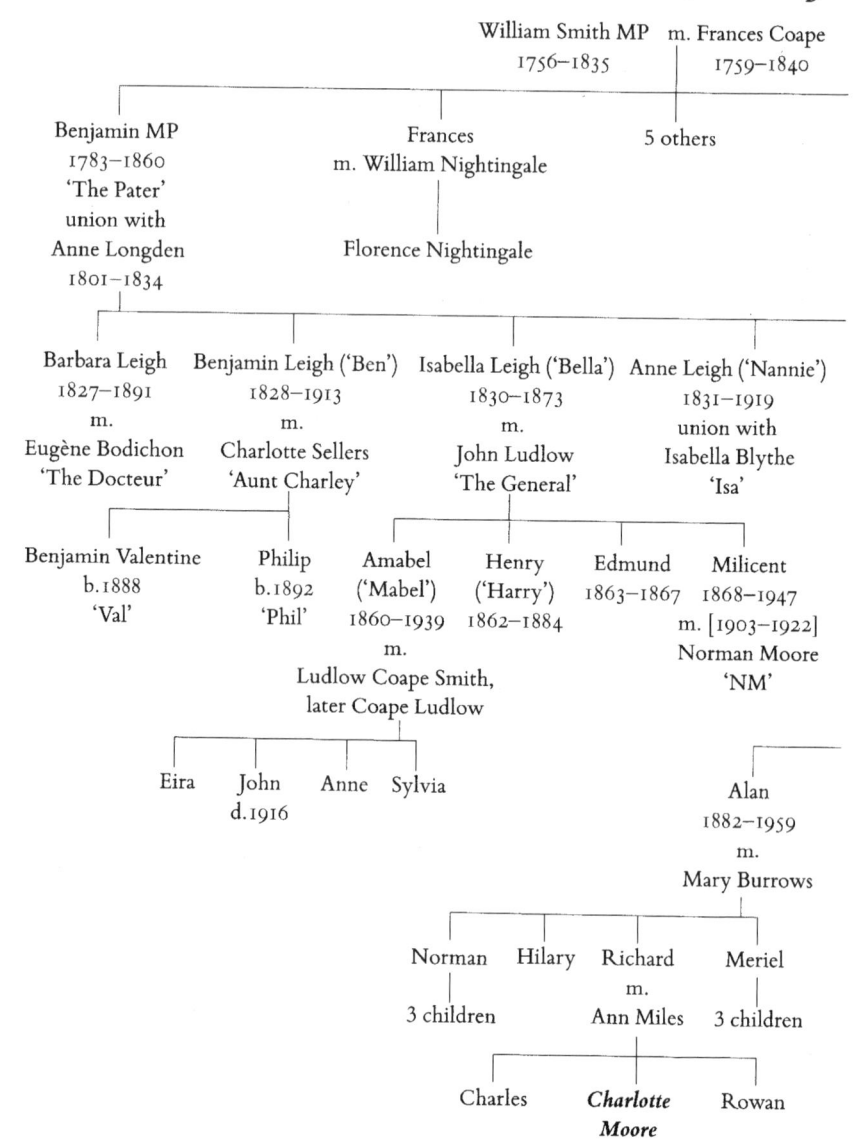

William Smith MP m. Frances Coape
1756–1835　　　　1759–1840

- **Benjamin MP** 1783–1860 'The Pater' union with Anne Longden 1801–1834
- **Frances** m. William Nightingale
  - Florence Nightingale
- **5 others**

Children of Benjamin and Anne Longden:

- **Barbara Leigh** 1827–1891 m. Eugène Bodichon 'The Docteur'
- **Benjamin Leigh ('Ben')** 1828–1913 m. Charlotte Sellers 'Aunt Charley'
- **Isabella Leigh ('Bella')** 1830–1873 m. John Ludlow 'The General'
- **Anne Leigh ('Nannie')** 1831–1919 union with Isabella Blythe 'Isa'

Children:

- **Benjamin Valentine** b. 1888 'Val' (son of Ben)
- **Philip** b. 1892 'Phil' (son of Ben)
- **Amabel ('Mabel')** 1860–1939 m. Ludlow Coape Smith, later Coape Ludlow
- **Henry ('Harry')** 1862–1884
- **Edmund** 1863–1867
- **Milicent** 1868–1947 m. [1903–1922] Norman Moore 'NM'

Children of Amabel and Ludlow Coape Smith:
- Eira
- John d. 1916
- Anne
- Sylvia

Children of Milicent and Norman Moore:
- **Alan** 1882–1959 m. Mary Burrows

Children of Alan and Mary Burrows:
- Norman — 3 children
- Hilary
- Richard m. Ann Miles
- Meriel — 3 children

Children of Richard and Ann Miles:
- Charles
- **Charlotte Moore**
- Rowan

Tree

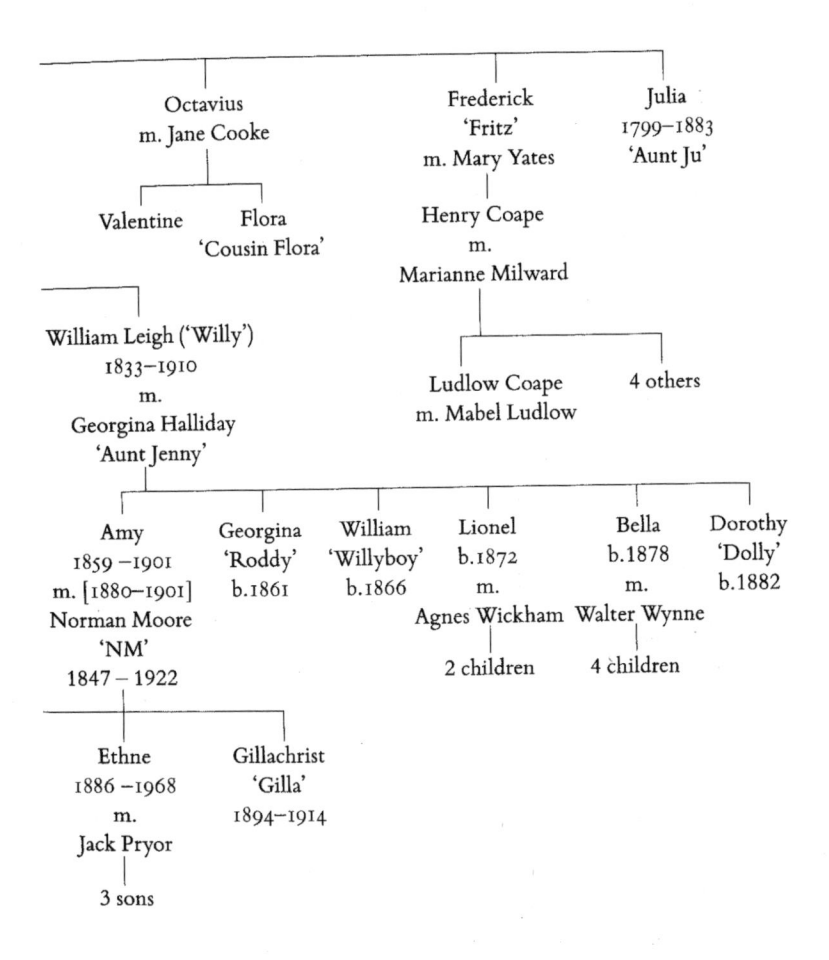

```
                    |                              |                |
                Octavius                        Frederick         Julia
              m. Jane Cooke                      'Fritz'        1799–1883
                    |                         m. Mary Yates    'Aunt Ju'
          |—————————————|                          |
      Valentine      Flora                   Henry Coape
                 'Cousin Flora'                    m.
                                              Marianne Milward
          |                                        |
  William Leigh ('Willy')                   |—————————————|
        1833–1910                      Ludlow Coape      4 others
           m.                          m. Mabel Ludlow
    Georgina Halliday
       'Aunt Jenny'
```

Amy	Georgina	William	Lionel	Bella	Dorothy
1859–1901	'Roddy'	'Willyboy'	b.1872	b.1878	'Dolly'
m. [1880–1901]	b.1861	b.1866	m.	m.	b.1882
Norman Moore			Agnes Wickham	Walter Wynne	
'NM'					
1847–1922			2 children	4 children	

Ethne	Gillachrist
1886–1968	'Gilla'
m.	1894–1914
Jack Pryor	
3 sons	

PROLOGUE

My name is Barbara Leigh Smith, a name I have earned. I am the oldest of five children and come from a long line of political reformers on my father's side, part of the liberal intelligentsia. Benjamin Smith, my father, was a Whig politician, an unconventional and somewhat eccentric character. Principles, rigorously upheld in pre-Victorian society, did not apply to him. Tall and handsome with reddish brown hair, he was a man I admired above all others. As a successful businessman, father was wealthy and a landowner, but before you leap to any conclusions, he was also a Unitarian and possessed a strong sense that he had to deserve his good fortune. He ensured that his children were well-informed regarding the grinding poverty most working people endure. I was made fully aware that children worked in the mines, women picked stones in the fields for a pittance and families could starve in lean years.

Father taught me that the only way to address such inequalities is by the provision of education. These were not empty words. He established the first infants' school in London where, every morning, children received a good wash and breakfast before embarking on the ladder of literacy and numeracy.

My mother, Anne Longden, came from the lower orders. She hailed from Derbyshire where she worked as a milliner. Her mother died in childbirth, leaving Anne to care for her father and younger sister Dolly. Slightly built with soft fair hair, she was still unmarried at the age of twenty-five when she met my father.

The Smith family were in no doubt that she was after father's money and, when she was with child, their worst fears were confirmed. However, in spite of these portents of doom, there was no doubt that this was a love match. Father told me that she was the least selfish and most gentle woman he had ever met. He spirited her down to Whatlington in Sussex, where she lived in a cottage on the edge of his large country estate.

I was born in April 1827, a sturdy child so I'm told, with reddish gold hair. The cottage stood on a small lane which led up to the church. Parishioners walked past on Sunday mornings. One old man in particular would raise his hat and say, 'Marnin miss.' Their wives were less friendly and would eye mother's girth, when she became swollen with brother, Ben. She was known in the village as Mrs Leigh. Much later I discovered the truth concerning her situation and understood the sly glances. Father didn't reside in the cottage but was a frequent visitor. He lived in a large country house, some five miles distant....

Chapter 1

To have lost my mother at such an early age had gouged a gaping hole in my memories of childhood. For many years I was unaware of this. I imagine that the shock and feelings of abandonment are so profound that one quickly finds a substitute mother and a way to survive without that one special person closest to your existence. It wasn't until I reached the age of fifteen that father came to my room one evening and presented me with a rather battered looking leather portfolio. 'I've kept these for you my dear,' he'd said gently. They are all I have left of your mother's possessions and I know that she would have wanted you to have them, now that you are of an age to understand something of her life. The large portfolio sat by my bed for some days until I'd found the courage to open it. Instinctively I knew that opening it would have a big impact on my equilibrium. Of course, I had often thought of mother over the years since she died, but her memory had faded and was lost in the heady process of living. If I am honest with myself, I feared probing into that black hole; she was dead and nothing would change that. Better to wrap that part of me up and hide it away, I'd thought. But now, at fifteen years of age, curiosity and a need to know overcame me; I slid back the catch and inside I found layer upon layer of letters tied with ribbon and diaries wrapped in a soft silk scarf. I'd forced myself not to recoil and one by one placed the neat bundles on my bedside table and with some trepidation opened the first diary. It was dated 1831.

I knew that, at that time, we had been living in a cottage in Whatlington. To see mother's handwriting on the page was disturbing, but slowly I became immersed in her careful record of events and surprised to find that pictures emerged in my mind of a time that had remained unexplored.

Her first entry described how father had visited the cottage one evening and told her that he was considering taking the family to America. Obviously, at four years of age, I couldn't remember his actual words but reading her diary I could remember a distinct feeling that mother was alarmed and not happy with this suggestion. Ben would have been a small child, maybe two years old. I can vaguely recall mother tucking me into bed that evening and asking her, 'What is America?' She didn't answer me but looked sad and tearful. The next entry described how father had returned in the morning wanting to know if she had read the pamphlets he had left her concerning the *Moravian Society*, written by a Mr Birkbeck. Apparently, he was a member of an organisation in America that father was interested in. On a single page mother had listed her worries: the distance from England, how the people in this new society may not accept them. She described our family as outlaws in England and could also be seen as outlaws in America. I didn't understand what she meant by this. She wrote how she had pleaded with father to keep the lease on the cottage in case things didn't work out. But he declined. I found reading all this rather upsetting, the pages were smudged with what could only be tears.

I have dim but pleasant memories of our cottage in Whatlington and I can now sense from her writing that mother was frightened of leaving her lovely home. She must have protected me from this as all I can recall is a feeling of excitement. I clearly remember mother saying, 'We are going on an adventure, Barbara.'

Chapter 1

We are now living in Hastings. I can see the sea from my bedroom window and hear the gulls fighting over scraps left by the fishermen on the beach. I realise that, in reading mother's diaries, I would have to allow her back into my life. The account I was about to read included me. I was there with her when these words were written and the decisions about to be taken by my parents would affect me profoundly. Over the next weeks reading mother's diaries took over much of my time. I concealed this from Ben; he was not interested anyway. I felt proud that father thought me grown-up enough to read them and understand something of mother and their life together.

Chapter 2

The next entry described leaving the cottage and the journey from Sussex to Liverpool; apparently we had travelled in a bumpy uncomfortable coach which took forever. All I can remember of it now was standing on the dock after we arrived watching hundreds of people running in all directions. To my child's eye, I recalled that giant men were loading trunks and carrying crates of squawking chickens aboard the ship. I remember stumbling up the gangway; it felt like climbing a cliff. We were met by a friendly man at the top, dressed in sailors' uniform. Ben and I had shared a large cabin with my parents; this was unusual and made a big impression. I remember snuggling down into my bunk on the first night at sea and cuddling up to Ben.

Mother was right, it was an adventure. Her words were now bringing alive things I had completely forgotten. I loved being on the boat. She had packed all of my drawing and painting things and had taught me how to sew. The best of it for me was sitting on the poop deck with Father. He would tell me exciting stories about America and, if it was very calm, we'd creep up there at night to look at the stars. I can remember sitting close to him, the smell of tobacco and the coarse feel of his wool topcoat. But the journey was dreadful for my poor mother. She described in her diary how little Ben was trapped, like a bee caught in a jar and, although he could walk steadily on land, he couldn't be left to run on deck as it was too slippery. The frustration of being confined had driven him to drum his heels with frustration. It was my first and only memory of

Chapter 2

mother getting really angry and shouting at father. She wrote how the weather deteriorated; huge storms swept in from the north-west. Sitting on deck was impossible. The ship had rolled and tossed; all the passengers were ordered to stay below decks. She described the wind roaring through the rigging and the creak of timbers bending on the swell; this made her fearful they would split and we would all sink to the bottom of the sea. I just remember lying in my bunk feeling frightened, fingers squeezed into my ears.

Reading through the lines I could see that Mother had become desperate. This was reflected in her writing which became erratic. She described how Ben grizzled constantly and refused to eat. Sea sickness plagued her, she spent hours hanging over a bucket and couldn't keep food in her stomach. The pungent smell of vomit brings these images back and still upsets me. I remember mother screaming, 'Benjamin, I need help, he's getting impossible,' I had never seen her so distraught: it was horrid. After this outburst, father had approached the Captain and asked if any of the young girls in steerage would help, for a small remuneration. According to the diary, there was no shortage of volunteers. Violet seemed like a grown woman to me, but mother told me later that she was fifteen and travelling with her parents to a new life in America. I have a hazy memory of her as plump and smiley. She spoke differently and called me Bab. Violet was happy to join us. I know that because she was such fun. She soon found ways to make Ben eat some food by making up songs and whistling tunes. She told me that her cabin was packed like sardines, I've never forgotten that: it made me laugh.

Another three weeks passed; mother had marked each day off in the diary. One morning a shout went up: 'Land ahoy.' I remember running up on deck with father to watch the approaching coastline. It slowly changed from a blurred smudge to one where I could see the palm trees he had told me about and the waves crashing on the shore. Mother joined us looking pale and exhausted. Holding on to father's arm, I remember her saying, 'I can't wait to get my feet on dry land.'

Pulling alongside Savannah dock is a sight I still recall vividly. We were standing on deck staring into a throng of people rushing about and shouting. I held my hands over my ears and hid behind mother's skirts, unable to make sense of it all. Just as father had told me, there were black faces everywhere. They looked angry or frightened, I didn't know which. I remember the heat wrapping around me like a damp sheet, my clothes heavy and clinging. The air smelt different: a bit like the compost heap in our garden at the cottage, mixed with something sweet. Mother held onto my hand tightly as we made our way down the gangway, greatly hindered by her billowing skirts; father came behind carrying little Ben on his shoulders. It felt like entering another world. Loud, colourful and more strange than anything I could ever have imagined. Whatlington and our tiny cottage had felt very far away.

By now I couldn't stop reading. It was thrilling but upsetting for me to remember a time when mother was in my life, alongside me at all times. Now, engrossed in her diaries the memories came flooding back into my mind. Her soft loving intimacy could never be replicated, or so I thought. At fifteen years of age I know so little of life.

Chapter 3

I could now sense from the tone of mother's writing that she was unsettled. This wasn't explicitly written about and she concealed it in letters home to her sister, Dolly. She described the large airy Plantation house we were living in and the gardens which were well cared for. But it was obvious that everything in her life was, as she described it, out of kilter. She disliked the oak trees which were festooned with Spanish moss and unlike her beloved oak trees at home. She felt discomfited by everything around her. The tree frogs haunted her dreams. She couldn't sleep due to the heat and the cacophony of noise from the cicadas. Father had employed six freed slaves but mother was unused to having servants and her diary clearly illustrated how she felt distinctly uncomfortable with the idea of it. I could sense that she was becoming seriously unhappy.

I was fascinated to read her account of a conversation she'd had with Grace, our black servant. Apparently, mother had been sitting on the veranda and Grace had said, 'Can I get you a cool drink Miss Anne? I made fresh lemonade this marnin', it taste good.' Mother described how she had looked up at Grace, shaken out of her dreary thoughts and said, 'Thank you, Grace, you're so kind.'

The next exchange she wrote verbatim, trying to catch the way Grace spoke. She was understandably astonished by her revelations and asked lots of questions. 'Can I ask you a personal question Grace? I'm not happy with the situation here concerning the slaves whom I see working in the fields. I would like to know how you became free.' Grace had laughed and replied, 'I was lucky, Miss Anne.

My owner was a Miss Gilbertson, she owned a big school for white chillun. She died last year and in her will she gave me, my husband and chillun our freedom.' Mother described how tears had welled in her eyes and replied, 'That is the nicest thing I've heard since we got here, Grace. I would like you to know that the children are so happy to play with your girls. Barbara never stops talking about Harriet and Chloe and all the new things they are teaching her.'

This exchange had obviously made a big impact on mother, she went on to describe how Grace had brought her the lemonade and she'd walked slowly around the verandah, her thoughts racing. *I must be more active. I'll ask some of the neighbours over for tea. The very thought makes me anxious, they are all so strong and sure of themselves.* The next line saddened me. *After talking to Grace, the day stretched ahead of me, empty and pointless.*

Reading this account I was left in no doubt that mother was nearing a breakdown, while I was having a wonderful time. Ben and I had adapted to life in America like ducks to water. We loved the freedom and the novelty of living in a warm and exciting place. Ben was a child who loved the outdoors and that was how we then spent our lives, outdoors, playing with Grace's children. Not a care in the world.

Maybe I caught a little of what mother was feeling when father came home one evening. He joined her on the veranda and, unknown to them, I was playing nearby in the garden with Chloe. Suddenly I became aware that mother was sobbing. Father had put his arms around her and was stroking her hair. That is a fleeting memory but reading her diaries so many years later it became much clearer.

Following on from this outburst, mother had related to father her conversation with Grace and the effect it

Chapter 3

had had on her. To her surprise, father sympathised. She wrote that he also was finding it hard to settle and had become disappointed and distressed at the lack of appetite for abolition in the Southern States. He feared they were seen as dissenters and was aware that it had been commented on that they employed freed slaves. He'd told her that although it may be acceptable to hold anti-slavery views further north, here he'd found it downright dangerous. Far from upsetting mother, this disclosure had reassured her.

Father had then gone on to tell mother that he'd made contact with Mr Birkbeck at the the *Moravian Society* and intended to visit him next month. He asked mother to accompany him. She wrote in her diary that she now felt less alone and relieved that father knew how she felt about things.

'I RESOLVE TO TRY HARDER AND ENJOY THE TRIP TO SEE MR BIRKBECK,' she wrote in capital letters.

The next entry was more positive. She was looking forward to the trip and listed the good things she had read in the pamphlets: tolerance: doing good through service to others: It was possible that they were anti-slavery: they teach their children in shared classes, boys and girls together: She intended telling Grace that she was going on a visit with her husband and the children would be staying at home.

In bold print she had written, **A reminder to myself.** *Things are different here. In Whatlington I also didn't mix with the neighbours, or ever got invited out to tea. Here, invitations are extended, which I appreciate, but find that I have a myriad of new customs to accept. People ask me direct and sometimes personal questions on first meeting; this is difficult. They want to know about my family, where I come from, and what I think of America. What can I say? It sounds weak to complain that the climate is too hot for*

11

my disposition, and I feel homesick for England. The huge subject to avoid is anything in relation to slavery. I can never admit that I feel oppressed by the huge plantations, which contain hundreds of slaves who live in cabins and are treated like animals. This dreadful misuse of our fellow humans is completely abhorrent to me, but I have to stay silent, to even mention such a thing would be considered offensive. In order to conceal my feelings I will have to bury my thoughts, I'll smile and make pleasantries; if necessary, I will lie about my family situation.

I read this entry several times. It told me something of mother that I couldn't have seen as a child. She was thoughtful and resilient but obviously faced with a challenging change of culture. Now that father was aware of her feelings she had some support and was able to face the future with him by her side.

One evening father came to tuck me up in bed and I have a distinct memory of our bedtime talk. Most of our talks seemed to blend into each other but there was something special about the way he asked me questions. Now, thinking back, I can see that he had been affected by his conversation with mother and the realisation that she was unhappy living in America.

He sat on my bed and looked at my collection of shells and pressed flowers. Then he told me that he was going on a visit with mother to a place called North Carolina. 'Are you happy here in America?' he said suddenly. The question took me by surprise. 'Yes, yes, I am, I love it here.' I'd told him. 'Remember when we were on the ship, you told me about black people? You said I should never be rude or ask about the colour of their skin. I love playing with Harriet and Chloe, its such fun. They

Chapter 3

don't mind when I ask if I can touch their hair, they stroke mine too.' Father had kissed me on my nose and said. 'Do you ever stop talking, my beautiful brave girl? Goodnight and sweet dreams.'

Remembering this night-time talk brought a swell of emotion. My father was then and still remains the sure steady place in my life, as he was for my mother.

I can see from mother's notes that she was determined to keep a record of the trip to the *Moravians*. She was nervous about it but was boosting her confidence by ordering new clothes and she described her positive mood.... *I have asked Grace to find a local needlewoman, as my wardrobe needs to be more in keeping with the climate. My dresses should be in a lighter fabric, muslin or cotton, with short sleeves and a lower-cut neckline. Maybe this will help me to stay cool. Of course, it is entirely unacceptable to throw off the corset, but some tea gowns to wear around the house would be a solution to that problem. I have just three weeks to prepare for the visit....*

I remember sitting on her bed as Grace was helping mother get ready for their trip. Mother said that they were travelling by paddle steamer. I laughed when Grace's mouth dropped open in amazement and she said, 'That's farther than I've ever been ma'am an I ain't never been on no boat.' I clearly recall mother's reply, 'Well, Grace, I came all the way from England on a boat and hoped that I would never set foot on one again. But Mr Smith told me that it will be different this time and far more comfortable than a stagecoach.' Mother had looked at me and smiled. 'Do you remember the boat from England, Barbara? That storm was terrible.' I nodded but could barely remember anything about England or the boat journey. I watched as Grace vigorously laced up mother's corset before she stepped into a freshly ironed lemon-coloured dress. She said, 'You sure look good Miss Anne and you'se smilin.' Mother had laughed and said, 'You don't miss a thing Grace.'

Sitting here in Hastings I'd read entranced as mother described their boat trip up the river. My obsession with travel is still to be realised, but my curious nature leant itself to a future in which I, too, could visit foreign lands. How I wish I could have known my dear mother. We were different, I could see that, but it would be wonderful to hear what she had really thought about things and not through this filtered careful diary.

21st April 1833

Standing on the deck of the Georgia Queen, *I noted that, thankfully, the water was calm, and the banks were clearly visible. It was invigorating to have the breeze in my hair and a change of scene. Benjamin had booked a comfortable cabin, and we planned to have dinner aboard, although it would be possible to disembark at Hilton Head Island and sleep ashore, if we so wished. The waiter that evening introduced us to a local beverage, Mint Julep, and he kindly gave us the recipe: 2½ ounces Kentucky bourbon, ½ ounce syrup and 2 sprigs of mint, plus some garnish, mix together with a little crushed ice.*

The river is wide and swift-flowing edged with dense vegetation. Large black alligators loll on the banks, sliding into the water as we pass. I struggle with revulsion and distract myself with the pelicans. They stand on the marker poles and dive like arrows into the river to catch fish. The challenge of coming to this country has given me a measure of my complete lack of experience outside an English country village. The climate in England is more temperate and the countryside less wild and raw. When I remember the green fields and leafy lanes of Sussex my throat tightens and tears threaten. I can see that the journey left me exhausted and adjusting to this 'new world' has been harder than I could ever have imagined.

We had been advised to take a carriage out to the colony and, riding through Charleston, I was impressed. The streets are wide with paved walkways shaded in a blue haze of jacaranda trees. Grand houses, with wide, airy verandas, sit in immaculate lawns. On the edge of town, stall holders were selling produce brought in from the countryside. At last we turned into a long drive which took us through fields of corn, cotton and tobacco, until we drew up outside a modest wooden farmhouse. Mrs Birkbeck was standing on the front porch. She waved and smiling broadly gave us a warm welcome. 'Mr Birkbeck will be along later; he's helping to load some grain.' She called for the maid to bring us some mint tea and biscuits she had made especially.

After finishing our tea Mr Birkbeck arrived, and we set out to tour the colony. Proudly we were shown the rows of beautifully tended vegetables, well-cared-for livestock and a solidly built school, of which any village in England would be proud. I could see the boys and girls sitting in rows and enthusiastically engaged in a Spelling Bee. Our tour ended with a short church service, held at the end of every working day, where we were introduced as Mr and Mrs Smith, newly arrived from England. I noticed during the service that marriage and the family was a central theme in the sermon and the sanctity of marriage is considered paramount to the success of the community. Mrs Birkbeck led the hymns and joining us afterwards, invited me to meet her sewing group. Benjamin left to tour the cotton fields with Mr Birkbeck.

'You have two children?' The women gathered around me, eager with curiosity. I nodded. 'A daughter, Barbara and my son, Ben. I've left them with Grace, their nurse.'

I wore a wedding ring in order to avoid questions, but felt like an imposter. The inquisitive women standing before me gave credence to my fears. If truth be known, I would be considered a fallen woman. This is something Benjamin and I rarely discuss. He remains adamant that marriage is not something he approves of under current laws, which deny women any rights. I understand his viewpoint, but the social consequences of such a stand are considerable, both here and in England. I kept smiling and fielded the more intrusive questions. We stayed for two more days and by the end of the second day, I could sense a change in Benjamin's usually ebullient enthusiasm. This observation would have to wait until we reached home, I thought.

On our arrival back in Savannah we took an open carriage and arrived home in style. The children came racing up the drive to greet us bursting with excitement: they'd found a snake behind the barn. Grace had prepared a light evening meal and we sat sipping a cool drink on the veranda waiting for it to be served. 'Well, what did you make of it all?' I put the question lightly, not wanting to betray my feelings. Benjamin looked pensive. 'It's given me much to think over, Anne. I came away feeling uneasy. Each time I broached the subject of abolition I was gently deflected and could gain no knowledge as to how it was viewed in the colony. I expect you saw that there were many negroes working in the fields, but once again I got no answer as to whether they were free or not. My guess is that, were they free, Birkbeck would have been more forthcoming. You asked me what I made of it? Well, I am not convinced that our family would be accepted, or that we would feel comfortable with their beliefs.' I leant against Benjamin's shoulder. 'Let's sleep on it.' I said quietly. He sat back, weighing my response. 'Maybe sleep isn't what we need, my love.'

Chapter 3

Coming to the end of this account I was shaken to realise that, at this point, my life was about to change dramatically. Mother was in poor health and, I realise now, with child. I can remember the piercing sadness when father told me that we were leaving America and going back to England. I was little more than five years old. The sadness of leaving my friends Harriet and Chloe still stays with me.

Chapter 4

Nine months passed. I have a clear picture in my mind of mother leaning on the rail of the ship as it approached Liverpool docks, her belly swollen with child. The voyage had been terrifying, not an adventure at all. Storms battered us all the way back, making the journey twice as long and halfway across little Ben became ill with fever. By the time we docked, father was so worried that he had left the ship as soon as he could, to arrange suitable transport for mother and a doctor for Ben.

I remember physically shaking with fearfulness as I watched a porter carry little Ben down the gangway, wrapped in woollen blankets, his face red and puffy. Mother was standing alongside me quietly. I knew she was in pain, as she grasped my hand tightly every now and again, whimpering like a small child. Without warning, a stevedore appeared alongside us and, gathering mother up in his arms, set off down the ramp. She shouted over his shoulder. 'Barbara, wait for your father.' Standing on the quay was a carriage and the man placed mother gently inside. I could hear her wailing when, to my dismay, the driver cracked his whip over the horses and off they sped, leaving me alone.

What will I do if father doesn't come back? The thought made my chest feel tight. From the deck I could see nothing but crowds of people milling around. *I must not cry.* I remember scrunching up my hands until, at last, I saw him pushing through the crowds, waving to me. I will never forget the relief when he swept me up into his arms. In a state of anguish, we reached rooms in Crosby, a small village along the coast from Liverpool. My little

Chapter 4

sister, Isabella, had been born and Ben was tucked into a cot in the care of a nursemaid.

It took mother a month or so to recover from giving birth: the day she sat up in bed and smiled was wonderful. I climbed up beside her and snuggled close. We laughed at Isabella's wrinkled tiny face. 'Barbara, my darling girl, we are back in England, and I am more relieved than I can ever say.' America had not been an adventure for my poor mother; but for me, it remained a bright jewel in my memory and one I would never forget.

Father now couldn't wait to get back to his old life and mother commenced writing her diaries. She described leaving Crosby and setting out for Browns, a large farmhouse on father's estate. We were travelling in all the comfort father could muster, which included several carriages and half a dozen servants. After several days we entered the rolling green countryside of Sussex and sang with joy. Little Ben had at last regained his health and Isabella was thriving. Mother's diary left me in no doubt that she was delighted to be back on familiar ground.

We quickly settled into Browns which, although far larger than the cottage in Whatlington, was comfortable and a good place for children to grow. Family life was full of fun and we were lucky enough to be provided with interesting activities, in line with my father's relaxed attitude to education. Mother's unease was not apparent to me until one evening I overheard a conversation they were having over dinner.

'I'm thankful that Ju and Dolly see fit to visit us, Benjamin. No doubt it has not passed your notice that we get a chilly response from the rest of your family.' Mother's voice was sad and strained. I listened more intently and grasped the nettle that my parent's irregular relationship was unacceptable in the Smith family. I heard father pour himself a glass of brandy. 'I recently came across the words 'shameless and brazen' in a letter between my sisters Fanny and Patty,' father murmured, he sounded tetchy. 'They are insufferable. I try to shield you from them Anne, but it's difficult. Let's concentrate on the many people who are broad enough in their thinking to accept a more liberal viewpoint on marriage. Maybe one day, when the laws for married women change, I will feel differently. Until then I shall stick to my guns, as the saying goes.'

Much of this interchange was a mystery to me but, being a curious child, it resonated and now, reading mother's diary from that time, I am beginning to understand so much more. Aunt Ju was my father's sister, and I had become aware that she was the only relative to whom we were ever introduced on the Smith side of the family. Aunt Dolly was mother's sister, and her only living relative.

Despite this underlying tension, of which I remained blithely unaware most of the time, life for us children felt secure and invigorating. We had endless fields to roam in and either Aunt Ju or Aunt Dolly would take us on excursions to the sea. Father had lots of friends who visited, and the house was always full of music and laughter. Over the next two years another sister named Anne (known as Nannie), and a brother, William, were born. In celebration, Father planted five fir trees in front of the house, trees he wished to grow straight and true. 'What I wish for my children,' he'd said to Mother, as he firmly tamped down the soil.

This bucolic idyll did not last; a cloud had appeared on the horizon. Mother's health was failing. In order that she would benefit from the sea breezes, father had leased a house in Pelham Crescent, Hastings. I loved this house; it was directly opposite the beach and looked out to sea. Mother now had a live-in nurse and father

Chapter 4

had bought her an invalid carriage. It stood in the hall, large and cumbersome. Aunt Ju said that Mother had consumption; she looked sad when she told me. Each day she was given warm baths followed by plunges into cold water. The nurse wheeled her along the sea front in the chair, wrapped up in soft woollen rugs.

I remember worrying at night. Mother's breathing kept me awake, it sounded ragged; she was very weak. I worried even more for my father. He was distracted and looked anxious, we didn't spend time together like we used to. One day he came home with a woman called Hannah Walker, who moved into Pelham Crescent and would be our nursemaid and companion. Father had also mentioned that we were to have a home tutor. Hastings was paradise. Ben and I went out with Hannah every day exploring the beach and would wave to the fishing smacks, just offshore. Little Ben loved it, he would have spent all day and every day down by the harbour if he could. The fishermen were friendly and let him climb up into their boats. His biggest dream was going out with them to catch some fish.

One of my best treats was exploring a place called *America Ground*. Hannah told me that it's called this because it was, in some way, separate from Hastings Town and resembled the newly independent country of America. It lay close to Pelham Crescent and held a complete fascination for me and Ben. Several lime kilns stood at the base of the cliffs. The smell when they were burning the lime was horrible. Hannah told us that, when she was a young woman, a child had fallen into a kiln and the body was never found. This story grabbed my imagination. I wanted it told time and time again with all the gory details. 'They are dangerous, them kilns,' Hannah used her strong voice when warning us that we should never go there alone. That made it all the more enticing. Another favourite place was the Black Hole nearly opposite our house. Hannah told us that captured smugglers' boats were kept there, either to be sold or cut in half, preventing further use. Some were used to make small houses. Ben and I wove endless stories around this place and filled our drawings with terrifying storms and shipwrecks. At night when the wind was whining around the chimneys, it was easy to imagine the smugglers creeping ashore and loading up the pack ponies with barrels of brandy bound for London.

Father took mother to Ryde on the Isle of Wight for a few days. He'd said the change of air may help her breathe more easily. We had been staying at Browns for a while, but something was not right and I didn't know what it was. There had been no word from father. One evening, following a long ramble with Nursie, (that's what we call Hannah), we were back at the house when the creak and jingle of harness and the snort of horses as they turned into the lane sent us racing for the front door.

'He's back.' Little Ben threw himself at father as he stepped down onto the drive. I stood back, waiting. Although only a child, my antenna was well developed, and I knew that something felt wrong. 'Where's mother?' I asked. 'Let's get inside shall we. That was a long bumpy ride.' Father wearily handed his hat to Hannah. 'A glass of something would be most welcome.' He smiled but avoided our questions. 'It's such a long time since I saw you,' I whispered. He gently put his arm around my shoulder. 'Let's get ourselves some cordial.' Sitting in the drawing-room sipping our drinks, he gathered us around him and asked Hannah to stay. Looking straight into my eyes he said, 'I'm sorry, my dear, but I have sad news: your mother died yesterday morning.' Ben's mouth dropped open emitting a wail which reverberated throughout the house and from numb fingers his glass slipped, shattering

Chapter 4

on the flagstones.

Although only seven years of age I'd known this was coming, but now I felt the space. That mother-empty space inside me, which I knew would never be filled. Aunt Ju told me later that mother was buried on the Isle of Wight. Father was grief-stricken, and we rarely saw him. He had buried himself in work and stayed at his London house in Blandford Square.

Days and weeks passed since mother left us, turning slowly into years. Contrary to expectations, my world did not end after she died, as I had feared it might. Nursie continued to take us on rambles over to Fairlight Glen, where she would find blind-worms and deaf-adders, as she called them. Many birthdays passed and I was happy enough, but there will always be a missing piece in my life. Nursie did her best to make up for the loss, she taught me some of the old local songs and how to dance The Galop. She was my constant companion, and I have developed a soft Sussex burr, much to father's amusement.

Ben and I were inseparable. We were allowed to roam the countryside and grew up with a strong feeling of independence. At the age of seven he was sent to a Unitarian school in Brede as a weekly boarder. He came home at weekends. School had not improved his manners in the slightest and he behaved insufferably, so we often argued. A Nanny was employed to care for Bella, Anne and Willy. I was head of the family when father was away, or so I liked to believe. This was often disputed by Ben of course.

Father's family had had ample ammunition to fuel their belief that we'd grown up wild. We received little discipline from any of our carers, who all related to us on our level, other than imposing any adult expectations. When father was down from London, Ben and I were often included in family dinners, where anything and everything was discussed without restraint. The Smith family, other than Aunt Ju, rarely visited and I was increasingly conscious that we were somehow not considered respectable. I didn't know why, but I heard it said at the dinner table when the conversation was in full flow. I had come to realise that father was unusual, very different from my friends' fathers who were serious and formal. We were all allowed a large measure of freedom and had permission to study whatever interests we might have, no matter how obscure. At the time I remember being obsessed with reading *The Arabian Nights*. It provided me with a cornucopia of treats for my imagination, on which no boundaries were ever imposed.

Chapter 5

Father inherited my grandfather's house in Blandford Square, Marylebone, shortly after mother died. Around the age of nine I lived there for a while and attended various schools in London, most of which I found rather trying. The worst was a Unitarian secondary school in Upper Clapton. It was run by two sisters, the Misses Wood. They really did try to make me happy, but the art of teaching had entirely passed them by, and it left me bored and listless. Lessons were carried out by rote and applied without imagination or skill. The best thing that happened there was meeting my friend Bessie Parkes when we were both ten years old. This educational experiment didn't last long, and I returned to Hastings, where life continued in a rather haphazard fashion. Unfortunately, this state of affairs could not be allowed to continue, and on one memorable day our promised tutor arrived at Pelham Crescent, Mr Buchanan. From that day learning took on an entirely different pace.

I remembered Mr Buchanan from some years back when visiting Westminster Infants School, the primary school founded by my father. The poor children there adored Mr Buchanan and clung to his legs like hiving bees. I found him a very interesting man; some people described him as a 'queer fish,' probably because he was a follower of Emanuel Swedenborg. The only comment Mr Buchanan made about his Swedenborgian beliefs to us children, was that God is never angry, judging or punishing. This I'd found very comforting and felt free to explore with him any thoughts I had had on religion. I'd realised very quickly that he held strong views on how children should be taught. Glad to say, I felt comfortable with his ideas, as they closely aligned with my father's. We had few formal classes, as he believed that children learn best by experimentation and discussion. Mr B, as we called him, read to the younger ones constantly, covering a wide range of subjects, but every day, no matter the weather, we would all go out on nature expeditions and explore the rock pools at low tide. I'm afraid we teased him mercilessly, but he tolerated our impertinent behaviour with much generosity of spirit and a humorous zest for life.

As the oldest, I had developed a more grown-up relationship with Mr Buchanan. He took my love of art seriously and understood that it was central to my being. He helped me to focus and channel my creativity and I was often introduced to artists I'd previously never come across. Hastings attracted many painters. Mr William Turner was a frequent visitor to Pelham Crescent, as was Mr Holman Hunt, who lived in a small cottage nearby. They were all very fond of our dear tutor, who ensured that my daubs were given serious appraisal.

Chapter 6

Father was now recovering a little from losing mother and in 1837 decided to stand as an MP in my grandfather's old constituency of Norwich and Sudbury. He admired his father's work in relation to moderate reforms and his passionate views on the abolition of slavery. Father asked me if I would support him on a campaign rally, where I was to wear a buff sash, the Whig Party colour. The following month we travelled to Norwich, and I will never forget the roar of the crowds as I stood beside him on the podium. I didn't really understand all of his speech, but it was received with such enthusiasm by the people that I could sense the rightness of what he was saying. He was vigorously supporting the Anti-Corn Law Association and, later, to help me appreciate his stand, he'd taken me to Ireland. The appalling poverty and starvation I witnessed there, more than anything in my life so far, convinced me that the fight for free trade should never be abandoned.

Becoming an MP entailed father travelling to London and Norwich on a regular basis, and because of this commitment, he'd had a magnificent sprung carriage built. It seated eight people and was made in Hastings. The hullabaloo could be heard along the beach when it arrived, driven by Stephen our coachman and drawn by four horses. It was painted a rich blue, the seats were stuffed with the best horsehair, upholstered with soft padding and silk-covered cushions, 'Come along children, climb up, climb up.' father shouted like a stagecoach driver. We all scrambled aboard accompanied by Hannah and set off down the road towards Robertsbridge. It was glorious, and people left their houses to see us pass, waving and calling greetings. How I wished mother could have been with us, bowling along, surrounded by her unruly brood.

The loss of my dear mother will always be painful, and on occasions such as that she often came into my mind. My hazy memory of her is one of patience and constant affection. But I can see now that her life with my father contained thorns. To my childlike eyes this had never been obvious, but now approaching fifteen years of age, I could see things more clearly. No doubt producing five children in seven years and then developing consumption presented an enormous assault on her physical wellbeing. Her early demise at thirty-two years of age was the result. We still travel frequently between Hastings and my father's estate in Robertsbridge. But it is in Hastings, where a liberal and accepting society thrives, that I felt most at ease. Genteel family life was not for me, and we were lucky enough to meet people there and in London, who valued the freedom to live as they chose, rather than as dictated by church or class.

A change occurred this month, forcing an awareness that I am leaving my childhood behind. I have started to menstruate. Aunt Ju has bravely set out to instruct me on the workings of female bodies and suggests I use napkins to protect my clothing. The whole business is an abomination. I couldn't believe it when she told me that it would happen every month and continue until I was in my fifties. Thank goodness she is here to give me some guidance. I took the opportunity to ask her about conception, but she was very reticent indeed and not being married, has little experience of intimate relations.

Chapter 6

She described the fundamentals, which were of no more use than those I have already gleaned from some of my more informed friends.

At times like these I miss mother acutely. Who can one ask about such things? It is of vital importance that I know what happens between men and women, both physically and emotionally. Why is it such a mystery? Nothing more was said on the subject and I continue to grow through my early womanhood in a state of ignorance. Should I ever have a daughter, I would make sure that she would be educated in these matters and not left in the dark. In a way that's hard to explain, reading mother's diaries has given me something to hold onto. Now I can reflect on her in a more adult way, I see that her life was far, far harder than mine is likely to be. Knowing this straightens my back bone, but I still would like some practical information on some of the things which are apparently unmentionable.

I have had several tempestuous arguments with Aunt Ju recently, which is unusual. This particular disagreement erupted because of the stupid clothes I am expected to wear. I love walking in the woods and hills with my box of paints: how am I expected to manage this in ludicrous skirts and tight bodices? Mine are always getting ripped and covered in mud. I was planning to have the bottom cut off one of my skirts, but Aunt Ju was outraged, and backed up by Aunt Dolly. I should have the right to decide what I want to wear. There is no law in place, as yet, dictating what women should wear and I am determined to dress as I please. I wrote to father....

Dear Pater, That well known patron of all liberal institutions, residing at, 'Liberty Hall,' 5 Blandford Square.

"Oh! Isn't it jolly

*To cast away folly
And cut all one's clothes a peg shorter
(A good many pegs)
And rejoice in one's legs
Like a free-minded Albion's Daughter."*

As with most of my furies I soon calmed down and we agreed to compromise in some way. When visiting Guestling church one day walking with Aunt Ju, we met a woman called Mary Howitt. Her family are grieving, having lost a son following a riding accident. His freshly dug grave, still covered in spring flowers, gave a welcome splash of colour. We all walked on together through the lanes and I was interested to hear that Mrs Howitt is involved in the anti-slavery campaign. She told me of a plan they have to encourage housewives to give up sugar, as a way of objecting to slavery in the colonies. This is a splendid idea. Also, and this absolutely thrills me, she told me that there is a movement in progress to raise money for a fugitive slave called Frederick Douglass. He has come to England to escape the slave-catchers. I intend asking father for some money to support the fund.

Since our meeting I have met Mrs Howitt's eldest daughter Anna, who is attending art school, with the intention of becoming a professional artist. This is inspiring, and I am now determined to attend art classes. At this time I feel pulled between two passions, art and politics.

Chapter 7

Supporting the anti-slavery campaigns can attract a lot of disapproval in some quarters and I realize that I have to be more circumspect. That being said, I am meeting more older women who are interested in such movements which has emboldened me to write some articles concerning women's rights. These have been published in a local newspaper under the pen-name, Aesculapius. My father's political career continues to fascinate and influence me and, as I grow older, I can truly understand the causes which inspire him. When the Corn Laws were finally repealed in 1846 the celebration in Pelham Crescent was memorable. It gave me a valuable gift. I now understand that things can change and become better for working people when politicians are willing to help them fight for their rights. My passion for women's rights is growing by the day and I have learnt much from father's perseverance and solid belief.

 I am now approaching twenty-one years of age. Our house in Hastings is filled to bursting. Willy, my youngest brother, is to attend a new agricultural college in Cirencester and is receiving extra tuition. His tutor, Mr. Kingsford, is an expert in political economy and I find his clear and precise teaching style quite a revelation. In an attempt to improve my sketchy education I often join Willy's tutorials. It is my impression that I am far more interested in the subject than is Willy. Academia was never been his strong point; he prefers to spend his time hunting or meeting with friends in London. We are like chalk and cheese.

 I wrote to my friend Bessie Parkes as her brother is

unwell. Also, I wanted to tell her that a slight problem has arisen with Mr Kingsford. He appears to have fallen in love with me. What can I say? I really like him, but he is more like a brother than anything else.

Dearest Bessie,

12th April 1848

I am so sorry to hear the news concerning Priestley's health. Consumption is such a debilitating illness and I'm sure your parent's decision to move to Hastings is a wise one. The sea air is excellent for this condition, and he will be able to walk along the shore and build up his strength.

From my own selfish point of view I am delighted that you will be moving into Pelham Crescent and right next door. That's wonderful. I love my sisters, of course, and get along with Bella well enough but Nannie is so irritating. We are constantly getting into arguments. I am convinced she came from another planet. Having you next door will be perfect and the Smith clan will help your brother in any way we can.

Ben has just been accepted for Jesus College, Cambridge. I am pleased for him, through gritted teeth, but am furious that, even though I am his equal academically, I would not be allowed to join him there, because I'm a girl. This cannot be right or just. But when we are not allowed even to vote, I can see no way in which this dreadful wrong can be addressed. I get very agitated indeed about this state of affairs. They are conducting a census in Hastings soon and I intend to record my occupation as 'scholar at home.'

At last, I'm beginning to feel like an adult. On my twenty-first birthday father transferred the title deeds of Westminster Infant School into my name, and also gave me an allowance. This is so amazing. I cannot quite grasp the full extent of how it will affect my life.

Chapter 7

I long to put my ideas and thoughts concerning education into practice. Much work has to be done. As you know, I want my ideas seen in print and this may well now be possible with a little extra cash at my disposal. But, my dear friend, the printed word would expose my somewhat radical views to the world. I understand the temptation to play it safe and keep quiet, but that is not how I want to live. Most certainly women will not be given their rights, nor any of the proposed reforms become a reality, if we all remain silent. Strong-minded women will win the day!

One last adventure before Ben leaves for Cambridge. On Saturday we went to Greenwich Fair. I dressed in Turkish trousers, disguised as an orange seller. Ben dressed as a fisherman; it was great fun. I shall miss him. I love that feeling of taking risks and smelling the heady air of total freedom, Ben is certainly game for all of that. No doubt most of father's family would not approve.

I must stop now Bessie; we are going out for a walk and I want to do some sketching before the rain comes.

Fondest love, Barbara

My dear father can do no wrong in my eyes. I say this to reassure myself and reaffirm the strong bond we enjoy. But there remains unexplored territory between us, conundrums which I cannot find the way, or courage, to address. Why did my parents never marry? It becomes, as I grow older, a private battle. I often reflect on experiences which, at the time, I couldn't understand. Such as one which happened earlier in my childhood, when a family with whom we had become close, abruptly withdrew their friendship. Invitations were not accepted and the children in the family no longer joined us to play. Why this happened was never explained but as I grew older it became clearer that it was due to my parents not being married. The fierce protection I felt for my mother formed a shield for my own pain. I became aware of this when I received a letter from Bessie in which she made an insensitive remark concerning milliners. I considered it disparaging and it cut me to the quick. Because of this I ignored her for weeks and really couldn't find a way to explain why.

I can never remember my mother or father discussing her background or the fact that she was employed as a milliner. I was very young and would not have understood the implications, but somehow I had picked up that mother was not considered *de rigueur* by most of my father's family. His eldest sister, Frances, had married into the Nightingale family and I was aware that my cousin Florence had never visited our house, or had anything at all to do with us.

Thank goodness for my female friends. I treasure them. They provide succour and partly fill that mother-empty space still tight within me. All of this means that I must find a way to smooth over my bruised feelings with Bessie. I am sure she was quite unaware of the hurt it has caused me and is probably at a loss as to why I have not contacted her. These wounds I ponder on but can't find a way to discuss with my father. I fear distressing him in any way and from a young adult's perspective, can see that losing mother is still hard for him to bear.

My dear Aunt Ju continues to shine like a beacon. Somehow, she has managed to extricate herself from her class-conscious family and is teaching me how to manage myself when participating in social events. One of her closest friends is Harriet Martineau, a beautiful, elegant woman, whose writing on society I greatly admire. Like Aunt Ju, she has never married, and that is another subject I would like to discuss, but feel too shy at the moment.

Harriet is very involved in fighting for causes which directly reflect on women's lives. As a practising

Unitarian, she wants women to be respected as rational creatures and believes this can only be achieved through education. I also believe this passionately but can see that our educational system is very narrow and leaves little room for wide-ranging discussion. I am encouraged by father to explore many political viewpoints and, although we are not an overly religious family, to discuss different forms of worship. I am concerned that Bessie is 'flirting' with Catholicism. Observing her relationships with people such as teachers, I can see that she has a need for a kind of idolatry which is alien to me.

Much to my discomfort, Father has asked his sister, Aunt Patty, to come down and care for the family over a period of six weeks. Unfortunately, Aunt Ju and Aunt Dolly have other arrangements. I am now of an age when I can be considered old enough to manage, with staff, but my eyes are giving cause for concern; a result, I'm told, of reading and painting in bright sunlight. I have only seen Aunt Patty briefly on one occasion, when she neither looked at nor spoke to me. I am determined that she should be made to feel uncomfortable and have borrowed a pair of blue-tinted spectacles from Anna which are intended to protect my eyes. Also, to my delight, they make me look distinctly odd. This should irritate Aunt Patty, or so I hope.

We stand hidden behind the draperies, in the upstairs drawing room waiting for her to arrive. At last a rather grand carriage pulls up, we stifle chortles of exuberant laughter as she stepped down onto the pavement, assisted by a footman. She looks even more forbidding than we'd imagined. Our maid opens the door and Aunt Patty stands as if frozen, when we tumble down the stairs. It quickly becomes apparent that she has had little to do with children, or at least young people in their natural state. By that I mean unrestrained and free to give opinions and engage with adults in an open and frank manner. Ten days into her visit, if it were possible, we all become even more boisterous and conduct ourselves outrageously. During one meal I read out a line of Frederika Bremer's, *Hertha*.

'What am I? What can I do? What ought I to do?'
I leap to my feet and throw my arms in the air,
'I do not want to have a wasted life. I want to study, to travel and work.'

At this line Aunt Patty's eyebrows shoot up and her face crumples as if she'd bitten a lemon. But I continue undeterred....

'We have some brains among our Sex, our own...
You should not seek another word to prove it.
I need but name a Martineau and Howitt.'

These are Bessie's words not mine, but they proclaim so loudly my own feelings that I use them to stake my claim for freedom of thought and independence. Aunt Patty leaves soon after. I find it hard to imagine how she can be so different from Aunt Ju and my father. It is as if they belong to entirely different parents. No doubt our reputation in the family has now fallen off a cliff. One positive thing came out of her visit. It fired my determination to apply for a place at Bedford College in Bloomsbury. I need to concentrate entirely on art if I am to achieve any measure of success. It is amusing, I am gratified to find, that Elizabeth Reid, who founded the college, is also a great believer in women's emancipation. In fact, she likens her courses to the Underground Railway: the secret route to Canada taken by black

Chapter 7

American slaves when trying to gain their freedom. The image, she suggests, is that of female reformers gaining a secret route to the professions through education. I love this analogy. It makes me want to laugh and shout from the top of Fairlight. 'We are here, we are not going to remain silent.'

I wait daily for the post, and one morning to my delight, a letter arrivs offering me a place to start at Bedford on 23rd April 1849. I so hope this opportunity will mean that, in future, my art will be taken seriously.

Chapter 8

I cannot deny that my first weeks at Bedford were daunting. I had to confront my lack of formal training, and set about imbuing the discipline that will, I am assured, improve the quality of my work. I carry books wherever I go, and for hours at a time sketch anything and everything that catches my interest. My tutor advises me to put away my colour box and focus my attention on form. Over the next six months I threw myself into mastering this technique and slowly I improve. Despite finding critiques of my efforts hard to take, I exult in realizing that this exercise can only take me further up the ladder to becoming a professional artist.

In the early spring I plan painting expeditions to the Lake District and Wales. Naturally, I will continue to explore my beloved Sussex which has never failed to inspire me. All of my life I have embraced the outdoors: this is where I feel most free. I so want to capture that beauty on canvas, it brings me such joy. Aunt Ju berates me for not taking enough rest and fears I will, once again, strain my eyes. But I am obsessed.

Poets, I believe, can find the words, and in Shelley's, 'Queen Mab' he personifies for me the all-inspiring, 'Spirit of Nature.'

Giving it a feminine twist, I attempt a piece of my own called, 'A Parable. Filia.' It is my attempt to capture the relationship between female artist and nature. This is not the whole text but it begins ....

'She saw that every tree had its leaves written over with beautiful hymns and poems and every flower had a

Chapter 8

song written on its open petals, every stone was engraved with tales of wonder. On the mountain cliffs were written histories of deepest wisdom, and on the sand under her feet were traced tales of the old world ...'

It was sad to hear from Anna Howitt this morning that she has been refused a place in the Royal Academy school. This is infuriating. Anna is one of the most accomplished women painters I know. It seems that we have a mountain to climb if we are to break through male domination in the Arts. Women provide so much that is of importance in this world it must be recognised. I am glad to hear that this set-back has not deterred her and she has applied to continue her studies with Friedrich Kaulbach in Munich. This fits in very well with a scheme I've been hatching for six months. During the summer I would like to go on a walking trip with Bessie. Poor girl, she is grieving the loss of her brother, Priestly. I have the funds and it would do Bessie the world of good to get away. I'll write to her parents and assure them that I'll keep their daughter safe and be her chaperone throughout the journey. My plan is to travel down through Belgium, Germany, Austria and Switzerland. I am confident that this would help Bessie, and we can visit Anna in Munich.

My persuasive letter to Mr and Mrs Parkes has met with a positive response and sealed an agreement that we will all meet up in Munich. Father is, as expected, entirely in favour of the proposed trip. He promises to provide us with a list of friends and acquaintances in each country through which we intend to travel, where hospitality is likely to be extended.

I sense a change in myself since attending Bedford College. I know what I am doing and where I am going. Mary Howitt has described me as a 'modern Valkyrie,' which is very flattering. Anna asks if I will model for her. She is painting Boadicea, the warrior queen. I don't see myself in this way at all, but I am often described as strong-minded. I love the idea of this persona but know only too well that it is not considered a compliment by some members of the male-dominated press. It is an image which could rebound.

I recently published an article in the Hastings and St Leonards newspaper, which restates Mary Wollstonecraft's argument that, '*Enforced feminine innocence, which is really ignorance, effectively denies women citizenship.*' This stirring battle cry is followed by a subject dear to my heart, '*The Foolishness of Fashion.*'

My articles are published under a *nom-de-plume*, which provides me with some protection from attempts to denigrate and present, in an ugly fashion, women who dare to challenge their lack of rights.

With great excitement Bessie and I set about planning our trip and adapting our wardrobes. Skirts are shortened by four inches and I order two pairs of ankle-length Balmoral boots, sporting coloured laces. Into my travel bag go a large floppy hat, blue-tinted glasses to protect my eyes, sketch pad and water colours. Pirouetting in front of the mirror we admire our appearance: no doubt, heads will turn. I hire a carriage to take us to Dover, from where we will board ship for Belgium. We intend to walk, ride where possible, and take stagecoaches when necessary.

Approaching the Belgian coastline we stand on deck, arms linked, giggling like schoolgirls. 'You look absolutely amazing.' Bessie spluttered and dances a little jig around me. The passengers waiting to disembark politely ignore the sight of two apparently respectable young women dressed in such unacceptable attire and, furthermore, unaccompanied. Their stern faces increase our hilarity.

Chapter 9

We spend out first night in a small tavern outside Ostend. I am not a stranger to travelling and request that our meal of fish stew with large hunks of fresh bread and a bottle of Burgundy red, be served in our room. This gives us time to relax, away from curious eyes, where we can map out the next stage of our journey. I suggest we start in the direction of Bruxelles. 'Let's not rush,' says Bessie. 'We've plenty of time.' I arrange with the innkeeper to send our luggage on, to an address provided by my father.

Early in the morning we set off, taking a well signposted footpath. 'I feel safe with you, Barbara, you're so confident, where does it come from?' This light remark from Bessie gave me food for thought, because I really don't know. I suppose being the oldest child is part of it, but also father pours unconditional love into his children and gives us the belief that we can do anything we set our minds to. What a gift! Taking a rest along the way to eat some bread and fruit and replenish our water bottles, I notice a signpost to Bruges and suggest we take a small detour.

Bruges proves to be entrancing. The winding canals captivate my desire to catch the sparkle of water on canvas. Each morning, we spread our materials on the ancient coping stones and breakfast on delicious fresh bread and cheese. Bessie concentrates on the medieval and Gothic architecture, patiently tracing the intricate images etched against a clear blue sky. We leave reluctantly, some days later, on the early morning stagecoach for Ghent. After finding an inn for the night, we continue our journey on foot. Reaching the outskirts of Bruxelles, we shamelessly beg rides on farm wagons. The latter gives us much cause for merriment, when we imagine the blistering disapproval I would encounter from some of the Smith family. Undoubtedly, Bessie's parents would feel appalled at their darling daughter using such a rough mode of travel. The freedom from all restraints is exhilarating.

After collecting our luggage we rest for two days in a small house attached to the British embassy, leased to a friend of father's. The odorous streets of Bruxelles soon lose their appeal and after talking with fellow travellers we are advised that Vaalserberg should not be missed. It is the highest point in the Netherlands, where it's possible to view the meeting point of three countries. A coach ticket to Maastricht includes overnight accommodation in a small Gasthaus, and we can, if we so wish, stay over for two nights and catch the next available coach. This suits our needs admirably. Few things are perfect, however. We find that the coaches are crammed with tradesmen, all smoking pipes, or cheroots, filling the carriages with the most noxious fumes. Other hazards soon become apparent. The thoroughfare is well used and the coach crashes and clatters over rutted surfaces full of potholes, constantly in danger of tipping over into ditches, often full of stagnant water. We fear for our lives. Small rivers are navigated and we are near to getting dunked on one occasion when a wheel sheers right off. This disaster holds us up for half a day while repairs are carried out in a nearby staging post.

At last we arrive in Maastricht and after a quiet evening and a good night's sleep decide to climb the berg in the early morning. It is well worth the effort. The day is clear and reaching the top, we could trace our ongoing route, winding below us down through the Rhineland.

That evening, after we had washed and enjoyed a

Chapter 9

change of clothing, the landlord comes to check that we are well catered for. Using my execrable French, I enquire whether hiring horses to take us on to the border is possible. The landlord initially looks doubtful. 'But mademoiselle, this will be risky. How well do you ride?' I laugh. 'We have been riding since we could walk, Monsieur, taught by some of the best trainers in England.' At this he looks somewhat mollified and suggests we look over the horses he has available. 'If you so wish, I can arrange for a boy to come with you and he'll return the horses, also I can recommend clean and comfortable coach inns along the way.' I nod. 'How long will it take?' The man holds up three fingers. 'Three days, if you take the pretty route through Vise. It's easy riding. The boy will take care of the horses at night, feed and water them. He knows the way; he's done this many times.' We shake hands and agree the price.

Repacking our luggage fills up the rest of the evening and we experiment with how to retain our modesty when removing the split riding skirts, made for us before leaving England. They allow us to ride astride. This is not a practice widely approved of, as ladies are expected to ride side-saddle. How ridiculous! We find them to be practical and comfortable, but they are definitely not considered respectable, even in the backwoods of the Rhineland. To solve this predicament, we are willing to compromise. Each evening we intend to dismount and change into something more presentable before entering a town or village, hence the need to practise disrobing behind a bush, without attracting too much attention.

The next morning we set off at dawn. Bessie is smiling and delighted with her horse, which she called B. I feel grateful to have such an interesting companion, one who is embracing all the vicissitudes and challenges of travel without complaint. Michel, our guide and stable boy, removes any anxiety of missing the bridle path, which takes us up hill and down dale, through tiny hamlets until arriving without difficulty at the Gasthaus in Vise, recommended by the innkeeper.

The changing of our attire becomes one of the most fraught parts of the journey for Michel. No matter how careful we are of his sensibilities, he is entirely nonplussed by the procedure. Hampered by the lack of a shared language, we need to signal graphically our intentions. On each occasion he spurs his horse into a canter and disappears along the track, only to reappear when we catch up with him looking respectable. Bessie and I fluctuate between feeling sorry for the poor lad and a devilish urge to tease him. Cast-down eyes and red cheeks are more suited to a young damsel, no doubt this adds to his discomfort. On reaching Aachen and depositing us in a busy coaching inn, we bid him farewell with many thanks and a generous gratuity. He looks relieved to be free of his spirited travellers, as he trots off with our trusty steeds tethered behind him. At a safe distance he turns and waves, shouting, 'Au revoir Mesdemoiselles. Bonne chance.'

Chapter 10

That evening we explored Aachen. It is by far the most beautiful city we have visited thus far. The cathedral is a masterpiece of medieval architecture, set amongst a captivating old quarter with narrow, winding lanes and crooked timber buildings. We agree that we should stay some days so that Bessie can attempt to sketch the cathedral and I can spend time experimenting with my paints. We also want to make use of the health-giving thermal waters and to rest, before setting out on the next stage of our journey south.

After much discussion with the innkeeper and fellow travellers, we find that the route to the Swiss border is well signposted, and an established network of coaching inns are available all the way. It is agreed that the innkeeper will take us the next morning to a nearby staging post, where we can hire horses. The estimated travelling time is three to four weeks. Riding at an easy pace we should reach the border town of Stein am Rhein, with some time to spare, before we procede on to Austria. I arrange for the bulk of our luggage to be sent on to our hosts in Bregenz, informing them of our route and when to expect us.

At the staging post we, once again, demonstrate our expertise with horses and reassure the ostler that his mounts will be in safe hands. I also give him sight of a letter written by my father. It gives us an introduction to an eminent family in Bregenz. This written confirmation of our standing proves to be convincing and ensures that we are given all the assistance needed thereafter. I do wonder if men are obliged to authenticate their skills, before their word is accepted.

The next morning, rested and well prepared, we set off through the busy streets with our luggage packed in strong, leather side panniers, containing all that we need for the journey. Our equine companions are well acquainted with the bustle and noise, calmly making their way without any sign of alarm. Good for them! Bessie and I are heartily relieved to reach the quiet agrarian countryside surrounding the city without suffering any mishaps. I name my horse, a beautiful chestnut filly, Bella, after my dear sister. Bessie is struggling with a frisky mare, who takes a while to settle down.

In the next days our journey takes on a blissful quality. We are now well acquainted with Bella and Rip, (Bessie's name for her spirited mount). The paths are well used but not over-crowded, which gives us ample time to enjoy the flower-filled meandering bridleways. The fields, stretching on either side, are well planted with crops, farmhands briefly cease their labours to wave and call, '*Guten Morgen Fräulein*'. The verdant hillsides bring back memories of England.

After each day's riding, having washed and changed out of our horse-smelling clothes, we explore the small German villages. Our perambulations cause a stir in the more remote areas. Young men, standing around in the evening with little to do, are fascinated by us. Two attractive young women travelling alone and dressed in such a strange fashion is an unusual sight, and quite a diversion. The biggest source of amusement is our prized Balmoral boots and, of course, our shorter skirts. Some young men are quite bold and want to know where we have come from. Their awestruck reactions, on hearing that we had travelled alone from England are hilarious and we take advantage to spin fantastic tales using a mixture of mime and fractured German.

In this carefree manner we make our way down through the Rhineland staying overnight in coaching inns and Gasthäuser, changing horses every three days. This method of travel is probably more arduous than travelling by coach, but it gives us the experience of being close to the land and the opportunity to observe the daily life of the local people. Rarely, if ever, do we feel threatened and are usually met with good humour and intense curiosity. We often purchase milk and cheese from small farms and attempt conversation. Few people speak English but with a great deal of gesticulation we make ourselves understood and certainly never starve.

Late one evening we cross the river at Horb am Neckar and continue on into the lower Schwarzwald. We sense a change in pace. The scenery changes from smooth paths and an open landscape to a more mountainous terrain. Wooded ravines and wildly tumbling streams demand all of our equestrian skills. The dense forests give us some of the most startling moments in the journey when we come across wild boar unexpectedly. Also, and this is far more alarming, small platoons of heavily armed mounted soldiers appear on the trail before us and roughly push us aside, showing no manners or concern for our safety. We receive no acknowledgement, other than raucous bursts of laughter at our distress, or a disdainful sideways glance.

To our relief, the dark coniferous forests eventually give way to cleared pastures; large wooden farmhouses are scattered over the hills, their windowsills decked with bright red geraniums. A reassuring sight. The houses are melded into the hillsides, providing accommodation for the family in the upper levels. Farm animals are sheltered in the cavernous, sweet-smelling barns beneath the house. The surrounding mountains, some still tipped with snow, inspire sketching and painting sessions which last for hours. But move on we must.

It is now ten weeks since we left England and it seems to me that Bessie is greatly benefiting from our adventure. Her dear brother will never be forgotten but tears are no longer on her cheeks and laughter once more erupts when we make up songs and outlandish ditties.

Feeling rather weary we at last reach the border and follow the signpost to Stein am Rhein. The staging post is a welcome sight and dismounting makes us aware that our muscles are screaming for soft feather beds. This has been the longest journey on horseback that either of us has ever attempted, 'I think this achievement demands a reward, Bessie.' After paying our dues for the horses, we asked to be directed to the best hotel in the town. Thankfully it is sited nearby and on arrival we order hot baths and a substantial meal to be served in our suite, together with two bottles of their best Moselle Riesling. That evening we raised a toast to the horses, ate until we were full to bursting, then slept like babes.

The following morning, after a long lazy breakfast, we explore the town. Nothing prepares us for the beauty of its setting and the sight of the painted houses, each one a unique piece of art. This is a perfect place to rest and reflect on our journey so far. I find it extraordinary that Bessie and I have not had a cross word since leaving England. Although she is my closest friend, this is the first time I have spent such a length of uninterrupted time with her. She is, and will always be, a person I must have in my life.

Gentle walks through the peaceful Swiss countryside soon help to relax our sore muscles. Local guides advise us on easy walking routes and we calculate that it is entirely possible for us to walk to Konstanz and board a ferry to Bregenz. This would give us an agreeable mode of travel for entering Austria.

Chapter 11

Our arrival in Austria hits us like a blast of cold air. Armed guards stand on the quay watching passengers disembark and searching travellers' belongings. For no reason that we can ascertain, our bags are ignored. We take a horse-drawn cab to the address provided by my father, still struggling to understand why we feel so unwelcome and ill at ease. The cab pulls to a halt outside a rather grand house, sporting a corner turret with an onion-shaped dome. To our utmost relief, we are welcomed with open arms. Our host, Herr Von Schmerling, who speaks impeccable English, is a man who has been a close friend of my father's over some years, frequently visiting our house in Blandford Square. His charming wife, who also speaks English, makes us most comfortable and after giving us time to refresh ourselves, in a rather splendid suite of rooms, invites us to join them for dinner.

As we enjoy our pre-dinner glasses of wine, Herr Von Schmerling gently quizzes us about our travels, but it soon becomes apparent that he has other things on his mind. 'Have you visited Austria before?' he asks politely. I say that we have not. 'Well, I must be frank with you, ladies, this country is not safe to travel in at present. I don't know if you have heard this while on your way down through Germany, but there have been worrying political demonstrations in Vienna. People have been killed and wounded; I must warn you that the whole country is in a state of unrest. Police surveillance has been increased and suspicion of anti-government plots is rife.'

This information clearly explains the military presence we witnessed in Bregenz and the cool welcome we received

49

on entering the country. On describing the situation, our kind host explains, 'This behaviour is not because people in Austria are unfriendly but because they are frightened. Corporal punishment is being used indiscriminately and people are in fear of their lives.' He shakes his head, looking grave. This news is saddening. Both Bessie and I are politically minded and acutely aware that many countries in Europe are unstable, following events in France. We had intended to visit Vienna, but Herr Von Schmerling suggests that, at this time, he would not recommend it. We stay with our hospitable hosts for two more days. Wandering through the streets of Bregenz, we now perceive our cool reception as something else. Suspicion and fear. We can see that people are under the domination of the sword, which in 1850 has taken the place of law. We leave Herr Von Schmerling and his warm-hearted wife with regret. He is a fair-minded man and can see that social reform is needed but wise enough to know that this is rarely achieved without bloodshed. One can only hope that compromises will be found, and outright revolution avoided.

We are now approaching the end of our trip and our meeting with Anna Howitt beckons. Taking our hosts' advice we decide to take carriages all the way to Munich, breaking the journey in Augsburg.

Arriving in Munich is quite a relief. The streets are bustling and filled with shops overloaded with produce and smartly dressed burghers looking prosperous. Feeling much in need of a rest and a change of clothing, we find some well-appointed rooms in a comfortable hotel. A quiet knock on the door presents a young chambermaid. After some miming and the use of the few German words at our disposal, we understand her to be asking if we want hot water and fresh towels. Hot water will be most welcome and whatever food your cook recommends. These are the words I want to say, but no doubt my version is barely recognisable. I accompany my request with much gesticulation. 'Wir sind sehr hungrich.' Bessie chuckles, rubbing her stomach and attempts to put the maid at ease by slipping a coin into her hand. 'Is it possible for our clothes to be washed?' She held up the grubby bundle, pointing and holding her nose, much to the poor maid's embarrassment.

On waking the following morning, rested and ready for breakfast, our washed and brushed clothes are delivered by a housemaid, together with our boots, well buffed with goose fat. Prolonging our luxurious sojourn, fragrant coffee and delicious pancakes with honey are served in our room. Now replete, I ring for the maid to clear away the detritus. She receives a warm embrace from Bessie for her endeavours, which causes her to blush in confusion. 'Which direction do we take for Marienplatz?' I am trying to decipher the crude map sent to us from England by Anna. The maid leans out of the window and, understanding one word, points in the direction of the main square.

Marienplatz is easy enough to find, but we quickly become lost when trying to make sense of the street names. I approach a local merchant and say in desperation, 'Miss Anne Howitt, English lady.' To my amazement he nods, and with vigorous arm-waving, gives us directions. The house in which Anne is living belongs to Herr Kaulbach, and is situated down a narrow side street, the finding of which causes us much confusion. We stand outside and call her name. Within seconds, one of the attic windows flies open and there she is, dearest Anna, waving and calling out to us.

The next day or so is filled with catching up on news from England and pouring over sketches and paintings. Anna is full of information about her course and generously demonstrates the new techniques she is acquiring. It is delightful to see her again. Anna shares a room in the house with another artist called Jane Benham, who works as a book illustrator. I know that Anne has no fixed income, and that my father has discretely funded her training for some while; due to this, we do not wish to prevail on her hospitality and every morning visit the market for provisions.

Before leaving for Germany she had become engaged to an illustrator called Edward Bateman. The couple had agreed on the importance of Anna completing her art studies and, shortly after her departure for Germany, he left for Australia to follow a gold rush taking place in the state of Victoria. I find it strange that he is barely mentioned during our many jovial meals. Our conversation ranges over so many topics in which Anna's future plans and return to England are discussed at length. Edward doesn't seem to be much in her thoughts.

After our visits with Anna, I found that plans for my own artistic development, which I have put on hold during our holiday, are surfacing. Every spare moment on our journey I have spent studying the landscape, trying to catch the vagaries of each scene, depending on light and angle. My studies at Bedford College have been useful and, after visiting Anna, I can see that with a little extra effort, maybe one or two of my paintings might, perhaps, be improved sufficiently for exhibition at the Royal Academy.

Imperceptibly the desire to return home creeps up on me and I find my thoughts turning to several reform projects which are in progress. They say that travel broadens the mind, and our travels through continental

Chapter 11

Europe have crystallised for me the urgent need for political reform in my beloved Albion.

Bessie's parents are ensconced in a comfortable house on the outskirts of Munich. Now rested and looking presentable, we set out to visit them and plan the long carriage journey home.

Chapter 12

On arriving back in England, I find my post-box full of invitations and enthusiastic letters from father. He is planning an outing for the whole family. As a Unitarian, he believes wholeheartedly in technological and scientific progress and has bought tickets for an exhibition in London, which is to be held at the Crystal Palace in Hyde Park. The building is constructed both in iron and glass, as a symbol of practical skill and to illustrate the romance of industrialisation. In addition to this prestigious affair, he has invited a party of twenty friends, which includes several German, French and Hungarian refugees, to be passengers on the first steam train to travel between London and Cambridge. Once there, we are to meet up with brother Ben and six of his friends for a slap-up lunch at *The Bull*.

As a family we are now widely spread. Father has decided to give up the lease on Pelham Crescent, a decision I find most painful. Hastings provided me with a perfect place to spend my early childhood and I am determined that, when the time is right, I will build a home of my own in the vicinity. Sussex is my base and my comfort. Willy lives at Crowham Manor, in Westfield, an estate my father acquired. He has now completed his studies at agricultural college and father has appointed him Estates Manager. Willy and I have little in common and I rarely see him, but I like to have family members close by and settled in my beloved Sussex.

Blandford Square, Marylebone, has become my principal home and I find that living in London provides regular contact with groups of people I have known

Chapter 12

over many years. Gabriel Rossetti, a member of the Pre-Raphaelite Brotherhood, has become a favourite and a considerable inspiration. Anna Howitt has now returned from Munich and is living in the Hermitage, a tiny house in Highgate. We have set up a group called The Folio, so named from a rather handsome book I've purchased. Each month we contribute examples of art or poetry, on a particular theme, which are then inserted into the folio for critical appraisal by the group. Lizzie Siddal, an actress and poet, is also a member. An entrancing creature with clouds of red hair, it is hard not to feel like a clod hopper in her presence. Her tall slender body looks fragile and elegant, but I fear she is not long for this earth. Gabriel adores Lizzie to distraction and worries constantly for her health. I suggest that a period of convalescence may help, and accommodation can be arranged in Hastings with the Elphicks, a family I have known since childhood. They offer clean and comfortable lodgings in the High Street and have traditionally supported the theatrical profession over many years. I am confident Lizzie will receive a warm welcome there and hopefully the sea air will restore her health.

In London, life is an unending social whirl. I was recently introduced to a woman called Marian Evans. We took to each other instantly and in a matter of weeks it is as if I'd known her all my life. My first impression is of a highly intelligent person who holds considered views on many subjects. Bessie suggests that she may fit into our group. She has moved to London from Warwickshire and is employed on the *Westminster Review*. All I can say is, that I hope she steers clear of John Chapman who runs the *Review*. The gossip in London salons is that he's a charmer and not to be trusted.

Sadly, as often happens in life, events take another turn. Marian has now left for Germany with George

Lewes, a man with whom she has been working on a translation of Feuerbach's *Das Wesen Christenhaus*. This has been completed and apparently Lewes is now researching the life of Goethe in preparation for a book: hence the visit to Germany.

Lewes is a married man, but I have heard that the marriage is not a happy one. So many rumours are circulating: some are unrestrainedly hostile towards Marian. I am determined to wait and see what happens. My view on marital relationships is, one could say, rather limited. I spent a few days with them in Tenby before they departed and I am left with the impression that they are extremely happy and well suited. Marian assures me that she holds George in the highest regard and that he treats her well.

This sequence of developments gives me much food for thought. I am in the process of researching for a paper on the most important laws concerning women. It is clear to me that better legislation is needed to protect women within marriage. Alongside this is my belief that, to have a successful marriage, it is necessary to have a strong bond, which is equal in its clarity and intent. This does not always seem to be the case following a legal union, according to current laws. Lewes is showing a strong commitment to financially supporting the children of his marriage. As a fairly new friend I can only respect that, and hope that it is an indication that he is an honourable man. When they return from Germany I wish to resume our budding friendship.

Before Marian left, we discovered a shared philosophy, based on stories we had gleaned from *The Arabian Nights* during our childhood. These stories give us an intimate understanding of each other. The story of *Perie-zadeh*, in which a daughter's triumph restores the honour of her disgraced mother, spoke to us both. Female ambition

Chapter 12

should serve women rather than betray them. I want that security of being surrounded by women or men of like mind, who are able to exist outside convention and can see beyond the petty requirements which make one 'acceptable' in our society. This need is my lifeblood. I am determined that, once back in London, Marian will be welcomed into the sisterhood.

My glorious adventure with Bessie has clarified my objectives. I must with all determination keep them clear in my mind. One project which has given me a great deal of work, along with much satisfaction of late, is having published *A Brief Summary, in Plain Language, of the Most Important Laws Concerning Women*. This article was published by the *Hastings and St Leonard News*, under Aesculapius, of course.

Chapter 13

Receiving the title deeds to Westminster Infants School has opened up a new avenue of ideas. I visit the school often and can't help noticing that in recent years the standard of teaching has declined. If my first teacher, Mr Buchanan taught me anything, it was the necessity of understanding how children learn. Physical surroundings are important, as are teachers able to bring alive academic subjects which can be insufferably dull. I think the school needs fresh blood and embark on finding a new Principal. I believe that with the 'right' person in charge, a school develops an ethos which is communicated to its pupils by osmosis.

My priorities are to provide sufficient space in which children can learn through play, art and discussion with teachers who are open-minded and kind. I hold no truck with the idea that children must be controlled through fear and the cane will not be a feature in any classroom of mine. As a way of broadening my perspective I have visited many schools around London and the Home Counties from which I have defined my priorities. Religion will not be part of the curriculum. I know this will be frowned upon, but I want children to understand the necessity of developing compassion, understanding and love for their fellow human beings by example. An understanding and experience of nature is also top of the curriculum. This will be achieved by daily exercise in outside spaces and visits to places of interest in the vicinity of the school.

I have found a possible Principal: her name is Elizabeth Whitehead. I also suggest to some of my friends such as Bessie and Jessie White that they act as volunteers and provide lessons in subjects where they have expertise. Jessie agrees to teach physiology and the laws of health. Another friend of Bessie's, Octavia Hill, wants to help out with French and drawing lessons. This is such an inspiring enterprise and one which has taken up much of my time, but I fear for its future. There are so many hurdles, not least that of finding women who are willing to train as teachers. It is seen as a lowly profession in middle-class society and, due to financial restraints, unavailable to working-class women to whom it would provide an excellent way up the ladder. How to shift the obstacles which prevent women from taking more control of their lives is a difficult rock to crack and that is how it feels at the moment: a rock, impenetrable. Bessie has just published *Remarks on the Education of Girls*, a book in which she calls for various reforms. This has been met with derision in the Press where it is suggested that she is somehow not feminine. I despair!

Mary Wollstonecraft was brave enough to push for the emancipation of women in a time when the very idea was considered outlandish, if not criminal. In fact, she described women as, 'outlaws of the world,' where neither women nor children are protected by the law. This state of affairs I am determined to change. I have completed the first draft of a petition to Parliament designed to change married women's property laws. I am encouraged by the example of Caroline Norton who challenged the 'right' of fathers gaining custody of their children, regardless of the circumstances.

Because of my own family background, I have given much thought to this and can see that father was only too aware of the burden he'd placed on us children. I now read this ruling, with understanding for our family situation. *The rights of an illegitimate child are only such as he can acquire; he can inherit nothing, being in law looked upon as nobody's son, but he may acquire property by devise or bequest. He may acquire a surname by reputation but does not inherit one.*

It's plain to see that father set out to provide us with all we needed to combat this dogma. But it still does not fully explain to me why he chose to put us in this situation, knowing the difficulties it would present us with. He taught me to think politically, a skill which has stood me in good stead. And because of this, I can see that I must start at a place where I am most likely to succeed. Presently, the law does provide some protection for single women who own property and pay taxes to the State. Obviously, this ideal situation only applies to a very small section of women in our society, leaving huge gaping holes for all the others. When one takes into consideration that a woman is seen as the 'property' of her father and husband, this gives a measure of how far we have to travel before any semblance of emancipation is achieved. And, did I mention 'the vote'?...

I have sent the petition to various people of influence, and I am amused to read the comment from one recipient in particular, which warns me that I may be laughed at. Despite this terrifying possibility, I am supported by an army of energetic friends and have acquired twenty-six thousand signatures in a few months. Not all of my women acquaintances are supportive. Some make the excuse that they disapprove of other signatories on the list. Others comment that, although admiring my ambition, they consider that the circumstances of my birth make me too strong a fighter against established opinion. For this reason they believe me to be less rational. I will not allow this ill-informed opinion of my character to affect me in the least. But I would be dishonest not to acknowledge that it hurts. I hear many harrowing stories relating to my staunch supporters during the campaign,

Chapter 13

the most touching one is of a very old lady on her death bed, whose last ever signature was written on my petition.

The Bill was brought before Parliament with the aim of establishing married women in the same position as single women in respect to property. But it procedes no further than the first reading. The Whig government are defeated in the next election and my hopes are dashed.

After this defeat I am in sore need of balm for my wounds and turn to Bessie. She is a bottomless pit of interesting contacts and inspiration. After a weekend of walking and sketching, she introduces me to her cousin, Elizabeth Blackwell.

Elizabeth is the first women to qualify as a doctor, at present visiting from America. She is tiny, barely five feet tall with wispy blonde hair and only one eye. She emigrated with her family from Bristol when, after the death of her father, she ran a small school to help the family financially. That alone is enough to arouse my interest, but following this she attended medical college in Geneva, New York State. It's hard to comprehend, but during her two years' residence in Geneva not one lady would call or speak to her. Despite this cruel display of social exclusion, she graduated as a Doctor of Medicine head of her class and was afforded top honours in every subject. From there she moved to France to study midwifery where she contracted ophthalmia and lost the sight of one eye. Her ambition had been to specialise in female diseases but, for reasons which are inexplicable, this was one area of medicine from which she was barred. I am most impressed with this woman who has entered the medical profession against all odds. At present we have no women doctors in England, but no doubt there is a huge need for them.

A hospital for women in London. Would this ever be possible? The very thought of it thrills me.

Chapter 14

I am staggering under what feels like a near mortal blow. My father, whom I have made no secret is the man I admire and love above all others, is not the man I thought him to be. By the most awkward coincidence I have discovered that he has been in a relationship with a woman called Jane Buss for several years. Up to this day I had no glimmer that this woman existed. It came about when I was asked by father's solicitor to sign a codicil in his will. To my dismay it laid down that his money is to be divided up into equal parts between the Leigh Smith children and three other children by the names of Alexander, Henry and Jane Bentley Smith. Calculating by the age of the eldest child, Alexander, I can only deduce that father took a mistress just two years after mother died. Later I discover that he had hidden her away in Fulham under the name of Mrs Bentley, just as he had done with mother in Whatlington, under the name of Mrs Leigh.

After making some enquiries, I found that the three children are being educated in Hampshire and Kent, no doubt at father's expense. No place of residence is noted in the Will for Mrs Bentley or Jane Buss and the only address mentioned is that of the children's schools. I presume their mother has passed away. I swing between rage and despair. How can I ever feel able to trust anyone again after this betrayal? I am unable to speak about it, either to him or any of my siblings.

The only person I feel safe with now is Bessie. I decide to write her a letter and maybe we can find a way to make sense of it all. We both seem to be going through

Chapter 14

a peculiar time. Bessie recently met a man called Robert Lacey who, after only two occasions of meeting her in company, proposed marriage. Shocking! Her parents are aghast and it has probably confirmed their fears that she needs to be safely married to a suitable man, as soon as possible.

I suspect that the rather conventional Mr and Mrs Parkes are uneasy with Bessie's choice of friends and their outspoken views and agree with none of them. I find it extraordinary to witness the formality conducted in the Parkes' household. Bessie is one of the most high spirited and free-thinking people I know, but she endured restrictions throughout her childhood that I would have found intolerable. When first visiting Pelham Crescent in the early years, she can recall my father kneeling down and buttoning up my boots. This casual intimacy amazed her and is one of the reasons she loved visiting 'Liberty Hall' as she called it. 'I could not imagine such a thing ever occurring in our household,' she expostulates. 'The nanny would never have allowed me out of the nursery with unbuttoned boots and father would never have thought it right that he should button them up.'

Listening to these anecdotes I can see that an ease of manner and tolerance emanates from father, but not in every circumstance. I had a letter from Ben last week. Apparently, he is in dispute with father in regard to his future prospects. Father wants Ben to train as a lawyer, with a view to a parliamentary career. This is ludicrous: Ben is not in the least interested or suited for such a profession. He wants to train as a mining engineer or possibly join the navy. I find it difficult to sympathise as, here am I, unable to consider any career at all due to being born a woman. I feel hollow and out of sorts.

Bessie's parents have obviously sent out for reinforcements and her cousin Elizabeth (now Head of my infants school) is corralled into the fray, with the aim of finding Bessie a husband. Without further ado she has put forward a suitor by the name of Sam Blackwell. Apparently, Mr Blackwell is a rich industrialist and a widower. Bessie, who is very outspoken and never holds back from expressing her opinions, wrote to her cousin and described her lack of fitness for marriage. 'I hate the idea of domestic life. The very thought of it I find abhorrent. No one could measure up to Barbara for intellectual stimulation or breadth of mind.'

What on earth Elizabeth made of this frank admission is hard to imagine. I can only be a sounding board for Bessie. We are both of an age when, if marriage is our goal, we should make moves before it is too late. So far, I have not met anyone who remotely appeals to me. I think it better that we avoid making any big decisions and plan another trip. Bessie suggests a cottage in Wales. I have so much editing and proof-reading to complete that a quiet cottage, with no interruptions, is perfect.

The small stone cottage tucked into the side of a tussocky hillside gives us just the place to escape. We arrive in a carriage packed with food, wine and all the writing, painting and drawing equipment we need for the next week or so. I soon have a coal fire glowing in the slate fireplace and a pan of soup heating for our evening meal. A change of scene never fails to provide me with peace of mind and the simpler the surroundings the better. I love looking out over hillsides, with no sound other than the bleating of sheep and a musical stream cascading down the hillside.

We spend our evenings discussing Bessie's overprotective parents and their determination to see her safely married. Some things, we agree, would never change and have to be accepted, but one of their expectations has to be resisted. They must stop searching for what they

Chapter 14

consider to be suitable men and Bessie must be free to choose her own husband at a time when she is ready.

I find that talking through my father's deception with my dear friend, helps me to find a rational way to deal with the shock and betrayal. There is no possibility at present that I can just dismiss it and forgive father out of hand. I will, however, separate my life from his and accept that, despite his inexplicable behaviour, he has given me more love and more of just about everything than I could ever have hoped for. He is liberally minded. I can't value that in the man and then reject it when it doesn't suit me. It is the not knowing, or naively thinking that I knew everything about him when I did not, that I am struggling with. Our relationship has been so close since mother died; my rock proves to be flawed.

Wandering around the Welsh hillsides I came to accept that I have three half-siblings. I may find the pluck to see if their mother is still alive, but then, I may not. At some time I must discuss the situation with father, but he's now grown old and feeble. Should I let him be or confront him face to face? A sudden thought hits me after one of my talks with Bessie, that Ben may also be aware of father's other family. This isn't a matter which he would willingly discuss with me, not being the communicative type. No doubt I will continue to cogitate.

As the days pass in our secret paradise, nature works its magic and I immerse myself in trying to capture the subtle shades of blue and grey in the Welsh hillsides. We swim naked in the lake and sing our hearts out, rejoicing in the beauty around us. Bessie helps me to see that the world has not been destroyed. I am still Barbara Leigh Smith.

Our carefully laid-out strategy for Bessie's future takes a jolt this morning when a letter arrived addressed to Miss Bessie Parkes. Apparently, on Cousin Elizabeth's suggestion, Mr Blackwell is to pay us a visit and, closely chaperoned, the couple should attempt to find some common ground. The letter states that he will arrive the next day at noon. Bessie is furious. Luckily we have some time to clear up our mess and agree that they will walk around the lake together and discuss the matter. Bessie intends to be straightforward and to put her case that she will not be coerced into a relationship against her will.

Mr Blackwell arrives bearing gifts. A large bouquet of flowers precedes him from the carriage, while the coachman hauls out a hamper crammed with delectable treats. Bessie offers him a place to freshen up after the long journey, followed by a cup of tea and biscuits. I suggest a walk around Landewin lake and we set out, I in the role of chaperone.

While walking I have plenty of time to observe Mr Blackwell. He must be a good decade or more older than Bessie and not in robust health. I can see that he walks with a limp and his sparse grey hair does little to flatter his rather plump countenance. Bessie looks like a young girl walking beside her grandfather. We arrive back at the cottage and prepared a delicious dinner with the contents of the hamper. Mr Blackwell looks flushed and jolly after the walk. The conversation ranges over a number of topics and, although not a man I would choose for a husband, I can see that he is of a considerate disposition and very much enamoured of Bessie. At last he departs, intending to break his journey in Bristol where he has business to attend to. We discuss their meeting at length after he leaves. 'I have sympathy for his situation as a widower but, is sympathy sufficient foundation for a happy marriage?' From this thoughtful observation I can see that Bessie is unconvinced. He obviously evokes no physical attraction or feelings of affection in her.

My thoughts are decidedly mixed and not all shared

Chapter 14

with Bessie. I can see that marrying a rich industrialist would give her the freedom to engage in her passion for social work and campaigning for government reform, but I hate to think of Bessie's vibrant nature being restricted, her youth cut short.

We now prepare to leave for London and while packing up our canvases and boxes of paints, Bessie drops a thunderbolt. I note a change in her during the morning but think it due to her reluctance to leave. Without preamble, she says, 'Barbara. I have decided to accept Sam Blackwell's offer of marriage. Before you say a word, it is on the condition that we have a very long engagement.' I must look astonished as she laughs and says, 'I sent him a letter, he should receive it by the time we reach London.'

Bessie's decision gives me much food for thought. I can see on reflection that being engaged actually gives her more freedom, placates her parents, and prevents her from being pestered by other unwelcome suitors. Clever Bessie!

Chapter 15

Back in London I am once again swept along by events. I receive the sad news that Phillip Kingsford has died of consumption. He was Willy's tutor some years back, and the first man who proposed to me. Obviously I didn't accept as he wasn't a man I could love romantically, but we always enjoyed an affectionate friendship and I will miss his wonderfully informative letters. I have now received another marriage proposal from a man who, once again, is interesting and of good character, but no spark has been ignited. What is happening? I feel as if I've become a magnet for men looking for a wife. But domestic bliss is not something I yearn for and maybe I am not suitable marriage material.

Nannie, my youngest sister, decides to live in Rome for a while. She is studying painting. I have a cautious and distant relationship with her. She has always been – how can I say this? – argumentative and difficult. Maybe a gap naturally exists between older and younger sisters. After all, even though being born into the same family gives us so much in common, one's actual nature may be very different. And Nannie is different. Rome offers her an alternative society to that found in London. I have often wondered if this is likely to come about when, not feeling entirely at ease in one's own society, an alternative lifestyle can be found abroad. Away from family it may be possible to be oneself, without attracting condemnation or be the subject of much speculation. I don't know if this applies to Nannie, but I consider it likely.

I make no secret of the fact that my closest relationships

Chapter 15

are with women, but the society Nannie has joined in Rome is of a very different calibre. They are women who like to dress, act and behave like men and, while I also like to engage in what can be seen as male pursuits, I feel predominantly female. How lucky I am to dip in and out of these variables, without being obliged to conform to either male or female shibboleths. It seems to me that human beings are complex and, if left to their own inclinations, can evolve in many different ways. The society we have now, with all its rules and expectations, is designed to control human nature and human sexuality in a way which I believe is repressive and not at all conducive to happiness.

But, for all my intellectual probing into the relationships of others, I now find myself in a situation which is unfathomable. I have for the past year submitted articles for publication in the *Westminster Review* and, because of this, have been in contact with John Chapman, a man for whom in the past I have had little respect. He is a philanderer, but despite being in full knowledge of this, I find myself in love with him. It feels like a sickness and one which is making me deeply ill at ease. His presence is totally distracting.

I first met John when I was just fourteen years old. I can't remember him making any impact upon me at the time, but even then his nickname was 'Byron.' This I can see now was apt. He is so handsome and his manner allows for a freedom of discourse that I find extraordinarily attractive. Together with his family he has now moved to a house in Blandford Square, and far from this easing the situation, it has made matters worse.

My health has been problematic for a while and I consulted a physician in Brook Street concerning a difficulty I have with swallowing. He suggests that this may be connected with a personal condition I suffer from:

that of irregular menstruation. How I came to discuss this diagnosis with John Chapman I cannot imagine. He is loosely connected with the medical world through his father who is a chemist and it seemed appropriate at the time. He proceded to carry out extensive research on my condition and is of the opinion that sitting in a piping hot hip bath, in which mustard has been diluted, will bring about an increase in the menstrual flow. According to John's advice, I should wear horsehair socks by day, and loose-fitting lambs-wool socks to sleep in. Tight boots should never be worn. All of these methods he assures me will improve my circulation and hence my menstrual problems. I am somewhat reassured that he is also treating Anna Howitt for a similar condition and is prescribing, 'Olei juniperi Sabine.' I cannot see any evidence that John has the medical knowledge or training to do such a thing, but he is so caring and reassuring that I trust he has our best interests at heart.

Due to this I am feeling under the weather and suggest to Anna Howitt that we leave London for a while. Hastings has always provided a sanctuary when I have needed one and we arrange to visit a farm just outside the town, where we can paint uninterrupted. The countryside helps me to relax and it is inspiring that Holman Hunt also used this farm when painting *Our English Coasts*. Poor Anna is having little success with her exhibitions and has been cast down by several negative reviews. I do wonder if her sadness impacts on her paintings which are beautifully executed but of a gloomy nature. Her relationship with Edward Bateman has finally come to an end and she is in a dark phase of her life.

While at the farm I receive letters daily from John. He is of the opinion that celibacy is unnatural and may be damaging my physical health. This point of view evokes extreme reactions in me. I don't consider myself

Chapter 15

abnormal in any way, but I do have a fear of being dominated by sexual needs. To my mind they make a woman vulnerable and prey to irrationality. In each letter he is becoming more explicit and when I consult him on the physical effects of marriage, he positively jumps off the page. He recommends married life as a cure for every female complaint imaginable. The pressure is beginning to tell on me, particularly as he now claims that Susanna, his wife, is aware of our love and that father also knows of our relationship. I resolve to take things slowly and John has to be patient, but each day I am assailed with words of undying love and his passionate belief that sexual union will confer benefits to my health.

Just how father and also Ben became aware of my feelings for John Chapman I have yet to discover, maybe from London gossip. Whatever the source, it provoked an extreme reaction. Father is furious. To my chagrin, Ben has taken it upon himself to investigate John's business affairs and confronts me with some unwelcome facts. Apparently he has enormous debts and is in imminent danger of bankruptcy. How I hate to receive such news about a man for whom I have developed such an intense attraction and to whom I willingly provide so many intimate disclosures. Ben did not hold back in giving his opinion that John was attempting to seduce me into a committed relationship. The humiliation is unbearable and I am desperate to find that they are mistaken, but each day Ben produces further evidence that I can't ignore. Today brings the final straw. It appears that my sister Bella has also consulted John on health matters, something of which I was not aware. I can no longer ignore Ben's opinion that John is a parasite and is determined to find a way into our family through one daughter or another.

Bella is so vulnerable; she suffers from melancholia,

the root causes of which are unclear. This may not be relevant, but I notice that she has become extremely distressed around our brother Ben and accuses him of not being respectful to her women friends. I suspect that her recent breakdown may have been caused by a failed love affair, with whom I have no idea, and fear that Chapman may have manipulated her emotionally. No one seems to be willing to delve into such delicate matters at this point but something has to be done. There is no doubt that she is not improving and needs a complete change of scene. Father is desperate to find ways to help both of us. He has looked into taking his three daughters to Algeria. This is a country I've never visited, but is recommended for people with lung problems. The very thought of such a trip lightens my mood.

I have recently been in touch with Marian Lewes. She's shown me such genuine compassion during this difficult time and invites me to visit them in Tenby before we depart.

Chapter 16

In preparation for our trip I've been reading anything I can find about Algeria. It is unlike any other country I have visited. Different in religion, customs and climate. For some time life at home has been fraught. Sharp disagreements are bubbling up from so many quarters and I am hoping that a visit to exotic-sounding Algeria will calm the waters. I am still smarting from my foray into emotional upheaval with John Chapman. It is hard to condemn him absolutely, but a constant stream of evidence has penetrated my blindness and helped to wean me off the drug of total infatuation. I've long been uneasy with the idea of such a condition and believe that the Greeks were right to call it 'love sickness.' My behaviour, when 'under the influence,' was not rational.

I am interested to see how we, by that I mean father and his three daughters, get on together in Algeria. I am uneasy that Nannie will be her usual irritating self, but I pray she becomes more amenable and considerate of Bella's fragility. The journey itself holds a whiff of adventure about it. Firstly, we take the boat from Dover to Calais then, after staying overnight in Paris, we board a train to Marseilles. This mode of travel will be quite a new experience. After arriving in Marseilles, a city I have never visited previously, we intend to rest for some days before boarding a boat for Algiers. I understand that Algiers is quite a modern city, having been re-modelled by the French. I am surprised to read of the number of people travelling there and that the country is becoming a fashionable destination.

I hope that the climate will suit Bella. I've spent much

time with her of late and realize that she struggles with demons which are entirely imaginary. I sympathise with her condition. I always like to see myself as resilient and strong-thinking, but the experience with Chapman has left me feeling vulnerable and fearful that my one chance of true love has been lost. A letter arrives from Bessie. She is such a loyal friend and is very concerned for my state of mind; I'd love her to join us in the new year. Her fiancé is generous and happy for her to travel in the company of friends.

My painting materials are packed, I hope that a different landscape will inspire me; also my walking boots, as the countryside around Algiers sounds interesting. I've exhibited at the Royal Academy on two occasions now and received very encouraging reviews, but I wonder if my many interests has prevented me from receiving greater acclaim as an artist. Perhaps I should devote myself full time to achieving a higher standard? So many things get in the way of it: my interest in politics, education and women's emancipation are a huge drain on my time. Hopefully this trip will give me more opportunity to reflect on my direction.

Failed love affairs and family squabbles seem insignificant when reading of the ridiculous war which has broken out in the Crimea. My cousin Florence Nightingale has been sponsored by the government to take a band of nurses to assist with the horrific injuries inflicted on the soldiers. She has established a medical base in Scutari and is being hailed as a heroine of the fight. I get these snippets of news from letters that Florence writes to others in our family who are considered respectable and from the newspapers who have lionised her. Ben has been at a loose end since leaving Cambridge and has become attracted by the 'grand theatre of war,' as described in *The Times*. However, something has arisen that could

Chapter 16

distract him from this folly. Uncle Jo, father's brother, has mining interests in Algeria and has asked Ben if he will investigate possibilities for investment there. Reading the newspapers, which describe the horrific conditions in Crimea, I am mightily relieved that Ben has agreed to take up this offer. The war has taken a disastrous turn and the number of casualties is alarming.

At last we leave Langham Place; father's carriage is packed tight. The staff gather at the door and wave us off with cries of Bon Voyage. We are all buoyed up, even Bella is animated; peeping out of her soft woollen blankets, she looks pale and childlike. The crossing from Dover is lively but one I have done often. Father reserved a cabin and we settle down to eat a picnic packed for us by his housekeeper. The coach journey is uncomfortable and, by the time we arrive in Paris, we are all feeling weary and in need of a soft bed. As a treat, father booked us into Le Meurice, a splendid hotel near to the Tuileries where we prepare ourselves for the next stage of the journey and enjoy the delights of French cuisine.

The journey down to Marseilles is quite remarkable. It is the first long train journey I have made and sitting in comfort while watching the scenes of rural France pass by outside the window convinces me that this will, in future, be my preferred mode of travel. Father reserved a private carriage where we could spread out to play cards and tell stories. At each small station people arrive just to see the train: each stop feels like a celebration. On departure, the driver gives an ear shattering blast of the whistle as we plunge under bridges laden with waving natives who are soon enveloped in clouds of steam. Despite the windows being closed tight, we arrive in Marseilles begrimed and smelling of soot. The station is noisy and full of coach drivers seeking passengers. We pile into a carriage and soon arrive at a harbourside hotel. Looking through the windows at the blue Mediterranean revives us and brings that first whiff of a foreign land. Rough seas keeps the boat in Marseilles harbour for a few days longer than we expected, but boarding on the third day our spirits are high and the crossing smooth. Hanging over the rails we wait full of anticipation to espy the coast of Algeria. It does not disappoint.

The bay of Algiers is shaped like an amphitheatre. A pale November sun gives a gentle rose tint to the white Moorish buildings scrambling up the hillsides decked with blue painted shutters. At the very top, silhouetted against a clear cobalt sky, stands the golden domes of two large mosques. We are delighted with the picturesque scene spread before us. The quay is crowded with shouting traders, all offering transport and help with luggage. Father speaks to a man offering accommodation and is alarmed to find that all the hotels in Algiers are full. 'Don't worry, Monsieur,' the man, whose name we later learned is Philippe, offers us a room for the night. We have little option but to accept. The room has mattresses on the floor, a sight which reduces us to hysterical laughter. Father, although amused by our hilarity, looks weary. Pulling out my guide to Algiers I can see that we are very close to the central area. 'I suggest we get some mint tea and pay a visit to a bath house.' Father holds up his hand. 'I'll join you for tea, but I intend to find a barber for a shave and freshen up.'

It is with some trepidation that we step through the towering archway leading into the Hammam. We are met with a scene straight out of the *Arabian Nights*. Belle, Nannie and I stand, looking nonplussed, when a veiled woman appears and leads us into a courtyard. The bath house stands open to the sky, green foliage cascades down the walls and below us sits a steaming thermal pool, surrounded by ancient pillars. The woman indicates that

Chapter 16

we must undress and gives us three light cotton robes. Nothing I imagine could delight me more than this experience, but Bella and Nannie are quite dismayed. Bella sits down on a stone bench refusing to remove her clothes. 'Look around you Bella,' I entreat her, 'There are only women here, they can't possibly harm you.' The veiled woman waits impassively. 'I'll go in first.' I pull my travel-stained dress over my head and slip comfortably into the cotton robe. My gasp of pleasure as the water closes over my shoulders at last persuades my hesitant sisters to join me. 'This is heaven,' I groan with joy. All around us, women are talking, laughing, and enjoying the experience of complete relaxation. After several hours we leave feeling rejuvenated and ready for whatever delights Algiers has to offer. True to his word, by the morning, Philippe has located a perfectly acceptable house available for rent throughout the winter. As is usual with most rented accommodation, it is sparsely furnished and rather musty. We open the windows and with the help of two maids, set about brushing the floors and dusting the heavy furniture. Father leaves us to our own devices. He intends meeting up with Ben, with the hope of repairing the rifts which have arisen between them concerning Ben's future career.

This may be the only thing we have in common, but Nannie and I share the same home-making drive. Under our vigorous attack of washing, brushing and polishing, the house is transformed and has taken on a more welcoming ambiance. From the maids we glean advice on where to purchase fabrics and set off for the nearest souk. Nothing prepares me for the visceral pleasure of entering an Arab souk for the first time. I am hit by a wave of colour which bombards my senses in a glorious cornucopia. This sight, combined with the delicious perfume of spices mixed with roses, provides a feast for the senses. It is impossible for us to communicate with the women traders who threaten to overwhelm us in their determination to sell their wares. The intricate designs and embroidery make me feel positively intoxicated and with a mixture of pointing and a few words of French, bargains are negotiated. We return to our new home following carts laden with cushions and swathes of soft muslin to dress the windows and hand-woven rugs for the floors. By the following week, we have flowering plants on the balconies and a well-stocked kitchen. While Bella is happy to sit in the sun and rest, Nannie and I go on sketching expeditions and collect cyclamen, heliotrope and violets to paint. Soon the house resembles a mix between a bazaar and an artist's studio. The only thing I miss about England so far is Bessie. I know she would love this place; I wonder if I can tempt her to visit?

Dear Bessie,

November 1856

I am sitting in the garden of our rented house and thinking of you my dear. The views are superb, swooping down the hillside over the roof tops of the old quarter, and out to Algiers Bay. In the far distance you can see the Atlas mountains, edging the horizon with a smudge of deep ochre. Some are already tipped with snow. It is testing my writing skills to give justice to the feel of this place.

Bella is recovering her health, greatly aided by the warm sun and dry air. Nannie and I explore the countryside, painting and sketching. Much as I love to be out in nature, the city of Algiers provides inspiration on every corner. The architecture is quite simple but attractive to our eyes. Smothered in mystery. We wake every morning to the sound of the Iman calling Muslims to prayer. Not being religious

Chapter 16

myself this does not tempt me, but it evokes a sense of ancient ritual which is intriguing.

It is difficult for me to communicate with people I meet in the town. My Arabic is non-existent, and my French is scanty. I really must do something about this. I would love to talk with the women and hear their views on life here. Walking around the alleyways Nannie and I are viewed with interest, but I rarely feel uneasy or in any danger. The population consists of a huge variety of disparate individuals brought here by the burgeoning French colony. Some of the military personnel are exiled from France, as they would not sign the oath of allegiance to Napoleon. There are Berbers, Turks, emancipated slaves and Jews who have fled Spain. A veritable pot-pourri of nationalities.

Father has seen a lot of Ben who is working to the south of the country. I do hope this is providing them with time to sort out their disagreements. Father is not a man to give up easily and I fear he will continue his drive to push Ben into the legal profession. Ben is an outdoors man, surely that is obvious to anyone who knows him. I am not a parent but strongly believe that it is wrong to dictate a son's profession.

Please write soon, Bessie, and if you can find the time, why not consider a visit? I promise you would be entranced. I have lots of secrets which I don't want to divulge in a letter but would love to talk over with you face to face. How is your engagement with Mr Blackwell progressing?

Much Love from your dearest friend,
Barbara

Chapter 17

I didn't mention this to Bessie in my letter, but one person in particular has attracted my attention since I arrived in Algiers. Previous to our getting here, father had made contact with some English residents of his acquaintance and last weekend they invited us to their home. The gathering consisted of visiting French and local people of note in the area, who give informal lectures. One such, who hails by the name of Dr Eugène Bodichon, gave an extremely interesting talk on the flora and fauna to be found in the surrounding countryside. Later in the evening our hosts introduced us.

What an interesting man! He is most intrigued to meet an English family and suggests that, if we are interested to join him, he would be happy to act as our guide. We all jump at the invitation, and the following week, together with the doctor and two servants, we spend a most jolly afternoon exploring the wadis and sand dunes to the south of the city. He is very well-informed and, despite his limited English, I learn so much from him. All the afternoon I watch him closely and I can say, in all honesty, that he is the most unusual man I have ever come across in my life.

This evening, while resting in my room, I draw some cartoons in which I try to catch his, how can I describe it? – strangeness. I'll send them to Marian in the next post and note on the back that the doctor will not wear a hat. This is because he says, the hair, if cultivated to grow like fur, is the best protection against the sun. While on our walk he wears Arab dress, a long, flowing burnous and stout leather sandals. I am bewitched!

Chapter 17

Eugène and I are now meeting daily and spend hours engaged in philosophical discussion, all conducted in a mixture of French and English. This is accompanied by a great deal of excited arm waving. He is a well-educated man, who studied at the *École de Médicine de Paris*. Public health issues were central in his studies and, when he graduated, he joined the medical corps as an army surgeon. We agree on so many things, not least the importance of nature and how necessary it is to make it a huge part of our lives. He believes that '*the naturist will be the theologian of the future.*' It is becoming clear that Eugène and I want to become more closely acquainted and, needless to say, a flurry of alarm is spreading through the family like wildfire.

I find it thrilling to meet another human being who has the same passion for the natural world that I enjoy. Here is a man who gathers flowers daily. Who, accompanied by his tame jackal, walks twenty miles to hear the hyenas laugh and, watch the sun set over the desert. These attributes are often considered feminine, but he is super male and powerful. I am not a tiny creature by any means, but Eugène can carry me across a river in flood. He is forty-six but shows no signs of ageing. His hair is black and thick, a tall man. Some people think he is ugly, but I think he is the handsomest and most fascinating man I have ever had the pleasure to meet.

Bessie is arriving next week on the post boat from Marseilles. I just cannot wait to introduce her to Eugène. We've been in Algiers for over three months now. I can see that the holiday has done Bella the world of good. She walks every day and it seems that her anxiety has diminished. Nannie has fallen totally in love with Algiers and is intending to stay when we leave. I can see that she doesn't share my affection for Eugène and makes little secret of the fact. As usual, we argue and get quite irritated with one another. I also have some opposition from Ben. In fact, quite violent arguments erupt, particularly when I find out that he had made enquiries through the French authorities concerning Eugène's background and character. How impertinent! I can assure him that Eugène's credentials are excellent. He is a descendant of an old Breton family, Bonapartist on his father's side and Royalist and Catholic on his mother's. None of this is of the least importance to me. Ben paints Eugène as an eccentric nonconformist who would never fit into English society, and is casting aspersions as to his intentions. Quite what he means by this I have no idea. If he imagines that Eugène is a fortune hunter, then he is far from the truth. Maybe they are still worried after my experience with John Chapman. The two men could not be more different. Eugène is without pretensions and has little or no interest in material matters. I find it incomprehensible that Ben is making such a fuss and exerting considerable influence on father, from whom I would have expected a more liberal attitude. But apparently not. Maybe liberal attitudes shrivel when applied to daughters.

I feel that everyone in the family is in league against me, apart from Bella. This is very upsetting but I remain determined that I will not be dictated to. I know that there are aspects to Eugène's nature and beliefs that some people might find worrying. For instance, he is considered to be a subversive in France. This is mainly due to a book he wrote called *De l'Humanité*, which is banned. The book puts forward the argument that Napoleon, while purporting to fight for liberty and equality, in fact, suppressed them. Eugène's whole being is committed to meritocracy and public health, so similar to my own, and, I should have thought, father's political standpoint.

Chapter 17

Bessie stays for two weeks. It is wonderful to spend time with her and she enjoys the countryside outside Algiers as much as I do. During her visit the subject of my relationship with Eugène comes up many times. We try to find common ground, but Bessie is determined to stay on the fence, and respects my right to make my own decisions. Her engagement is progressing at, one could say, a snail-like pace. Now back in England she is, as ever, very busy with social work. Mr Blackwell does little to impede this. In her last letter she describes a meeting with Matilda Hayes, a woman with a colourful reputation, and has discussed with her our idea of starting a feminist journal. Even though I will be absent for a while, I want to keep in close contact with my friends in London and Hastings. I like the idea of a feminist journal and intend to support it when I return. In the meantime I continue to write articles and pamphlets. There is a good postal service between Algiers and London, and I am eternally grateful to William Ransom; his newspaper, the *Hastings and St. Leonards News,* has given me a voice. I still write under a pen-name but at least my views are heard. My last article, *The Education of Woman,* caused quite a stir.

During Bessie's visit we write an article called, '*An Englishwoman's Notion of Algiers.*' I do three illustrations and it is published in the *Illustrated Times*. Bessie suggests that we open a shop in London and sell books, papers, stationery, etc. This would give me an excellent outlet for my publications but I can see that most of the work will fall on Bessie's shoulders. Since the success of our article in the *Illustrated Times* we have made some enquiries about setting up *The English Women's Journal*. With a viable outlet, from which we can sell, I am convinced this could be a profitable undertaking.

It has become a habit to walk with Eugène in the evenings. We both enjoy the opportunity to be alone together. Last evening's walk is one I will remember forever. A well-used mule path takes us away from the town and within a short time we reach a winding track leading us up into the sand dunes. Eugène carried a rush mat to sit on, a basket containing glasses and a chilled bottle of wine. This is unusual.

Sitting alone in the wind-sculpted dunes, silence cocoons us as a soft breeze ruffles our clothes. Streaks of violet touch the far hills, beyond which lies a desert wilderness. We watch in awe as the sun sinks low in the sky, blood red. Without warning Eugène softly says the words, 'Barbara, can we marry? I wish for you to be my wife.' A deep stillness washes over me. Without hesitation I reply. 'I want you as my husband, Eugène.' Later, I explain to Eugène, that it is usual in our culture to make a request for my hand in marriage to my father and warn that his reaction will likely be negative. As I foresee, this is the case.

Many nights of heated discussion follow Eugène's proposal. Eventually father capitulates. It would be untrue to say that he gives us his blessing, but as I am now thirty years of age, long past the age of consent, he has no grounds on which to forbid the marriage. Each day, or so it seems, I am approached by someone in the family or someone the family has co-opted, who wants to discuss my decision to marry Eugène. They make little attempt to cover their disapproval, and I have yet to discover exactly of what it is they disapprove. Possibly it's because Eugène is not British. All I can say is that their determination to find evidence against him strengthens my desire to marry him, despite all opposition. They will not break me.

What is happening to my lovely liberal family, that

Chapter 17

they behave like patriarchal tyrants? To my absolute horror, Ben has now fallen out with Bella over this matter. I cannot describe how it disturbs me that, far from being pleased that I have found a man with whom I can share my life, the family seems set on destroying my one chance of happiness. I find it difficult and embarrassing to discuss this situation with Eugène, but to his credit he seems determined to ignore the chill and we continue to enjoy each other's company.

Chapter 18

In an effort to calm this volatile situation Eugène agrees to return to London with the family in May. He's not invited to stay at Blandford Square but has found rooms in Paddington, as dismal a place as one can imagine after sunlit Algiers. This snub, I am convinced, is an effort to dampen Eugène's desire to become my husband. I try to shield him as much as possible from the froideur which surrounds our attempts to integrate into the wider family. I intend to organise all manner of treats on our return.

Thankfully, I have some friends who are welcoming and able to accommodate Eugène's natural eccentricity. The Sunday after we return to England, Marian and George Lewes invites us for lunch at their house in Richmond; what a lovely couple they are. I have no doubt that they have experienced social ostracism and disapproval due to their unmarried state. It gives one a measure of the narrow spite which ripples beneath the surface, from people who, should the truth be known, are themselves far from flawless.

After hearing our news, they give us their blessing and will attend the wedding, much to my relief. It will be a quiet affair. Most members of the extended family decline invitations but, true to their abiding loyalty, Aunt Ju and Aunt Dolly are standing by me. This day, which I always imagined would be joyous, is destined to be restrained. We continue to have good wishes from many friends, but my family remain grudging and convinced that I am making the biggest mistake of my life.

The more time Eugène and I spend together the surer I become that we will form a solid bond. I am the very

Chapter 18

opposite to him in temperament, but not in values. I fully understand why people find it hard to read us. After all, I am a middle-class English woman and he, despite his French origin, is deeply immersed in Algerian culture. That in itself is a challenging mix. A large part of me delights in the differences between us and the disquiet it evokes in the more stuffy family members.

We arrange for our marriage to take place in July at the Unitarian Chapel in Portland Street. Father and Ben will witness the marriage, no doubt with heavy hearts. I am no longer in the bloom of youth and chose a simple ivory silk wedding dress, cut on classic lines. My veil is of Honiton lace and I will carry a spray of purple and white lilac. Aunt Dolly has given me green ribbons as a wedding gift, which I shall weave into my hair.

At last the big day arrives. When I walk down the aisle on father's arm and see Eugène waiting for me, my heart leaps. He looks magnificent in a grey tailored morning suit, set off by a richly embroidered waistcoat especially made for him in Algiers. In his buttonhole he wears a purple Iris.

The ceremony passes in a blur. There are too many pockets of tension, too many pin-pricks of sadness. How I wish mother could have been there. I cannot begin to imagine what she would make of it all, but I like to think she would support me. When I write, 'Artist', on the marriage certificate, in a clear bold hand, I feel her presence and a strong sense of justification. My paintings are now exhibited by the Royal Society of British Artists and in the Crystal Palace Exhibitions. I can only hope that they will sell in large numbers; this will help to validate my work and supplement our somewhat depleted incomes.

I cannot say that the wedding or the formal dinner which followed are celebratory affairs, but for both of us the day has a profound significance. We are now joined by law and will endeavour to stand side by side through whatever life throws at us.

In a final attempt to protect me, as he saw it, father puts my assets in trust, with the stated caveat that I should use the income from my shares independently and exclusively of the said Dr. Eugène Bodichon. Any children of the marriage will benefit from the trust and, should there be no children, my assets will go to my sisters. This action means that I have less financial autonomy than I had at twenty-one years of age.

As a wedding present father made the Blandford Square house over to me to ensure that I have a London address. All of these legal manoeuvres leave me feeling frustrated. It appears that father is in favour of women's emancipation, but only on the condition that they conform to the old adage: that men hold the purse strings. I find this all very hard to swallow and the insult, indirectly aimed at Eugène, is humiliating.

Chapter 19

For the past three months we have been living in Blandford Square and are planning an extended honeymoon in America. This venture will give us uninterrupted time, far away from prying eyes. Our married life starts under the full gaze of friends and family, with which we are not altogether comfortable. Father tries to establish a closer rapport with Eugène but I can see that he still finds him an oddity and, of course, the gulf in language prevents any fluent discourse. Ben is noticeable by his absence and I've given up any hope that we will, once again, be a close and loving family. I am trying with every avenue at my disposal to make Eugène feel content in this country, but despite my efforts, it is proving to be a difficult task. The cultural differences seem insurmountable. I can see that my life before marriage was completely consumed by art and striving to establish political reform with my army of women friends and supporters. Where Eugène will fit into this rather crowded existence is hard to see. He has no work to engage in, or friends in this country with whom he can relax.

To my wry amusement, some of father's family are thawing, I am now seen as a respectable married woman, no longer an illegitimate daughter, but somebody's wife. This is galling and I find their prurient curiosity as unpleasant as their condescending acceptance of my newly acquired status. Anyone who follows my views on women's emancipation will be aware that becoming a wife is yet another adjustment I have to make. I am now Mrs Barbara Leigh Smith Bodichon. Every name is a statement and each one I have earned. This awkward acceptance of my marital status is a conundrum which finds little, if any, sympathy in the wider family.

Despite these teething problems, I am determined that Eugène and I will build a life together which is unique to us. It will be embroidered with all the intricacy of a fabulous adventure. We will take a leap into freedom. I am looking forward to extricating myself from this tangle of social labels and familial expectations.

If this all sounds rather gloomy, it is a state of mind which rarely descends on me when we are alone and without the strain of social intercourse. Eugène has taught me so much. We have many intimate evenings when the few staff we employ go off duty. At these times Eugène loves to explore the kitchen and concoct delicious meals for me to enjoy. He introduces me to some fine French wines and teaches me to appreciate the French style of cooking.

Also, and this is by far the most precious, my dear husband shows me what joy can be found with a partner who is sensitive and understands a woman's body. Why has it taken so long for me to become sensually alive? I am learning every day to shed my inhibitions and embrace the idea that physical love is a natural and wonderful part of married life.

In the bedroom we talk without restraint and Eugène is most amused by a fear I harboured for many years: that I might become consumed by a craven sexual appetite which could dominate my life and distract me entirely from accomplishing my life's work. I have few female relatives with whom I can discuss such intimate things and, in retrospect, can see that I gather slips of information, or misinformation, with which I cobble together half-baked ideas on the whole business. My one unfortunate experience with John Chapman made

Chapter 19

me realise that human sexuality is a drive which, if left to develop without any informed understanding, can become a trap. My ignorance and naïvety could easily have been my undoing.

If I have one disappointment in our marriage it is that Eugène has none, or very little, interest in art. All of my efforts to engage him have been in vain. 'Nature is my life force,' he declares. 'I have no wish to imitate its beauty with a dearth of talent. You, my dear, have the eye and the skill, I most certainly do not.' I have no intention of becoming a silent, compliant wife, and as our love is built on shared principles, I intend to persist with my interests and political ambitions. These first three months have submerged Eugène in my English life with all its complexities and the drives which are a huge part of me. I hope that our journey to America will help us to find a way of being together in a life where all of our many interests and ambitions are equally respected. Maybe then we can find a way to bridge the gulf between England and Algiers.

Arriving at Euston Station, we are delighted to find some friends and a few family members gathered to give us a good send-off. Long distance train travel is still a novelty and we look forward to taking the train to Manchester where we change onto a link train for Liverpool. Both of us breathe a sigh of relief as the train leaves the station. At last we can relax, free of the need to be on show and free from the barely concealed whispers. I have no doubt that there is little expectation in the family that our marriage will survive. At this stage in our relationship I feel too sore to discuss the dislike and disapproval my family have for Eugène. To his credit he ignores the slights and concentrates on those of my friends who accept him and whose company he enjoys. The further away we have travel from Ben and Nannie, to name just two, the more comfortable we are with each other and the more determined I am to prove them wrong in their narrow-minded opinions. Viewing the English landscape through the billowing steam from the engine brings us a feeling of excited anticipation for whatever the future may bring, despite their cynicism.

When we arrive at the Liverpool docks, I experience a flash of déjà vu as we climb the companionway leading up into the steamboat. The last time I took this journey was twenty-six years ago with mother and father and little Ben under sail. How had mother felt, leaving her beloved country for a land far beyond her imagination? And now, here am I, doing just the same thing, but with a bona fide husband, and aching to embrace the adventure stretching before us. Father paid for our passage as part of our wedding gifts. Due to his generosity, we enjoy a small suite of rooms where we can rest comfortably during the voyage.

My childhood memories of America are scant, but I still retain a sense of being somewhere very different from home. The heat made a big impression I recall. For this trip I have assembled a wardrobe suitable for the Southern States of loose, fine cotton dresses and brimmed hats to shield me from the sun. These items of dress lie deep in the confines of our luggage as New York in December is bitterly cold. Before leaving England, I had a thick woollen coat with an Astrakhan collar and matching hat made up for me in London.

The voyage to New York is blissful. It literally carries us away from England and the confines of the family, back to our early days in Algeria. We enjoy each other's company and spend lazy days on deck, I sketch and

Chapter 19

Eugène reads his collection of French journals. The boat is stuffed full of immigrants who travel third class, all hoping to start a fresh life in the new world. On arrival in New York I find it fascinating to watch them as they stream off the boat, carrying all their worldly goods. I admire their pluck. To set off for foreign lands with little but the clothes on your back takes courage and a great deal of luck.

Chapter 20

We check in to the Metropolitan Hotel in Manhattan, also paid for by my dear father. Being the best watering-hole in the city, it attracts only the most wealthy, or those who have recently struck gold. Little did we realize that all this apparent material ease was about to change. Entering the grand foyer the following morning on our way to breakfast, we are aware that the atmosphere feels tense. Those self-assured men with whom we had mingled the previous evening, are now standing in groups looking agitated and shouting orders at the waiters, who scuttle off in search of newspapers. We discover eventually that, overnight, two large banking houses have failed and the New York Stock Exchange is facing a crisis of confidence. This information is overheard from snippets of talk we glean over breakfast and from glimpses caught of newspaper headlines. There is little we can do but check that our funds are secure and that our ongoing travel plans are still feasible. Finishing a delicious breakfast of pan-fried steak and eggs, we walk to Penn Station and make enquiries. 'No problem, Ma'am, the first train leaving for Cincinnati will be the day after tomorrow. I'll book you a sleeper.'

Having made these arrangements, we spend the day exploring the city aided by Jo McNamara, a guide procured by the hotel. New York feels rough around the edges: a city in the making. We keep to the main thoroughfares which are lined with impressive buildings, some in the early stages of construction. Jo is a colourful character who left Dublin to make a new life in America some two years ago. He explains that parts of the city are divided up between nationalities. This occurs when immigrants set up tents and shelters when they arrive and a community builds around them. For example, places are identified as Chinatown or the Irish Quarter. The atmosphere in these areas is charged with an almost anarchic energy. The streets throng with bustling hawkers, urchins on the lookout for naïve visitors and women ready to sell themselves for a pittance. Jo wisely skirts the perimeters; it is plain to see that the police have little control over the volatile residents. Jo explains that the police themselves are in some disarray due to a rivalry between forces, which caused them to riot outside city hall in the week before our arrival. Despite this, his dream is to join the police and he tells us proudly that his name is already on the list.

Our short stay in the Metropolitan Hotel is restorative. We thoroughly enjoy the luxury of hot baths and comfortable beds, but three days is enough. Not natural city lovers, we eagerly climb aboard the train to Cincinnati, looking forward to open countryside and clean air. Settling into our seats, our luggage stowed safely in our sleeping compartment, we see that every seat is occupied, and every tiny space filled with bags and packages. Amid a cacophony of blaring whistles and people shouting tearful farewells to their loved ones, the train leaves the station in clouds of steam.

We are about to discover that life is to become far less cushioned. Little of polite society exists in this transient populace and we find ourselves objects of considerable curiosity. Eugène travels in an Arab burnous, as he finds this mode of dress comfortable, but it doesn't lend itself to anonymity. When discovering that he speaks little English, he is left alone and the inquisitive enquiries switch to me. The ladies find my clothes and hat extraordinary, fingering the fabric and commenting on the quality. They make little effort to conceal their amusement. I have become used to this prying curiosity in England where, I must say, the frank disapproval is somewhat more disguised. My clothes are practical and simple, and I find it hard to imagine why women put up with flounces and fripperies, particularly in this challenging environment. My shorter skirts and sturdy boots aid my mobility, and my floppy hats are necessary to protect me from the sun or to keep my head warm. These explanations do nothing to impress my female fellow travellers, and the unwanted comments on my attire continues unabated.

Despite having booked a sleeping compartment, we arrive in Cincinnati exhausted and absolutely filthy after seven days. Much as I love train travel, the soot from the engine is insufferable, and the stink emanating from both us and our fellow travellers abominable. We take a short break in a decent guest house to clean ourselves up and for Eugène to find some warmer clothing. Tickets are booked on the *Baltic*, a Mississippi Steamer to take us down river to New Orleans.

It is now early January and the weather is bitingly cold. This is very hard for Eugène to tolerate and makes wandering around the sights in Cincinnati impossible. We are recommended to visit Shillito's Store. Its wares are advertised with the motto, 'Truth Only – Facts Only'. This sounds reassuring and after a quick foray around its extensive male clothing department, Eugène buys a wool fur-lined cloak. A useful item which can also double as a blanket.

The *Baltic* is a large and spacious boat which has plenty of seating areas where we can sit and talk to our fellow passengers during the day. Our cabin is comfortable enough, but during the night the temperature drops

Chapter 20

below freezing. Eugène's cloak has come in useful.

On the first day we strike up a conversation with two black women travelling to New Orleans. The oldest, whose name is Dorie, is a free woman. Her companion, Trixie, is working for her freedom. They speak openly and without rancour on a subject we find most disquieting. Apparently, Trixie's owner will sell her to herself for $60. This is my first encounter with a person who is enslaved. Her matter-of-fact way of describing her situation gives me much to chew over. Coming from a long line of abolitionists, I have strong views on the subject as does Eugène. We are, however, very aware that we are visitors in this country, and so take pains to keep our opinions to ourselves. There are so many questions I would like to ask Trixie but even the most innocuous feels too risky. I sense from the other passengers that we are already attracting attention by engaging with the negro women; perhaps even this mild contact is considered unacceptable here.

The first day aboard makes me aware of the complexities which exist in a society containing every nationality on this earth, or so it seems. It gives Eugène and me so much to talk about. Each evening we spend time exchanging the small experiences we had during the day while trying to communicate with our fellow travellers. Despite the boat being large, the upper decks are crowded, while the hold is packed with animals: horses, mules, cattle, turkeys – within a day the stench is disgusting. As we travel downriver the boat pulls in for people to disembark, taking with them some of these poor incarcerated animals. They are most often settlers who have set up small farms and purchased animals from country markets set up in the larger settlements.

Chapter 21

We have now travelled two hundred miles down the Ohio river and are stuck in dense fog: this has not been a pleasant journey so far. I amuse myself by reading and seeking out people with whom it may be possible to have informed conversation; unfortunately they are few and far between. One passenger in particular is causing me concern. He hails from Texas and, I fear, is unhinged. Addressed as the General, he is physically intimidating, nearly seven feet tall and strikingly handsome. During the long evenings we have taken to sitting on the upper deck. He often stands nearby, reading aloud his poems and letters to a small group of passengers, eager for entertainment. His intellect is impressive but the aura of aggression and violence around him is palpable. I confess to feeling nervous in his company and with due reason, as it turns out.

Eugène is the subject of much curiosity from the men on board. Many watch him intently but are loath to engage him in conversation. The General is well into his cups most evenings and, to my dismay, took it upon himself to assault Eugène violently on hearing that he is a doctor. Apparently, he was recently discharged from an asylum, considered to be cured. But now, able to imbibe alcohol freely, the General has once again become unstable. Admirably, Eugène stood his ground and threatened the man with a pistol if he would not back off. At this point the Captain appeared, accompanied by other passengers, who, to my astonishment, took the attacker's side. The Captain said he would put Eugène ashore if pistols are drawn before ladies again. No harm done, but it gave us a close encounter with the level of physical threat which can easily be aroused over trivialities. I think, on reflection, that it is Eugène's perceived eccentricity which inflames the Captain. The General, although not of sound mind, is obviously more acceptable on board than an odd stranger.

We leave the Ohio river at Cairo and join the Mississippi. The scenery is magnificent, with dense woodlands on each side covered in mistletoe. While sitting alone on the foredeck one evening and taking in this fascinating scene, the General comes up to me and says he wishes to apologise for his behaviour. At this point Eugène joins us and, noting the change in the General's demeanour, holds out his hand. 'I bear you no rancour,' he says, 'let us be friends.' After that we talk for hours and the General tells us his life story which is, as I expect, full of triumph and disaster. Later in the evening we are joined by a negro band. The music seems to calm the General who is now delighted with us. We celebrate our reconciliation by dancing two cotillions. How I wish all of life's difficulties and misunderstandings could be healed in such a pleasant and amicable way.

The river banks give us a sense of the rapidly developing country. Colonisation in action. Thousands of immigrants are making their way here with the promise of cheap fertile land. Starting out on such a life is never easy. I watch the men and women in the homesteads as we pass by, comfortably accommodated on our Mississippi steamer. They all work like navvies and their achievements are phenomenal. Out of the drained virgin swamp, they create houses which are strong and solidly built. Each homestead is protected by stout fences, designed to keep out wildlife and stake out the boundary.

Alongside the cleared areas stand barns, huge by English standards, which provide shelter for animals and storage for feed. All this activity is driven by the constant need to keep sufficient food on the table to feed their large families. The women fill their days with an endless round of caring for children, washing clothes, tending vegetable patches and preparing food. Some, I am pleased to observe, have pots of colourful flowers on the windowsills. Watching them, I am aware of my privileged life. All my material possessions just landed in my lap. These women are working alongside men and I can only hope that one day they will be given equal status.

Life onboard has taken on a rhythm unlike any we have experienced before. The weather is getting warmer, which makes being outside so much more comfortable for Eugène. Travelling with him is a joy, and I believe this to be a positive indication that we can find a way to live together. We are now well down into the Southern States and consequently the passengers have taken on different personae. Each day brings encounters with people with whom we have little in common, but who are, nevertheless, interesting company. As the sun slips down below the trees in the evening, Eugène and I love to sit and sip a Mint Julep.

However, it would be dishonest of me not to complain. The practicalities of travelling in such a fashion are often a source of irritation. It demands a great deal of tolerance from both of us. The food is basic and not always to our taste, the quarters cramped, and we have to share all toilet facilities. A trial indeed! I strive to embrace such challenges to my protected sensibilities and force myself to be innovative. My need to step outside the soft life, provided for me by my wealthy father, is strong. I believe I have an obligation to face the hardships experienced by others less fortunate.

That being said, I often find myself in conversations

Chapter 21

which test my ability to remain benevolent and objective. One such occurred yesterday afternoon while we were relaxing in the ladies' cabin, an area where husbands are allowed to join their wives. It concerned a newspaper cutting in which it was announced that a wedding would soon take place between a mulatto girl and a white man. An ejaculation of disapproval reverberated around the cabin. 'Is this a common occurrence?' I asked mildly, wanting to broaden the discussion. 'No thank God! Only permitted in Massachusetts and a few other states,' was the indignant reply from a woman called Rebecca, with whom I'd conversed pleasantly on other occasions.

This dip into a controversial subject was taken up by several men and women in the group and I heard a name I recognised, Lucy Stone. 'She was educated with people of colour,' I said. A snort of derision met this comment. 'She believes in womens' rights, voting and all that nonsense, and she's an atheist,' Rebecca snapped. A look of complete disdain distorted her otherwise charming countenance. At this point the discussion descended into a barrage of prejudicial views ranging from abolition to the generally held, ridiculous idea of education for negroes and women's emancipation. 'Do you not think they should be taught to read?' My straightforward question put a spark in the tinder box. A middle-aged woman who would not look out of place in the shires of England, spoke up. 'Take my word for it Mrs Bodichon, they will run away. In my opinion it makes them unhappy to learn to read. What use is it to them anyway?' Eugène and I exchange a glance and, saying our good nights, leave the group to take a walk around the deck.

Eugène looks quite despondent. 'This is so difficult,' I say, acknowledging his discomfort and not quite knowing how to manage my own. We'd had a discussion earlier about a book written by Harriet Beecher Stowe called

Uncle Tom's Cabin. I would have loved to have heard other opinions on this outstanding piece of literature, but thought better of it after I hear Rebecca state disparagingly, 'I hate that Mrs Beecher.' Eugène sighs, 'It is hard to understand why humans are so inhumane.' I tuck my arm into his and give it a squeeze. 'I think I put kindness at the very top of my chosen attributes, and you have it in abundance, my dear.'

Chapter 22

It is now early February. We reached New Orleans at last and decide to stay for a month. Hotels are not to our taste, so we've found two rooms in a large lodging house for the duration of our stay. The rooms are spacious and airy with wide verandas on which I can set up my easel and spread out my paints. This cannot be called a salubrious area; it's very close to the docks, but that suits us fine. I like to think of it as our first home. Eugène cooks for me. He has a skilful way of producing delicious morsels, which have included alligator tails, fried bananas and gumbo soup, all produced with little apparent effort. I confess to being a poor cook, this is an area in our marital relationship where we are happy to exchange roles.

Our unusual honeymoon is providing us with a novel way to embark on married life. Every day is different and in no way compares to life in Blandford Square. Our new abode is giving me yet another experience of living with Eugène; he is a most caring and thoughtful man. I feel cherished and loved. We have a sleeping arrangement which pleases us both and allows for romantic liaisons whenever the need arises. I find him so attractive in manner and appearance. He can't be more different from the men we spend time with, whether in polite society or in the rough and tumble we have experienced since leaving England. If I am 'cracked' then so is he. There is hardly an aspect of conventional life that he adheres to. He has no need to prove his masculinity by dominating others or make a display of his physical strength. These aspects of his character, I believe, help us fit so well with each other. I long for a child. Eugène would make a truly outstanding father, as he possesses many of the attributes of my own father. Kindness, and consideration for others is at the centre of their ethos.

Each day we go for a walk. This is not proving as easy in America as one might imagine. There are no signposted tracks as found in England. Eugène is a very strong walker and can cover twenty or so miles a day without resting; I also love to walk, but ten miles is my limit. We have now dropped into a comfortable routine in which Eugène goes to the area of swamp where I want to paint and then beats the ground with the intention of scaring away any snakes in the vicinity. When I am comfortably settled, he leaves me alone, while he explores the surrounding area, always carrying his Winchester rifle.

Sitting alone after Eugène leaves, the swamp feels alive. There is a constant hum of insects and strange creatures scuttling around me with no fear. The unworked soil has a rich, compost smell. It takes my memory back to my arrival on the Savannah dock at four years of age.

Those early morning or late evening excursions give me so much material. I have never experienced such vegetation. It is like staring into another world. The colour and texture of leaves and bark are all unfamiliar to me. Silver-tinted Spanish moss hangs from the cypress trees giving my surroundings a veiled mysterious atmosphere. In the early morning a soft mist drifts over the wetlands, touched with an apricot hue as the sun rises. The days fly past, while I am totally absorbed in capturing the changing scene before me. By the time Eugène returns the sun is low in the sky, casting a blaze over the water like molten gold.

Most of the people with whom I come into contact have little love or knowledge of art. They stare at my paintings and are pleased when they recognise something

Chapter 22

familiar in them, but have little appreciation. I find this curious as the trees and flowers are amazing in their abundance and I struggle to do them justice. Maybe a life of extreme physicality, for both men and women, does not lend itself to such pursuits, and it's only when some measure of security and comfort has been attained, that a person can indulge in leisure.

I continue to be an object of considerable amusement or, on occasions, outright disapproval by the women who inhabit the boarding house. They are of the 'Southern Belle' variety and spend countless hours primping and fussing over their hair and general apparel. When I return from the swamp after a day's painting, wearing my blue spectacles, muddy leather boots and large floppy hat, they snigger and make little effort to conceal their hilarity. One person who takes me as I am is Mrs Sillery. A woman completely at ease with herself, strong and resilient. She wastes no time in telling me her life story, which is a triumph of love over disaster. Although she is an American, her husband is an Englishman who lost all of his wealth through failed business transactions of one kind or another. While obviously living in circumstances far below those she was used to, Mrs Sillery now makes money through dress-making and any other respectable occupation which brings in cash. I have obviously made an impression as she often seeks me out and regales me with stories which I find unbelievable. One evening we are sitting on the veranda drinking mint tea and I admire her hair, which she wears piled on top of her head, secured by a braid of plaits. She looks delighted. 'Glad you like it, my dear, it belonged to my sister.' I look puzzled and she laughs. 'She died last year from the yellow fever. A lovely girl, the best sister you could ever wish for. After she passed on, I cut off her hair and made these plaits.' I conceal my revulsion at this disclosure. Keeping locks of hair, nicely concealed in a locket, has taken on another dimension.

Knowing Mrs Sillery, as I feel I do after a month or so, I can see that as an American she really is free. The society she lives in provides ample opportunity to accumulate and grow; a self-made man is revered. Land is freely available to those who can afford it and who are willing to work hard. In this country, there exists no social class of men with honours they have not earned and who are protected by inherited wealth. The social divisions lie between rich and poor and white over black.

It has taken me some time to recognise what true freedom looks like. Men are free here and celebrate that, sometimes in ways you wish they wouldn't, but women still have a long way to go as far as legal rights are concerned. Mrs Sillery is free in that no one will judge her by class; she sees herself as a survivor and as good as anyone. Even so, she still cannot vote and, of course, black slaves have no rights at all.

We are nearing the end of our time in New Orleans and I set myself two more challenges before we leave. I promised Aunt Ju that I would paint an alligator for her. Eugène captures a specimen and finds a way to tether it on the veranda. It seems I have set myself a dreadful task. I am morbidly obsessed with these creatures. While on the boat it was possible to view them on the shore, where they lie supine like logs, but in close proximity, the horrific idea that you are close to something evil can be unnerving.

Eugène often talks of his belief that the spirits of animals rise gradually into higher forms until they reach the spirit of man. This prehistoric vision before me, now firmly tied down, is most definitely in possession of a spirit. I sit very still, staring into its slitted yellow eyes. What kind of man will you become, should Eugène be

Chapter 22

right? My thoughts play into an overactive imagination and I can believe that I am in the room with the devil. Needless to say, capturing this spirit on canvas is too difficult and my painting skills fail me.

When Eugène returns my fears are confirmed. As he walks through the door, the alligator attempts to leap at him, but the tether holds fast and the creature bites its own tail, shrieking like an injured child. I find this difficult to describe, but there is something about the swamps of Louisiana which attack my soul. Somewhere between heaven and that other place.

Having failed in my promise to Aunt Ju, my second challenge is to attend a slave auction. I ask myself why I need to do this; I think it is something to do with the hypocrisy that we have listened to over the past month or so. I talk to negroes, both free and enslaved, but I have not met one who believes that it is good to be a slave. Many will laugh and smile and deflect but, when carefully questioned, the unhappiness is laid bare. Without exception, all the slaves I speak to, when asked, say they want to be free. This admission is only uttered with caution and accompanied by a plea that I will never disclose their words to a soul.

In my opinion, it is inhumane for a person, whether black or white, to be owned. During our travels we have spent time with some very kind people in the Southern States who are slave owners. Some wrestle with guilt and obviously battle with an uneasy conscience. These people allow their slaves to be educated and taught skills with which they can support themselves and thrive outside captivity. Others are blind to any awareness of their inhumanity. Their prime motivation is profit and the more slaves they own, the bigger that profit will be. Their bestial behaviour is concealed in faux beliefs, or a devil-may-care brutality which defies description.

Whipping and all manner of punishments are meted out with impunity. 'It's for their own good,' has became a statement I wish to wash from the face of the earth.

Chapter 23

I approach the Courthouse downtown with a feeling of dread, having read the posters that a slave auction will be held on this very day. As I cross the street, I hear the shouts of the drivers as they herd a large group of young men, women and children into the pens. There is an air of excitement, mixed with the smell of sweat, as people jostle each other in an attempt to view the merchandise. Many stalls edge the square in front of the Courthouse, with hawkers selling drinks and handing out pamphlets. When the first batch of men are brought up onto the platform, a roar goes up from the crowd. I feel the tension creeping through my body as the bids start. Not one person in the crowd appears to find this unpalatable. It is an event which takes place on a regular basis, this is business as usual.

I watch, feeling nauseated, as the auctioneer calls for 'lot' six. It consists of women and children. The first woman is pushed forward, a small girl hanging onto her skirts. 'Likely woman, Dora, comes with a girl aged four years and a strong boy age ten. Good cook, and healthy,' he shouts. 'Let's start at seven hundred dollars.' A man walks on to the podium and, without speaking, opens Dora's mouth, examins her teeth and, as if buying a horse, runs his hands over her body. Seven ten, seven twenty, the bids mount. Dora stands immobile; her eyes fixed on the floor. The buyer gives a nod, and then utters words which send a shiver down my back. 'I'll not take the boy.' A quick bargain is struck with the auctioneer as Dora's screams ricochet around the square. To my horror, she sinks to her knees and begs God to save her son. The crowd bellows and bangs the tables as she clings onto her daughter, tears streaming. The new owner grabs Dora by the scruff of her neck and manhandles her into a buggy. I watch, feeling helpless, as her son is dragged back to the pen. All my human and maternal instincts dictate that I should save him but how can I do that? The very idea of buying a human being makes me feel physically sick. I hurry away feeling soiled and desperate.

Our last night in New Orleans is spent discussing my visit to the slave market. Eugène had refused to go and is not in the least surprised that I found it to be traumatic. 'What did you expect?' he asks. 'These places are hell on earth. The very worst of humanity can be found there.' It's hard to explain why I needed to go to such a place. My conscience dictates that I should not avoid experiences which upset me. I believe I have to witness such atrocities in order to be true to myself. How can I justify living my privileged life if I don't truly understand the hardship of others and strive to bring about reform?

We are leaving for Mobile today on a steamboat called *Virginia*. I depart from New Orleans with a huge mixture of emotions. Maybe top of the list is relief. Open drains run through the streets and the stink hits your senses like a blast from hell. The east bank of the city is wild and full of extreme characters all, or so it seems, running away from something, be it the law, broken marriages or impoverished homelands. This produces a vibrant and fascinating population, but one that is on the edge; violence threatens near to the surface and can erupt at the curl of a lip.

Now on the delightful Alabama river I feel as if we are moving towards home again, going up rivers, rather than down. This sounds irrational, I'm sure, but it is only when you move away from someone or somewhere that you can see things more clearly. Eugène and I sit and talk this

Chapter 23

over endlessly. We are different in that I am an intensely social person. I love the stimulation of others through conversation, or sharing ideas on art, social issues, etc., while he is more self-possessed, and very caught up with his projects. His great love is physical exercise out in the open air, immersed in nature. I think this is where he feels most at peace.

This is the first time in my life that I have lived so intimately with someone. Of course, family life at home was intimate and close, but each of us are now treading our own paths. Bessie is the other person closest to me; I miss her acutely and would love to hear her opinions on some of the people we've met along the way. Much as I love Eugène's company, I get very homesick and, to my disappointment, receive few letters. I stifle the thought that I have been cast out by my family and, by marrying Eugène, they no longer include me in the charmed circle.

We intend to stop in Savannah. I have the address of the house I lived in briefly with father, mother and Ben. It was for a short time only: eighteen months, I believe. What a journey I have been on since mother died! I have so little memory of her, mostly gleaned from her diaries, but occasionally images surface in my mind and I can sense her presence. My belief in the afterlife is nebulous. While travelling through the Southern States, I have been conscious of the deep spirituality that supports many of the black people we have met. I can honestly say that some of my most uplifting times here have been in small country churches with a gospel choir, convincing me without doubt that there is another place: one that is waiting for us when we die. How clearly I can see that, even if this is not the case, the scorching belief that this could be true helps them to tolerate what otherwise would be an unbearable life on earth.

Chugging our way up the Savannah river, I once again

look in awe at the dense forests on either side of us and, standing on deck at night, the sparks from our engine give an elemental feel to our experience. Sad to say, my sentimental visit to my old home is a disappointment. The owner told me that Grace and Samuel left for Canada years ago, and no one we speak to remembers mother or father. As I stand before the house, I try to conjure up mother in my mind and imagine little Ben racing around looking for snakes, but the memories are obscure and tinged with a sense of loss. We catch a train in Savannah travelling north.

Chapter 24

I am reeling from culture shock. Arriving in Washington is like landing on another planet. We decide to book into a good hotel and I am aware that this may sound out of character, but I need to spend time reappraising my wardrobe and attending to my appearance. While travelling, I distanced myself from many of the white women I met in the South. I don't share their obsession with appearance and dress, being of a more practical nature, but Washington is a different matter. Suddenly I can see that my hair needs attention and my clothes are shabby and unsuitable. An exhibition of my Louisiana paintings has been arranged in a small gallery off the Smithsonian Institute; we will be attending a private viewing. Even I cannot turn up for that looking like an itinerant.

Suddenly I have surfaced. Galleries in Philadelphia and Boston have agreed to exhibit all of my paintings of the Southern States: I am delighted. Both Eugène and I feel full of beans and optimism. Maybe this also has something to do with a sight we spotted during our journey north, as we were rattling along in the train. Standing in the middle of a ploughed field was a white flag on a pole – the Mason–Dixon Line. This is the boundary between the slave states and the free. Perhaps it's my imagination, but the people we are meeting now are quite different, more open, more curious, and certainly glad to see us.

There is talk that my pamphlet, *Woman and Work,* is to be republished in New York. I will be interested to see what reaction it receives. Why it caused such a stir last time I can't imagine. Equality in education and work opportunities should surely be something all women can aspire to. Women need professions, of that I am sure. I want to be rid of the idea that women are only truly feminine when they are frivolous, silly and weak.

Following up an introduction through one of father's contacts, I attend a reception at the White House. A very mixed bag of people indeed. They range from diplomats and generals, right through to a moustachioed Turkish admiral. He looks resplendent in a magnificent gold-braided dress coat, decorated with rows of medals. and topped off with a red tasselled fez. Eugène refused to attend. I am rather disappointed as he could have made quite a splash dressed in Arab attire. I don't understand why he wouldn't come. His command of English is still shaky, maybe it was that, or perhaps he finds large crowds too much. I love it and feel quite in my element.

This morning I am attending a meeting of abolitionist campaigners. I will have quite a lot to say on this subject and will be interested to learn just how far their cause has progressed. From my experience in the South, there is still a long way to go before slaves will be freed, and not without a fight.

Our time in America is nearing an end. We still have people to meet in Philadelphia and Canada, but I can sense in myself a yearning for home. That being said, it only takes an evening, such as we had last night, to entrance me. We were invited to visit Lucretia Mott, a beautiful woman in every respect. Full of grace, is how I would describe her. She is seventy years old but full of ideas and enthusiasm for her causes, the most pressing of which is the Philadelphia Anti-Slavery Society. She has visited England and, by coincidence, met my father.

We discuss how women's emancipation is progressing in America. Her unrestrained and positive response is

Chapter 24

inspiring and leaves me in awe. To meet a rich woman like Lucretia who supports reform causes and who is still met with rotten eggs and abuse, is impressive. She gives me books and shows me notes from the lectures she has given. It puts the fire back in my belly. Eugène loved her instantly. Being a Quaker, she addresses him as Friend Bodichon and takes a great interest in his views on nature, while questioning him closely on his impressions of life below the Mason–Dixon Line.

We leave that evening feeling uplifted and totally stimulated by the open expression of opinions and the impression of people who really care about others, whether black or white. On returning to our hotel, Eugène prepares some tea. I note that he looks thoughtful and am not surprised when he tells me he has something on his mind. Suddenly he says, quietly but firmly, 'I must say this to you directly, Barbara. I do not want to live in England when we return.' This is something I did not expect. 'I do not feel welcome by many members of your family, and I don't think I could bear to spend the winter in such a cold and damp place.' After this jaw-dropping statement which he has obviously been preparing for some time, he sits quietly sipping his tea waiting for my response.

I had noticed that he is suffering from the change in temperature since leaving the South. 'What do you have in mind?' I look at him and see the determination in his eyes. He folds his arms. 'I propose that we spend the summer in England and winter in Algiers.' A ripple of relief goes through me: a compromise is possible. He continues, 'We will have to buy a larger house in Algiers, and now that the train network is working between Marseilles and Calais, this arrangement is certainly possible.'

We spend the night in the same bed and enjoy the

close and loving relationship we have nurtured over the past year. This journey has given us an intense and broad knowledge of each other. We have learned to live side by side, but separate. This is how I believe marriage should be. Knowing but not possessing; needing but not suffocating each other's development. Our love-making brings us such pleasure but each month I wait, and each month I am disappointed. There appears to be no answer as to why I am unable to conceive a child.

With some reluctance, we leave Washington for Niagara Falls. Father impressed upon us before we left England that it should not be missed, and indeed it is extraordinary. Crossing over into Canada is yet another profound experience; I see immediately that Eugène is happier here. This is partly because the French language is spoken in many areas, but also because he considers it to be a soundly moral place. All I can say is that the people impress me as being happier than in America. Why this should be is hard to tell. The population is smaller and I certainly feel that between religions there is more harmony and tolerance. Government is more prevalent here, as witnessed by the presence of community militia and soldiers, but we find this in no way oppressive.

We are now on the Quebec ferry on our way to Boston. The journey down the Richmond river has been spectacular, with blue mountains providing a backdrop enhanced by a dusting of snow on the peaks. I have to quell my homesickness and make sure that I fully enjoy these last few weeks. I receive a letter to say that Bella's health has improved and a marriage may be in the offing.

Boston is giving us a wonderful send-off before we make the long journey home. I sell two pictures in the British Exhibition and hear through the grapevine that *Women And Work* has created another storm in New York. I would love to have been there and joined in the debate. Who, I wonder, is causing the storm? For the life of me, I cannot understand why any parent would not wish to see their daughter educated alongside her brother, with the expectation that she is trained in a profession or trade. What better preparation for life could there be? There seems to be, particularly in the middle classes, a sublimation of women's natural intelligence, based on some perverse belief, that it is somehow unfeminine to work. Many women of my acquaintance have achieved handsomely in the professions. Florence Nightingale is but one. The need in society for trained nurses, teachers, doctors, watchmakers is acute. Once this blind prejudice is discarded, maybe fathers and mothers would see that a girl who is educated and trained for the workplace is given a gift beyond price. I see that this is an incendiary idea to many and my views are received with considerable disquiet, but I remain determined to fight for my beliefs until my dying day.

The lady artists of Boston are holding a soirée for me next Saturday and I can't think of a more fitting way to end our visit to America. Our tickets are booked on the SS *City of Boston*. This is a good time to leave as the heat is intense: the cool of England's countryside is a very attractive prospect.

Chapter 25

So much has happened in the family while we were touring in America. Willy, my youngest brother, married Georgina Mary Halliday, a distant relative of the Nightingale family. They intend making their home in Crowham Manor, Westfield, when the current tenant moves out. Bella has become engaged to Major-General John Ludlow and, I am glad to say, I will be there for the wedding in September.

General Ludlow comes from a long line of military people, but they fit in perfectly with our family, being enthusiastic reformers. When based in Jaipur, India, he successfully campaigned against the tradition of suttee, a horrendous practice whereby women throw themselves onto their husband's funeral pyre. Well done, Colonel Ludlow! Another triumph for the feminist cause.

I think Bella has made a good choice. He is a kind man and will take care of her as she is not robust; I worry about her physical and mental health. That leaves Nannie and Ben. I do wonder if Nannie is the marrying kind. She has really taken to Algeria and spends much of her time there. Ben is still fancy free. So ... the Smith family has taken on a different shape.

Since arriving back from America in June, we have lived in Blandford Square. Once again, we both feel on show and exposed to barely concealed curiosity. I am happy to say that we are now much more secure and able to fend off intrusive questions. To my irritation and sadness, some relatives have no qualms about hinting at the possibility of us starting a family. This discomfort helps to speed up our plans to return to Algiers and begin

Chapter 25

our search for another house.

I wouldn't be honest to myself if I didn't admit to feeling nervous at the prospect of splitting my life in this fashion. I have projects here which need my constant attention. If I am frequently absent things may progress without me. 'Nothing is constant but change.' Good old Heraclitus was right about that!

My travels in America have prepared me well for moving into Eugène's house. It is uncomfortable to say the least and I use all of my home-making skills to make it tolerable. Since returning, Eugène immerses himself in his medical work, and is in the process of writing several articles regarding the treatment of malaria. Together we start on a guidebook with the title, *Algeria Considered as a Winter Residence for the English*. We hope it may produce some income, as our resources are considerably depleted following the American adventure.

The English Women's Journal is now well established but I am not entirely sure that we are hitting the right note. I want it to be more directly political. That is the only way to make an impact. Bessie is not altogether in agreement with this. While I was away in America, a woman called Emily Davies became involved. She met with Nannie in Algeria where she was nursing her consumptive brother. Nannie introduced Emily to *The Langham Place Group* and I have a sense that she is very influential and ready to take over. I feel uneasy about this but really can't complain, as for six months of the year I will be absent.

Eugène has decided that he will not attend Bella's wedding in September due to work pressures, but Nannie and I will leave together within the next week. So much awaits my attention back in England: helping with Bella's wedding arrangements and consulting more directly with Bessie.

Nannie and I remain very different characters and yet there is a connection, which I suppose always exists in families with shared memories. She is in a deep friendship with a woman called Isabella Blythe. They are very close and I can see that Isabella makes Nannie happy. Quite an achievement! She is not of a confiding nature and the details of this arrangement are never discussed. I am only too happy that she is content. Nannie is not greatly fond of Eugène, and I decide that we need to separate our living arrangements as quickly as possible. This is something I will look into on my return.

We arrive at father's country house, Mountfield Park Farm, tired and weary after the long journey from Algiers. Waiting for us is a houseful of family and guests, all in pre-wedding celebratory mood. Father is sadly too ill to attend the wedding and is on strict bed rest. I am taken aback at the sight of my energetic and charismatic father lying prostrate, his face drawn and thin. On seeing me at the door of his room he rallies and holds out his arms. 'You're back,' he whispers. 'I have thought of you every day, my dear Barbara.'

I spend the afternoon lying on his bed. I have tea brought up and wafer-thin sandwiches to tempt his appetite. We talk of Savannah and my visit to the house. Thin tears creep down his sunken cheeks, but I manage to make him laugh with stories of my experience with the alligator. Not once does he ask after Eugène, but I make sure that he can see how contented I am with married life and the plans for our new house in Algiers. 'You must come to visit when you're stronger, the sunshine will do you good.' I stroke his face as he drifts off into sleep.

Over the next days, Nannie and I, helped by an army of

Chapter 25

servants, do a magnificent job decorating the house. It is filled with flowers and garlands and in the kitchen a feast is being prepared for the wedding reception. On the day, three carriages set out from two directions to Guestling Church. Bella, myself and Nannie in the first carriage, Aunt Ju and Aunt Dolly are in the second, followed by the Mountfield servants in the third. The lanes are lined with onlookers and when we reach the church, most of the parish is waiting to see the beautiful bride.

Coming from the direction of Glottenham is the Major-General, together with Ben, who will be standing in for father. In the second carriage is Willy, Georgina and Uncle Jo, father's brother. The third carriage is crammed with the Glottenham staff. It has been coordinated so that the groom will arrive just ten minutes before the bride.

The ceremony is sublime and the happy couple leave the church to cheers and handfuls of rice. Returning to Mountfield, we celebrate long into the night. How wonderful it is to see the family together, but how sad that father can't join in the dancing.

Chapter 26

I leave for Algiers with mixed feelings. The journey gives me time alone to contemplate the dilemmas my new life may present. One path could be to focus my artistic leanings on Algiers, and possibly form a colony of artists. In this way I can attract some of the bigger names in the international art world and thereby re-establish and maintain the contacts I already have in England.

Visiting London again after such a long absence makes it quite clear to me how easy it is to be forgotten and overlooked. My painting, *Louisiana Swamp,* is received with general acclaim and I was encouraged to approach Ruskin for his opinion. He is an eminent art critic but was most disparaging. He commented that it is not a subject worth displaying. The note which I receive later is damning: 'I don't like your *Ladies' Reading Room* either.'

This last statement convinces me that a male conspiracy exists to keep women's ambition in check. Craft is acceptable, but fine art, from the male perspective, is definitely considered to be beyond women's capabilities. There exists a snobbery and misogyny in the British art world of which I haven't been aware previously. Distance gives me clarity and it is obvious that I will have to work hard to make up the time lost while in America and Algiers. It is my friends that I'll have to rely on. We keep in touch through letters: they are so valuable to me and it's imperative that I do not neglect them.

Before leaving for Algiers, I meet up with Anne Howitt one afternoon in Highgate. Her sorry tale gives me some measure of the prejudice against women painters. Her

Chapter 26

current exhibition at the Crystal Palace was harshly criticised and some of the reviews smack of pure malice. She is distraught after having been, once again, rejected by people she admires and respects. Her anguish is given voice when she exclaims, 'Oh! How terribly do I long to be a man.' Having her work accepted for the exhibition had been a dream, but it was cruelly snatched from her. This makes me so angry. We have made such strides and yet far inferior work, produced by men, is lauded and given credit. Why is this credit never given to women?

Reaching Marseilles, I find a comfortable place to sit on the boat and re-focus on my return to Eugène. I note a lack of enquiries while in England as to his wellbeing, which is hurtful. I wonder if this situation is far more common than I previously realized. Families, at least in our level of society, go to great lengths to make good matches for their children. By marrying Eugène, I have avoided this manipulation and I can see that, for whatever reason, he is still not accepted.

Stepping off the boat in Algiers I determinedly shrug off my disquiet. Espying Eugène waiting on the quay, my spirits rise and we clamber up into the waiting carriage, already spilling out news and our pure delight at being together again.

Eugène has made enquiries about properties for sale in the outskirts of Algiers. This is a project high on our agenda, as his old house is too small to accommodate us, too uncomfortable and too close to Nannie. I have yet to discuss with him my plans for expanding my art interests into a more dynamic vision. A colony would certainly need larger facilities. I tell him of my anger and disappointment with the contact I had with Ruskin and about Anne Howitt's experience. He is very sympathetic to my cause and, with his encouragement, I set out to organise a campaign, all done through the wonderful postal service.

Within two months I gathered the signature of every significant woman known to me in the art world and write a strongly worded petition. The petition is delivered to the Royal Academy, an august establishment from whose portals women are barred. It is rejected within one month. The fury can be detected across the miles contained in the piles of letters which arrive in my overloaded Algiers post box. An explanation is demanded and received with much derision.

According to the Royal Academy it would not be acceptable for male and female artists to paint nude models in the same room.

If they think for one instant that this prudish statement will be the last of the matter, they are very much mistaken. We resort to subterfuge. Laura Herford, a fellow student of mine at Bedford College, submits a painting to the Royal Academy with the signature A.L. Herford. She is offered a place under the name of A.L. Herford, Esq. Caught in the act of specifically discriminating against women, the Academy capitulates. This success is met with huge joy and a large measure of vindication.

This turn-around by the Royal Academy fires my determination not to disappear from the London art scene and I set out to consolidate our success with an avalanche of letters to friends and family. I am here, I live in Algiers for six months of the year, but I will not be ignored.

As if to confirm this message, a huge piece of good news arrives in the morning post. Marian's book, *Adam Bede,* has been accepted for publication. There is a barb in this news however: she has made the decision to publish under the pseudonym of George Eliot. She tells me in her letter that she is worried that her book will not be read if it is known she is a woman and living in

Chapter 26

an unconventional relationship with a man who is still married. My reaction is, as you might expect, a mixture of delight for her success and white-hot determination to keep on fighting for the cause.

Chapter 27

April slips in with the news that father has died. *It was a peaceful death*, the letter informs me. I am bereft; one of my pillars has left this world. Eugène wraps me in his arms and rocks me like a child. He knows that nothing he can say will help. All day we drink mint tea and I regale him with stories of my childhood and how my father had always kept me strong.

One episode I didn't share with Eugène was my discovery of father's other family, and how it affected me. It's still too painful and remains one of the most devastating shocks of my life. My pain is all to do with deceit, a word I would have never, until that point, associated with my father. I regret that I am now unable to discuss it with him. Preceding this unwelcome knowledge, my feelings for father were of unadulterated adoration. He personified for me an ideal of how all men should be. He had been a link with mother, now albeit a slightly tarnished one. On thinking this over, I wonder if knowing that he was not perfect actually prepares me better for the ups and downs of life. He gave me unquantifiable gifts of enormous value: confidence in myself and sound political and social values, courage, and enough money to make some of my dreams come true. Uncomfortable as I am with wealth, I try to be generous and to bring about some improvement in the lives of people who are not so fortunate. All of these qualities he taught me by example.

With sadness Nannie and I leave Algiers to attend the funeral, which is to take place on the Isle of Wight; father is to be buried alongside mother. Since my

Chapter 27

arrival in England, Marian helps me to find the words for his memorial. As I stand by their graves, where they are together at last, I find some solace. It also gives me validation as a person, which is more difficult to explain.

Losing father has been a big blow to the family. Sorting out his affairs is taking some time, but it is been accompanied by a distraction. Bella is already with child and this news brings something to celebrate. The summer flies past, but my thoughts are now turning towards my dear husband.

Bessie is accompanying me on the journey. Nannie decides to take a detour around Switzerland and will arrive later. I always love Bessie's company and it is a long while since we've had such uninterrupted time together. We need to talk over what is happening with the Journal. We are still out of step on its fundamental message – moral or political. Surely, we can meet in the middle on this.

It is glorious to see the blue-grey coastline of Algiers come into view as we sit in the prow of the post boat. This time, arriving at my second home, has a slightly different feel to it. With father gone, a strong tie is been broken with England. Of course, I am still close to my family, but they are now all moving in different directions and I have my own life to lead.

Speaking of links to the past, it was lovely to meet up with Hannah Walker at father's funeral. She is now an old lady, seventy-five years old, I believe. She also attended Bella's wedding and we talked for hours about our time in Pelham Crescent and the walks we took over Fairlight. Hannah was my first mother substitute and, of course, she could remember the real one.

I find on returning that Eugène is gathering information on suitable properties and, after recovering from the journey which I find takes longer than it once did, I set out to take a look with Bessie. Nannie recently returned from her Swiss sojourn. She ducks out of this project altogether and I am not too displeased. She tends to have a different viewpoint on most things and that can be tedious. Maybe she will cheer up now that she is back with Isabella. It will be such fun looking at properties with Bessie. Eugène is interested but not excited at the prospect of moving from a house he has occupied for so many years.

The next day we take an omnibus out to Mustafa Superiores, an area I am told is one of the most exclusive in Algiers. It is strange how some houses talk to you and the very first one we look at does just that. It is rather run down and designed in the Moorish fashion, not at all grand, but I like that. It stands in the hills behind Algiers with spectacular views. We can just see the snow-tipped Atlas mountains on one side and the bay of Algiers on the other. The gardens are huge, wild and neglected; but can be easily tamed with some tender love and care. Father has left me funds which easily cover the cost of it all and after Eugène gives his approval, we will transform it into a home.

Unbelievably, post continues to arrive from England twice a week; I find this very comforting. I can see that spending so much time with my family during the funeral arrangements and tidying up father's affairs, has once more given me a voice in the family.

The next month is filled with moving into Campagne du Pavillon. This name is chosen by Eugène and comes from his original home in Brittany. I set to with Bessie, helped by our servant Hamet and two women from the village nearby. We lit a fire with cork and sprinkled rosemary on the floors. The scent is delightful. My intention is to have an English-style kitchen and Eugène

Chapter 27

plans to build me a small studio in the garden, where I can paint undisturbed. Apart from these two improvements, the remaining funds will be spent on furniture. The souk provides Bessie and me with endless pleasure, choosing carpets and hangings. Sadly, she will be leaving at the end of the week and I'll miss her company acutely. We make a resolution to write weekly and for me to send more articles for the Journal, which she's promised will be published unexpurgated.

All of this activity is disrupted by the morning's post, which brings a mixture of good and bad news from home. At the end of December Bella gave birth to a baby girl, to be named Amabel. But reading through a long letter I received from Hannah Walker, I see that things have not gone smoothly since the birth. Bella has suffered an emotional breakdown and has rejected the baby. It seems that she wants to move out of Glottenham Manor and return to Pelham Crescent.

Hannah says that Bella misses me. Ben is trying his best to help, but I have always been a mother-figure to Bella. At such times, my link between Algiers and Sussex is stretched to its limit and the miles taunt me like a reproach.

Chapter 28

Our life in Algiers settles into a comfortable pattern. Eugène is immersed in his work, and I am trying to find people nearby who are of like mind; so far, I am unsuccessful. There is a mix of nationalities in the vicinity and they are friendly enough, but I have a yearning for my old friends in London. I miss the frisson of intellectual challenge. Creative ideas are the stuff of life and continually bubble up in groups of people who are striving for reform and who are driven to question the status quo. So many of the expatriate French are shallow and not at all interested in art or any other cultural pursuits. To my discredit, my French is still at the infant school level and my Arabic is worse, certainly not up to any broad-ranging discussion. They seem to find me amusing enough, but overall I think the whole community find us a rather odd couple.

I decide to establish a weekly soirée for the over-wintering English. One couple who do sound promising are engaged in translating the works of Hafiz, a Persian poet. But the person who most excites me is a French woman called Madame Luce. She speaks fluent English and I invite her to join the group and give a talk on her work. She has struggled for years, using her own funds, to establish a Moorish girls' school in Algiers. This is a huge leap towards emancipation for women here: nothing like it has existed before. The French authorities make no effort to cater for Algerian girls' education in their budding colony and refuse to give her any assistance. Madame Luce teaches the girls to read, write and sew and pledges not to instruct the children in her own Christian religion. Despite this agreement, I am astonished that this is accepted in the Arab community. How clever she is to employ an Arab woman to give religious instruction! The wisdom in that makes my heart sing.

Eugène is aware that I am struggling socially, but there is little he can do about it. We talk endlessly and, amazingly, manage to communicate in our mangled version of both languages. I love him dearly, but how can I fill the gap which exists in our relationship? I am trying to find a way. I fill my days with art and working on saving examples of Arab crafts, which are in danger of being swamped by French imports. As part of this project I am drawing an exquisite piece of embroidery: this is a difficult task and does nothing to improve my eyesight.

Perhaps I have been rather spoiled. Growing up in a large and lively family provided me with lots of company and my friends more than satisfied my interests. I don't believe that love can, or should, take the place of work in a woman's life, but this is the situation I now find myself in: unemployed. I am engaged at a distance on the *The English Women's Journal*, but to my chagrin, Bessie and Emily are doing most of the donkey work. I believe that being a mother is a job of work. After all, mothers are providing future citizens who will contribute to the social and material fabric of the country. I am aware that such an idea strips the experience of motherhood, removing the intensity of maternal love, and making it sound more like a chore, but it is a highly skilled role. Sadly, this vocation is denied me. Each month I see the evidence that no child is forthcoming. Eugène and I mourn this loss, while constantly rationalising on how we must not let it dominate our lives. For me it is exquisitely painful and I have to avoid thinking of it too much. Meanwhile, Bella is expecting her second child. How can that be? She is frail and sickly, whereas I am healthy and strong.

There is no fairness in this world. Nannie presents me with another problem. She has bought a house next door to Campagne du Pavillon. This is far from ideal as she makes no effort to conceal her dislike for Eugène. She considers him beneath me which is ridiculous.

Eugène and I spend part of the spring travelling through Brittany in order to visit Eugène's family home at Mauves. We take the train and walk and walk. The countryside is unspoilt with rolling green fields, not too dissimilar to Sussex. As we stride up the steep tracks, we have plenty of time to talk. Eugène explains that his mother left the family estate some years earlier and a cousin, Amadée Le Grand, had bought the house, Campagne du Pavillon, and some of the land to keep it in the family. Emerging from a small coppice, I can see two lichen encrusted stone gate posts framing a long avenue of fine oak trees. Eugène stops abruptly; to my concern his eyes fill with tears. An ancient manor house stands at the end of a long drive.

As Eugène struggles to retain his composure, his voice grows hoarse with tension and he places his arm around my shoulder. 'I apologise, ma chérie; it is so long since I last visited this place. The memories are vivid, and some are not pleasant to recall.' We walk on slowly, Eugène drew my attention to small markings left from his childhood. His name carved into a tree; the remnants of a hut built from timber found on the estate. It is easy to imagine the young Eugène living here, quite isolated and totally immersed in nature. 'What can you remember of your parents?' I ask gently. Eugène has been quite reticent about his background, and I ask this question with care, not wanting him to feel that I am prying. He shakes his head. 'Not a great deal. My father died when I was seven years old, so I have little memory of him. Mother lived

Chapter 28

in this house for years with just the servants.' He glances towards the house. 'I have distinct memories of her from an early age. She came from a prominent French family who had business interests in St. Domingo, her maiden name was Antoinette Le Grand de la Pommeraye.' I laugh. 'What a wonderful name! Barbara Leigh Smith sounds bland in comparison.' To my relief Eugène smiles. 'She was a warm, loving and kind mother. Very similar to you, my dear. Sadly, after I left to study in Paris and later went into military service, I saw little of her. My posting to Algiers as an army surgeon made travelling difficult. Her religion was a great solace and although I didn't share her beliefs, she was tolerant and in sympathy with my values.'

All of these scraps of information help to fill in the hinterland of Eugène's life that I am slowly building over the years. His commitment to meritocracy and public health is closely aligned to Unitarian values and is one of the reasons why I feel in tune with him. To my mind, the tolerant way in which he manages the differences between English and French culture is to his credit. How dare Ben, or anyone else in the family, cast aspersions on his origins? There are more similarities than they will ever care to discover, if they look back far enough.

Our arrival at the house is signalled by the dogs, who guardedly watch our progress as we walk up the long drive. Amadée, Eugène's cousin, is standing at the door when we arrive. He gives us a warm welcome and instructs the maid to take us to our rooms where we can freshen up.

We stay for several days and I am impressed when Amadée's married daughter and her husband ride eighteen miles from their country house to meet us for lunch. The talk is mostly of the revolution and its aftermath but, due to my inadequate French, I am unable to understand most of it. Eugène explains to me afterwards that his family supported the royalists. I notice that he stayed silent throughout most of the discourse and he tells me afterwards that he no longer fits into this social environment. 'Near on six decades have now passed, Barbara, but it seems that every stone and every tree in this country is a subject for a bitter debate on the revolution. There was cruelty and injustice on both sides.' His face turns dark and troubled. There is no doubt that despite the welcome from his family, Eugène no longer feels comfortable in the country of his birth and Algeria has become his country of choice.

We travel on to Nantes to meet up with Eugène's friend Dr Guepins. I am looking forward to meeting this man who gave Eugène solid support in the past and a good character reference when father and Ben were intent on finding evidence to the contrary. He welcomes us with open arms, and his fondness for my husband is evident; a shared feeling which could only endear him to me. We stay overnight and enjoy an evening of delectable food and wine. His politics and values are very much my own. *La terreur* had been catastrophic for his family; some of his accounts I find hard to listen to.

This visit to Brittany gives me a greater understanding of my husband's character. I can see how his oddball nature was moulded. 'A man who treads his own path,' was how Dr Guepins describes him. How can father not have seen that Eugène would fit me so well?

Chapter 29

An idea is slowly forming in my mind since returning from France. It probably originates in Mauves when we were exploring the area around Eugène's old home. The countryside, so like Sussex, may have suggested to me that if we have a country house of our own in England, Eugène would feel more comfortable when visiting. The more I consider this option, the more certain I become that this will be a solution for both of us. After discussing it with Eugène, I send a letter to Ben, who, since father's death, has taken over the Glottenham Estate and suggests that I lease three acres of land on which I can build a cottage.

I wait impatiently for a reply and find to my surprise that Ben is happy to lease the land. Without delay we set about formalising the agreement. I envisage a home based on the lines of an old Sussex manor, not grand, but spacious enough for us to invite friends and accommodate our many and varied interests. I will need a studio, maybe upstairs to get the best light.

When the plans arrive from a local architect, we pour over them for hours. Like many manor houses, there will be no grand entrance hall and the stout front door is to open straight into the living-room. An image flares into my imagination. This room should welcome guests with a blaze of warmth: colourful fabrics for wall hangings, hand-crafted woollen rugs and our treasured books to line the walls. At long last my paintings will have a home. I do so hope our new abode will enable Eugène to feel comfortable and at ease in my beloved England. This project has found me a way to fill the gap in my life, and I dare to dream that with the new house, a new baby might just happen.

We moved into Scalands Gate in July 1863. From the outset Eugène is delighted with the location. He can walk in any direction for miles with our lively dogs and not meet a soul. I feel something settle inside me. We have found a way. We are very different and, of course, we have our differences of opinion, but for me this is part of the grit and challenge in our union. It makes me smile that we are both oddballs. Where is the wrong in that? We do no harm to people; in fact I believe that we do more good than most. So, oddball, eccentric, however people want to describe us, as long as we are happy, then fiddlesticks to them.

Our new nest is now complete and brings us much joy. The kitchen holds the lingering aroma of exotic spices from dishes Eugène prepares. The shelves are cluttered with my collection of Algerian pottery and all manner of bits and pieces we have picked up on our travels. At long last I have a place to which we can invite family and old friends and start to rebuild that easy familiarity I feared lost. I have striven to retain contact with them through frequent letters while in Algiers, but living away for six months of the year somehow detaches one from the swift current of up-to-date news. I've missed the casual conversations wherein one can sense the underlying drift of what is happening in people's lives.

Eugène, never a lover of London, no longer has to put up with it; while I can travel up weekly and stay for days on end, knowing that Eugène's many interests on the estate will occupy his time. A fundamental change is achieved. We've found a way to squeeze the best out of both countries and straddle the miles between Algiers

Chapter 29

and England. This is becoming so much easier now that the trains are running more frequently between Paris and Marseilles, and a regular train service has been established between Hastings and London.

Summer is now on the wane and, according to our arrangement, it is time to return to Algiers. Eugène leaves without me this time as I intend embarking on a short period of tutelage under Camille Corot in Paris. His work has interested me for some time and I can see the benefit from studying his technique which is considered quite avant-garde. In some circles he is described as the poet of the French landscape. Tonal contrasts rather than a formal drawing composition form the basis of his new approach and the effects of light on landscape and buildings are quite unique.

I enjoy the journey to Paris, and meeting Camille is pure pleasure. He emanates kindness and is full of jokes and anecdotes which put his pupils at ease immediately. From what I have read about him, he is very generous and supports many good causes in Paris, including one close to my heart: a day centre for impoverished children.

After spending a week here I feel totally inspired. His salon is filled with students and the atmosphere is uplifting. He gives me clear instruction on how to emulate his style. 'What I am looking for in a painting is the form, the whole and the value of the tones. The colour comes after.' I spend hours studying his painting, *The Little Bird Nesters*. It touches something in me. I love the subtlety and the way it captures his message. While there, I meet Charles Daubigny, a member of the Barbizon school. This school is based on the outskirts of the forest of Fontainebleau, and I decide to conclude my side-step into study with a short visit before I continue on my journey to Algiers. The school is set on the edge of the forest which has been left to grow wild. It is forbidden to graze cattle, light fires or cut wood. It has a primeval feel and reminds me of the swamps in Louisiana. Of course, there are huge differences in vegetation: the tall oaks are similar, but without the trailing Spanish moss and a welcome lack of alligators. I love the naturalness of it and, unlike Louisiana, I can wander safely with no need to beat away the snakes.

Once more I am on the train to Marseilles. My long journey gives me time to think about my week with Corot and read through the points I noted at the first meeting of *The Kensington Society*. I can't begin to describe the feeling of excited anticipation I felt when arriving at 44 Phillimore Gardens which is the home of the Indian scholar, Charlotte Manning. Seated in her spacious dining-room were a group of fifty women. Glancing around the circle, I register the thought that a more powerful group of women would be difficult to find. They were drawn from the fields of education, medicine and all manner of social reform. We set about preparing an agenda, which it is hoped will change women's lives forever.

Helen Taylor is a crucial member of the group. She is closely connected to a Liberal MP by the name of John Stuart Mill who, invited to stand for Parliament, campaigned on an election promise that he would bring women's suffrage to the attention of Westminster. This small nod of encouragement from the upper echelons set our dreams alight. I smile remembering that I campaigned for him by driving a carriage covered with colourful posters through the streets of London, accompanied by Bessie, Isa Craig and Emily Davies. Needless to say, Emily was concerned that our flamboyant behaviour might hinder Mill's election but, in the event, he was

Chapter 29

successful. The press were disparaging as we expected, but we are not to be silenced.

Sadly, my involvement with the Kensington Society is disrupted by my leaving for Algiers. I am determined to keep my voice heard and on my arrival at Campagne du Pavillon will post press articles in support of their cause. I am now writing a letter to the group promoting the employment of women and putting forward the suggestion to the Chairman, Helen Taylor, that we should do something immediately about attracting women voters. Despite the excellent postal service, I find being away from the action very frustrating. Eventually, a letter arrives from Helen agreeing with my proposals, but suggesting that we focus on small things, rather than aiming too high and failing. She informs me that John Mill intends to limit his appeal to single women and widows of property, who are being taxed without being represented. He is busily gathering solid support from various quarters. From this distance, I can only lend my written support and promise to make a significant contribution towards expenses.

We realize that many people who would like to play a part in our campaign tend to shrink back when the blinding spotlight of the press is focused upon them. I can sympathise with this. Lives can be ruined and businesses fail under such harsh scrutiny. I only hope there are sufficient numbers of women and eminent members in society out there who are brave enough to stand up and be counted. I notice that *The Spectator* has already suggested that the petition has been written by a man. This is infuriating!

I remember my efforts, made several years ago now, when petitioning for *Married Women's Property Laws*, and how that fell at the first fence. But, putting those negative thoughts aside, we must persist. I am encouraged that things are gathering pace and we have collected 1,500 signatures.

To my irritation, I am now suffering from a bronchial condition rendering me unable to travel. I had intended to be back in London to accompany Emily and Lizzie when taking the petition to Westminster, but Eugène is concerned that I could develop pneumonia when undertaking such a long and arduous journey.

The following week a letter arrives from Lizzie describing the hilarious situation which occurred when they took the unwieldy package to Westminster. Apparently they hid it under the stall of an apple vendor while Emily went into the lobby to look for assistance. My name, 'Barbara Leigh Smith Bodichon and others,' was printed boldly on the front. I hear later that Mill presented the petition to Parliament, but has yet to receive a response.

Encouraging women to support the cause is more difficult than one would imagine. I can understand their reticence. If you are unaccustomed to challenging men, then it can be unnerving. The reality of giving us their backing could have a direct effect on their material circumstances, should the husband be directly in opposition to women's emancipation. It is hard to remain steadfast in the face of marital strife, or worse, destitution. In this respect I constantly remind myself that I am wealthy in comparison to most women and have been fortunate in a father who was cognizant of women's vulnerability. Even though I have been raised to think independently and protected from poverty, the vastness of what we are trying to achieve is daunting.

Male domination has been in place since the dawn of time and, in our generation, it seems they have perfected the mechanics of control. Many middle-class women are wilfully blind in my opinion and agree with men that it

Chapter 29

is unfeminine to want a profession, or lack the necessary knowledge to vote on matters of state. These women accept their unequal status and can't see that it denies them any chance to expand their horizons. In essence they remain child-like. The very thought of living with such a constriction on my thoughts and actions makes me furious. Education and getting the vote is the only way out of this cul-de-sac.

What a long road we have before us. I am mortified to hear that Margaret Oliphant, a writer in *Blackwood's Magazine*, dismissed the signatories of the petition as, '*A mere twenty unnatural women malcontents, who, unlike the rest of their sex, refuse to content themselves with their divinely ordained domestic sphere.*' My first reaction to this disparaging article was one of exasperation. The magazine was conceived along conservative lines, and it was expected that contributors such as Oliphant should reflect this. Even so, I am disappointed that she takes such a negative stance and is willing to print inaccuracies, purely to make her point. I decide to ignore this and pen a pamphlet entitled, *Objections to the Enfranchisement Considered – 1866.*

After this, I write to her directly and counter her assertion that women do not want to vote by pointing out that the women who signed the petition most certainly do and, what's more, are willing to stand up and be counted. Furthermore, I suggest, it should be considered desirable that women should have a role to play outside the home, including duties to parish and state.

I am gratified to read that my paper has been read in Manchester by Lydia Becker who runs a Ladies' Literary Society. She sent me a very positive letter and has joined the Manchester Women's Suffrage Committee. This is very encouraging and convinces me that we can only be successful in our aims if we are confident and strong enough to stand up against ridicule and derision. I receive a wonderful piece of news today: Elizabeth Garret Anderson has become the first woman in England to be admitted to the Society of Apothecaries. That is thrilling!

But I cannot ignore the fact that women's emancipation is a hornets' nest and this is made manifest in unexpected ways. A row has been brewing as to whether men should be allowed onto the Kensington Society Committee. I am for men being included, but Helen Taylor is digging her heels in and is against it. The press are scrutinising our disagreements, and the last thing I want is for our dissension to be blown up and exaggerated. The *Saturday Review* subjects John Mill to a barrage of disrespectful comments and suggests that, while he is a man of principle, supporting votes for women is a joke. Emily, cautious as ever, decides to lower her profile on this issue, as she feels there is a risk it will damage her reform platform in the girls' education field. A clear and consistent voice is what we need. A strong female voice which will be heard and respected.

Chapter 30

I admit to feeling at a disadvantage in our campaign. The six months I spend in England fly past. So many demands are put on my time: visiting relatives, catching up with friends and organising painting exhibitions. The time left for attending meetings and establishing contacts with persons of influence is severely limited. There is no doubt that Emily is emerging as Queen Bee. What am I to do? The causes we are fighting for are so important to me and once again I find myself pulled in all directions. Being frequently absent diminishes my influence. Thank goodness Emily and I agree on this matter. I will just have to accept this situation.

My health is not robust. There are days when I feel low. I comment to Emily, 'You will go to vote on crutches, and I shall come out of my grave and vote in my winding sheet!' She dismisses this dreary comment, as well she should. One piece of news cheers me recently. The French Gallery in Pall Mall accepts a painting I completed in Fontainebleau.

I am amazed to realize that I have now spent nearly a decade in Algiers. On reflection, I can see that the decision to build Scalands and the fact that Eugène is willing to divide his time between the two countries has, and perhaps this is too dramatic a statement, saved our marriage. We love each other dearly but being such disparate individuals with an endless portfolio of causes and interests to distract us, it is important that we give some time to each other. Had we had a brood of children, this would no doubt have been a very different relationship. Believing as we do that children should be given time and attention by their parents, I can see that we would have had to relinquish many of our more demanding interests. Hmm! Interesting to wonder who would have sacrificed the most.

We have some inspiring visitors this winter who are a diversion. Matilda Betham-Edwards was introduced to us by a local artist, Lady Dunbar. Milly, as she is addressed by her friends, is fascinating and speaks fluent French, which is helpful for Eugène. I suggest she move to Campagne du Pavillon for the remainder of her visit. It is a delightful time; we spend our days writing poetry and discussing projects. The time passes too quickly, and she returns to England. Before leaving I suggest that she travel with me next winter, when I want to make a journey down through France and Spain visiting places of interest and seeking inspiration for paintings. Thankfully my health is improving. Eugène builds up my strength with daily exercise and a diet designed to boost my energy.

I receive a disturbing letter from Hilary, a cousin on my father's side of the family. She has always harboured aspirations to study painting but, as is often the case with single women, she has been corralled into caring for an ailing relative. This expectation has shaped Hilary's life. Her cousin Florence made good use of her but was quite ruthless in dispensing with her services when they were deemed unreliable through ill health.

Hilary is suffering from a loss of faith and a confusion of duty between her need to study and caring for others. How familiar this sounds to me. I have thought long and hard on how to reply. To experience such a profound crisis is painful, and careful words are needed to provide a tiny spark of light. I can only be honest with her and state that I am far from knowing what or where my faith stands. I do not understand God's ways in this world. I try to do my best for others and remember one of father's sayings, 'Direct your thoughts and you will save much suffering.' I plan my day and if I am feeling very low, I dress in something cheerful. I remind her that she has many friends, and that they are one's truest support in such times. I advise her to find a project, one which focuses on her own needs, and suggests some classes she can attend. One step at a time, my dear cousin, this is the only way. Find the courage to take the first step, inaction is fatal.

Receiving sad letters is often the experience of people who live far from friends and family. Months pass and little is heard, and then the letters arrive bringing with them grief and much reflection. I had just replied to Hilary's letter when I receive the news that Hannah Walker, my old nurse, has died. This did not come as a complete surprise, Hannah being eighty years old. Reaching such an advanced age was quite an achievement. My mind swooped back through the years, remembering our walks on Fairlight and our explorations of Hastings. Some places are etched in my mind with such clarity: those smells, sounds, and the brush of wind on my cheeks feel immediate. I like to remind myself that these memories are always with us, and even though death is inevitable the times spent together remain and are a source of strength and comfort.

Sadly, I rarely see or hear from either of my brothers. They have made it clear that they disapprove of Eugène, and I've been unable to find a way to build bridges. Sometimes I despair of my family. Poor Eugène, try as he might, cannot do any good in their eyes. It is ironic that, due to her love of Algeria, I have seen much more of Nannie over the past decade. This proximity has done nothing to bring us closer or to develop any deeper understanding of each other. Nannie continues to disparage my relationship with Eugène and has little insight into how it works. All she can see are the negatives, which she points out at regular intervals.

Her friendship with Isabella is never spoken of between us. They live together like man and wife and anyone spending time with them can see that they love each other dearly. Nannie's feelings for Isabella are clearly sexual. She depends on her entirely for her emotional and physical wellbeing but, of course, this is never openly acknowledged. While travelling, I meet many woman who prefer to live as men and I have no problem with this. I believe that human beings are complicated and to attempt to put everyone into little boxes complete with labels, is ridiculous. This liberal idea does not apply to Nannie. She lives in her bubble with Isabella and feels entitled to criticise anyone and everything with impunity. When they are apart, this trait becomes even more pronounced. Should we find ourselves together in England without our partners, she feels free to tell all and sundry just how annoying Eugène is to her, and that she considers him mad.

I devise a way of keeping our households as separate as possible, but I continue to feel discombobulated and affronted by her spite towards the man I love. This is not a comfortable state of affairs. Eugène is able to distance himself and continues in his work and pursues his experiments in total disregard of the situation. His long interest in the medicinal properties of plants has taken a different turn of late. Eucalyptus trees have grown in Algeria for some years and he has become convinced that the oil they produce can be used as an antiseptic treatment for nose and throat disorders. This would be a breakthrough in itself but, in addition, he is exploring the possibility that the oil could act as a prophylactic against malaria.

You would think that Nannie, being a chronic

hypochondriac, would be interested in such a theory, but no. Eugène has planted many of these trees on his property which Nannie now insists will ruin her view of Algiers Bay. As they reach a height of two to three hundred feet, she may well have reason for complaint. Once more I am caught in the middle, not a comfortable place to be. None of my attempts to point out the attractiveness of the trees, their aromatic scent or the possible health benefits, convince Nannie that they are anything other than an eyesore.

—⟶•⟵—

Life takes an unexpected turn. For a month I am assailed by a dreadful fever. Eugène diagnoses typhoid, an illness which is common in this part of the world. In the early stages he fears for my life, but I slowly recover, all due to his excellent care. My throat is still raw from coughing and my dear husband concocts a tincture of eucalyptus oil, boiled water and a drop of pure alcohol. It is soothing and I find inhaling the aroma helps me to breathe more easily. He makes a good nurse, one that believes in fresh air. My windows are always open and the view over the bay raises my spirits. Each day he helps me to walk the length of my room and sit for a while on the sunny terrace, where he brings tasty tidbits to tempt my appetite. For someone who generally enjoys good health, I am profoundly shocked at my loss of strength, but each week I get a little stronger. My determination to beat this malady will help me return to my former robust self.

My weekly post from England urges me to get well and stirs my curiosity with current gossip. This is so helpful and Bessie often includes small sketches of places we've visited in the past, all aiming to amuse and encourage positive thoughts. I am most cheered by one I had forgotten from the days when we travelled together down through Germany on horseback. It depicts us galloping across a flower-strewn Bavarian field, our hair flowing free, skirts hitched. Out of my horse's mouth, she had drawn a bubble containing the slogan – *Votes for Women*.

Chapter 31

Four months pass and I am once again feeling strong and able to travel. Eugène books me a ticket on the Post Boat, leaving next week. I intend to meet up with Bessie in Paris and we will rent a chalet between Versailles and St Germain. I feel in sore need of her company. She has always been more generous than any other friend or family member in her support of Eugène. She may not be entirely frank with me, but Bessie knows more than anyone that I am a demanding partner. It would take an unusual man or woman to accept my somewhat erratic nature and liberal views.

―――※―――

Bessie and I stay at the chalet for four weeks. It is perfect for me and helps me find some peace of mind and restores my physical wellbeing. I've always known that Bessie is unconventional in many respects, and I note that she is besotted with Madame Belloc, from whom we are renting the chalet. I can understand why. She is a beauty and possesses a charm which appeals to both men and women. My dear friend has a long and troubled romantic history. She broke off her long-term engagement to Sam Blackwell six months ago, and now feels entirely free of entanglements. She floats (that's the only way I can describe it) between her attraction to women and men. She is entirely comfortable in the company of women and falls in love with them quite easily, but men are a different matter. She struggles, desiring the security and protection they represent, but is uneasy with any display of overpowering masculinity.

I have some sympathy with Bessie's dilemma in this respect, although it is not a factor that intrudes in my relationship with Eugène. He has no need to dominate or impose his opinions. He is happy that I like to run my life somewhat independent of him. In fact, the more I am able to accept this, the happier we are. Vive la différence!

Maybe my illness has made me blind to what is under my nose, but today brings an astonishing turn of events. Bessie announces, without warning, that she has fallen in love with Louis Belloc, the son of our landlady. I am aghast! This news totally tips the axis upon which I view my friendship with her. What can she be thinking of? This man is a semi-invalid, and she will need to nurse him, or more likely mother him, as he is patently unable to care for himself. I believe she is throwing herself away in this marriage and will have to relinquish all the interests which give her so much pleasure. I write to her mother and express my disapproval in forceful terms. I've no concern that Bessie will read this letter, as I feel a desperate need for her to know my opinion and hope that perhaps it will dissuade her from this course. We exchange strong words and she is in no doubt that I consider her to be making a huge mistake. We are leaving for Scalands next week.

I am feeling low in mood and hope I can regain some of the composure I enjoyed before this awful news struck. The journey back to Sussex is a strained affair. I send word to the staff at Scalands to prepare the house for us and intend making Bessie's stay as comfortable and interesting as possible. I'm not ashamed to say that it is my attempt at seducing her back into rationality. She is obviously upset that I can't give them my blessing, and we dance around each other, trying to find a way to repair the rift in our friendship.

Bessie leaves for London this morning, her plans for marriage intact, but our friendship remains somewhat

Chapter 31

shaky. In order to distract myself from this seismic event in my life, I set about inviting friends and family to a gathering at Scalands. The house is looking wonderful in the April sunshine and I feel the need to fill it with people and reconnect with my local interests. This morning I take Eugène's favourite walk down through the grounds. The trees are greening up nicely and I remember back to the early days of my childhood experiencing the excitement when the first signs of spring appear in the hedgerows. It always seemed like a miracle to witness the force with which a plant such as cuckoo pint forced its fleshy spikes up through the soil and, as if celebrating the joy of life, spreads its leaves to the sun. I write to Eugène begging him to join me as soon as he is able to leave his work. I receive a letter by return post promising that he will be with me within a fortnight.

The summer passed in a whirl of picnics and visits to London. Eugène takes the opportunity to plant out a herb garden at Scalands and includes many of his healing plants. He brought with him a eucalyptus sapling which we have placed in a sheltered spot. He hopes to interest the Society of Apothecaries with the research he has carried out into its medicinal properties.

All of my efforts to dissuade Bessie from her path into matrimony have been in vain. A letter arrives from her this morning to say that her intended marriage has been brought forward and a date is set for September. It had been planned for next spring, but I can see that she is under so much pressure, from both her mother and many of her friends, that she has decided to make a clear statement of her intent. I have given much thought to my extreme reaction to Bessie's decision to marry. Is it that I believe Louis would be unable to provide her with a happy and satisfying relationship, or that she will be living in France, and I'd see less of her? I come to the conclusion that both reasons are presumptuous and selfish. If I am honest with myself, it has to do with the fact that Bessie is my closest friend. We've known each other since childhood and, although I am married to Eugène, she provides me with a love which is rare, something between that of a mother and daughter. We love each other, and I know that Bessie would agree with me about that. All I can say is that it has been a painful time and I've needed many hours at Scalands, filling my time with riding and painting, to enable me to find some acceptance of the situation.

Generous action is the only way to reach out, and I offer Louis and his mother the use of Blandford Square for the duration of the wedding celebrations. The couple are to be married in the Catholic church, Old Spanish Place, London. After which they will take up residence in the St Cloud chalet, where Bessie and I spent so many pleasant hours together.

I find myself under pressure to return to Algiers. Nannie in particular is relentless in her nagging for me to return. This really is irritating and I ignore her wheedling letters for a while. Eugène will be leaving immediately after Bessie's wedding and it would make sense for me to return with him, but I am loath to leave and will hang on here, building my strength.

Chapter 32

During the previous month my spirits took an upturn and I feel able to make the journey, Milly Bethan-Edwards is joining me. We intend to travel through France and on to Spain, as I especially want to visit the Prado Museum and take in various points of interest along the way. During my illness my artistic inspiration drained away. I painted little but had exhibitions in Birmingham and the Dudley Gallery in London. So I can't complain.

I find Milly very open-minded and still the cheery companion I remember from last year. We are so different in many ways. On arriving in Madrid she insists on attending a bullfight, despite me telling her that the gory spectacle had made father quite faint. But she is determined and I leave her to it. Out of curiosity I visit the stables behind the Playa de Toros. A more dismal place is hard to imagine. I see that the gladiatorial drama may appeal to the basic instincts, but for me, any residue of glamour is immediately extinguished by the scenes I witness. The Picadors look half-starved, their costumes grubby and garish. The scraggy uncared-for horses bring tears to my eyes. Wherever I look, all I see is squalor and misery, for both animals and humans. The poor bull is locked in a dark stable and every effort made to irritate its senses to produce a savage adversary for the matador. Such brutality is not for me. Listening to the crowd baying for blood, I am happy to forego the experience and seek out a quiet bodega where I enjoy the warm sun and sketch the scene parading before me. Later, Milly finds me happy and relaxed, while she is most out of sorts, feeling shocked and revolted by the spectacle she witnessed. I avoid saying, I told you so, and wave for a carafe of wine.

We leave the following morning for France, en route to Marseilles, and the journey took on a magical quality. I love travelling: it is one of the greatest pleasures in my life. There is something about the quality of the air in Spain which warms my blood and tickles my appetites. Now, in autumn, the sun has lost its ferocity and I bask in the sights and smells only to be found in the southern climes. Fruit trees, laden with oranges, lemons and pomegranates are scattered over parched brown hillsides. Grapes and olives are ready for picking and the countryside is alive with all the hands that can be mustered. Spain is famous for its festivals and all this bounty will be celebrated with exuberant gatherings and copious vats of wine. I feel my energy returning and the long pall of sickness leaving my body. It is only now, months later, that I recognise how low the typhoid brought me.

We are now near Marseilles, where I intend picking up some post. We will stay there overnight and catch the boat the next afternoon. It is exciting to see a pile of letters waiting for me at the Poste Restante. I can see several with Emily's distinctive handwriting.

For some years I have been interested in forming a women's university college and Emily has made no secret of the fact that she would like to join me in this endeavour. Raising funds is high on the agenda and this is one area in which I can help. During the last six months in England, we both put a great deal of time and energy into planning and researching the path to take in order to have our plans accepted by the educational establishment.

As part of our thinking, while languishing at Scalands I put together a paper on *Middle-class Schools for Girls*. It is to be presented to *The Social Science Association* which is soon to be meeting in Glasgow. The paper lays out my wish to create for girls an availability of grammar schools, equal to that enjoyed by boys. Middle-class boys receive a vigorous education, but the small number of girls who attend school go to private establishments run by wealthy benefactors. I have visited such places in the past but found the head mistresses reluctant to engage in any dialogue in relation to curriculum or ambition to establish a clear path towards higher education. My guess is that the scope is very limited. One can only dream of a nationwide system of education made available to all classes. Meanwhile, I will focus on what can be achieved, and use for my inspiration a piece taken from the poem 'Philip and Mildred' written by Adelaide Proctor.

> *Darker grew the clouds above her, and the slow conviction clearer,*
> *That he gave her home and pity, but that heart and soul and mind*
> *Were beyond her now; he loved her, and in youth he had been near her*
> *But he now had gone far onward, and had left her there behind.*

This sad little poem captures only too well that for men and women to live and work together, side by side as equals, equality of education is an imperative. How lucky I have been in this respect. Father made sure that doors which were closed to others were opened for me and I have been able to pursue my artistic and political interests unhindered. Cambridge excepted of course! At present, an examination exists for boys to gain entry to Oxford and Cambridge and Emily intends enquiring if the same can also be provided for girls. Oxford has already rejected her proposal, but Cambridge is considering it.

All our efforts fired us up. Before I left, we had gathered together a committee, gleaned from the Social Science members, with the intention of sending a petition to Cambridge. This could be the leap which would eventually enable women to be taken seriously and our intellectual achievements acknowledged. The petition consists of one thousand two hundred signatures and contains the names of of the most prestigious women of my acquaintance.

After some investigation, we earmarked a building site in the centre of Cambridge and I embark on negotiations with a lawyer of my acquaintance. It is quite frustrating to leave at this stage when such momentous decisions have to be made and swift action taken. Thank heavens for an efficient postal service! I put my trust in Emily; we have different ways of going about things, but I find her to be an excellent organiser. Before I leave we agree that she should set up a new committee to be called, *The London Schoolmistresses Association*. This will give us some *gravitas* and a strong platform from which to negotiate.

I open the first letter full of excitement and anticipation but after reading the first line an unexpected bolt of alarm hit my stomach. Without any consultation, Emily has decided not to put my name up for inclusion in the association. Her letter leaves me quite shocked. Struggling to clear my mind, I re-read the letter and register her reasons. In the first instance she states that, as I have been politically involved in supporting women's emancipation, I may be seen as undesirable by people outside this movement, whose support she wants to attract. By people, I imagine she means members of the Cambridge establishment who have made clear

Chapter 32

their views on women's emancipation. All of which are negative. As if this were not enough, she outlines her opinion that the university would be more likely to accept the establishment of the new college, if it is nominally Anglican.

I sit quite still, feeling stunned and wrestling with a mixture of betrayal and hurt. Would she have had the effrontery to behave in this fashion had I regained my strength and been residing in England? It feels like a stab in the back.

Milly soon notices my change in mood and questions me closely. Should I confide in her? I decide not, she is, after all, a fairly new friend. I mention a headache, say I feel a little tired and set about putting aside my bruised feelings. It will be so good to discuss this with Eugène. Suddenly he feels closer, and remembering his constant strength and support, I cannot wait to see him. Giving myself a shake, I resolve not to let this upset ruin the lovely time Milly and I are enjoying together.

We spend the evening exploring the colourful sights of Marseilles, a city I am now familiar with, and enjoy a simple meal on the quay, enhanced by a good bottle of claret. We agree that Velazquez is one of the greatest painters of all time and discuss the awe-inspiring art we enjoyed in the Prado. Raising a toast to artists and their endeavours, I find that my spirits have lifted and Emily's unthinking action is put aside for a while.

The Post Boat leaves the following morning and after an uneventful but pleasant crossing, we arrive in Algiers relaxed and glad to be home. This journey is never an easy one for me. I notice the pattern of my feelings since living here that, parting from loved ones and my precious projects, is akin to leaving part of myself behind. I depart from England with a heavy heart. However, at some point along the way I start to look towards Algiers, and

England fades a little. I doubt this painful process will ever get any easier, but it is one I have accepted as a condition of my marriage.

Chapter 33

As we enter Algiers harbour, the evening sun dips behind the purple-tinted hills. On the quay, standing alongside the carriage, are Eugène and our servant Hamet. They look delighted to see us, and we are all in a merry mood while bumping along the mule tracks leading up to Campagne du Pavillon. Pushing open the heavy front door I pause and note the transformation that takes place following my arrival. I so enjoy wandering through the house settling my mind back into this other life. So many things have happened to me since I was here last, and I need to familiarise myself with the scent and feel of the place. Hamet takes Milly straight to her friend's house nearby. This is intuitive as she sees that I need time alone with Eugène. I only wish my sister is as sensitive. A sharp knock on the window announces her arrival, after which I receive a cool welcome. Within a short time she is complaining about Eugène, the eucalyptus trees, the dogs barking, ad infinitum. I don't let this spoil my homecoming. After all, it is such a privilege to have two homes and, much as I love Scalands, it is chilly in the winter.

After the first week I settle into my old routine of painting, walking and answering the mountain of post which has been neglected. Another letter in the pile I collected in Marseilles was from Ben, to let me know that Aunt Dolly has passed away. I am determined not to let this upset me and will cheer myself up by remembering our good times together. According to Ben's letter, she died peacefully in her sleep after a short illness and, living well past her three score years and ten, had had a long and happy life. She was my last direct link with mother. Her kindness and gentle guidance, together with Aunt Ju, gave me the care I needed during my early years and adolescence. As usual there are questions I could have asked, but which don't seem important when you are a child. For instance, how did mother feel when leaving her life in rural Derbyshire? That cannot have been easy, particularly when most of the Smith family did not accept her.

Opening yet another letter, I see that, true to form, the disagreement concerning the religious allegiance of the proposed college continues. Emily is well aware that I have always taken a secular approach in any previous establishments that I'd financially supported and would like to continue with this stance. Her allegiance is political, as far as I can see, and has nothing to do with her religious leanings. She assures me that no obligation will be put on students to conform, but for the purposes of negotiation, she feels it best to keep our religious affiliations clear and simple. All I can do is keep a high profile with people who know me well and make sure they are informed of my views. I have made my feelings clear concerning my exclusion from the committee of *The London Schoolmistresses Association.* She is yet to acknowledge this. After a long and supportive discussion with Eugène concerning this matter, I decide to wait until I return to England. Once back on home territory, I shall make clear in no uncertain terms my displeasure at her disrespectful and somewhat arrogant decision.

The following week brings a huge disappointment. A letter arrives this morning to say that we have lost the Cambridge site. This is a considerable set back, and letters have been flying back and forth trying to find an alternative.

Chapter 33

A month passes and, after tortuously long debates via the postal service, it is agreed that we will lease Benslow House in Hitchin, from where we can start a small college. This pleasant small town is between London and Cambridge, which will enable us to move in either direction when a more suitable site is found. We have appointed Mrs Charlotte Manning as Mistress at Hitchin. She has health concerns but will be supported by her stepdaughter from a second marriage, who will provide secretarial assistance. I am not finding this an easy period. Negotiating leases and practical arrangements by post has made it frustratingly difficult.

Emily has arranged for an old friend of hers to set about preparing Benslow House for students. It has been empty for some time and is in dire need of airing and a good clean. I arrange for the funds to be put in place to stock the kitchen and for suitable furniture to be purchased. It will be a make-do affair to start with, but all of the students are aware that this is a pioneer project and everyone will need to pull their weight and knuckle down. Emily is determined that, from the outset, we model ourselves on Cambridge colleges and insist on a high table in the dining room. This is ridiculous at this stage, but I have to choose my battles. I am borrowing and begging books for the library and sending some of my own pictures to brighten up the walls. Benslow House is due to open on the 5th October 1869 with just five students. Progress at last.

I am pleased to say that, despite all my battles with Emily, the news is not all trouble and strife. Bessie sends me a cutting taken from *The Spectator* reporting on the new college … '*The college at Hitchin owes its origin to Madame Bodichon and has been achieved with her tremendous energy, and not least her gift of one thousand pounds.'* This complimentary recognition helps to soothe my ruffled feathers. I long to visit. Most things are progressing well, although I note that there are some irritated disputes between the students and lecturers. I am happy to see that at the end of the Michaelmas term the first five Hitchin students attempted and passed their 'Little-go' examination. *Punch* broadcast the news under the headline, *The Chignon at Cambridge.*

It is now five months since I arrived back from England and I am struggling to maintain my sense of purpose. Having one foot in England and one in Algiers is demanding. The latter foot is not on firm ground.

The sad, but not unexpected, news arrives today that Bella, my sister, has lost her little boy, Edmund, at only four years of age to a lung disorder. In times past I would have rushed back to comfort her but, and this may sound selfish, I have few reserves of physical or emotional strength. I walk in the hills around Campagne du Pavillon trying to stimulate my inspiration to paint, and keep up with my post. Two things slow a complete recovery: the lingering effects of the typhoid and Bessie's betrayal, as I continue to see it. These two events have drain my energy and zest for life. Oh God! I feel so low. Things can surely not get any worse, I thought. Then in the morning's post I have a letter from Bessie with the news that she is expecting a child and hopes that I will be in London for the birth. I should be overjoyed, but instead a creeping wave of grief is threatening to suffocate me. I will die childless. I will never know that ultimate experience of giving birth and holding a child close. Eugène and I will never see the fruits of our love. I have never felt more alone.

I am bored! The thought hits me one evening while

Chapter 33

sitting on the terrace watching the sunset. I must get back to England and make my presence felt. Take action – even if it is the wrong course – action brings about distraction from gloomy thoughts. This has always been my advice to people who are feeling low. I smile wryly to myself, reflecting on how easy it is to advise others. Physician heal thyself. I walk slowly into the house looking for Eugène who is, as usual, in his study poring over research results. I lean over his shoulder. 'I know it's a little early, my dear, but I have decided to leave for home, so many things need my attention.' As so often happens with Eugène, I am relieved and surprised at his easy response and willingness to give me all the freedom I need.

Willy, my youngest brother, invites me to stay at Crowham for a few days when I return. I am close to Amy, Willy's eldest daughter. She is a sweet girl and I am trying to find interests that will expand her education. Lord knows I have sufficient avenues of opportunity, although I sense a reluctance in her to engage in academia. She is a talented actress and maybe this could be developed. I'll make it a project to engage with her and see if I can encourage some cultural pursuits. I pop two letters in the post, one to Amy suggesting that we meet in London for a few weeks before I travel on down to Sussex; the other giving instructions to the staff at Scalands to prepare the house for my return. There! I have made a decision and already feel much better for it.

Chapter 34

My arrival back in England is met with a post box full of invitations and welcome back notes. It is so lovely to know that my friends are still supportive and desire my company. Emily is the first to arrive at Blandford Square. I see immediately that she has something on her mind. I insist we order tea, but before it arrives she launches into a diatribe of critical comments about the Hitchin students. Apparently, a group of them decided to enact some Shakespearean scenes for the pleasure of the dons and other students, after their triumphant success in the Cambridge examinations. However, this is not the reason for Emily's distress. Taking a breath she gasps, 'They dressed in male attire, Barbara. I've decided to take strong action, We cannot allow this type of behaviour. It will ruin Hitchin. If this were reported in the press it may well be the end of it, our reputation would be tarnished.' I listen, finding it hard not to laugh. How ridiculous that such harmless enjoyment should bring such a reaction, to the extent of threatening the pupils with disciplinary action.

I pause, waiting for Emily to calm down. 'Would you like me to have a word with them, Emily?' I ask, using my placating voice. She nods, tears filling her eyes. 'You must lay down the law, Barbara. Good behaviour is imperative if we are to maintain high standards.'

The following week I meet the girls in the library. I see from their expressions that they are expecting the worst and I set out to put them at their ease. 'What a pity I missed your performance.' I let the words sink in and smile. The next hour is enchanting as I hear all

Chapter 34

about their exam trials and the joy of success. What a wonderful example they are, high spirited, curious and brave. Later I overhear a comment made by one of the students. 'Madame Bodichon was charming. A case of the prophet coming to curse and remaining to bless.'

Despite Emily's exasperation, I smooth over the whole debacle and for the next year the college weathers many storms, the biggest being the death of Charlotte Manning, the Mistress.

At last our patience is rewarded. Emily finds a suitable site outside Cambridge, near to the village of Girton. At the moment it looks bleak and windswept, but we appoint an architect and give instructions for the style of building we envisage: Gothic Revival. Emily and I discuss the plans ad nauseam. We both want a building which looks impressive, but how to achieve this with our meagre funds is challenging. Mr Waterhouse, the architect, has a reputation for watching the budget and is well aware that we will need to make every penny count.

I want the whole site to be surrounded by a broad belt of trees that will screen the grounds from prying eyes and provide a solid wind break. The area is large enough to contain sports fields and flower gardens and I suggest a cottage garden in which to grow herbs and vegetables for the kitchens. My aim is to create a relaxed atmosphere, where the students can forget their studies for a while and enjoy walking in the fresh air.

Emily is already setting about raising funds, and I contact Lady Stanley of Alderney and several others of my acquaintance who are likely to be interested in supporting our new venture. The quotation we receive from Alfred Waterhouse for the building work is substantial and keeps me awake at night. Marian generously offeres the proceeds of her next book, *Middlemarch*, as her contribution.

Girton will, no doubt, be one of the most demanding projects I have ever undertaken. Emily and I are working every day of the week, fighting on every front. Slowly the funds are coming in and within the next month the first footings will be in place. I am on the Building Sub-Committee and have no problem with this. Emily is queen of the committees and appears to have endless patience, while they work through the minutiae of detail contained in founding a prestigious academic establishment. My forte is organising the practicalities. For instance, I am now discussing with Mr Waterhouse the best route for the coal carts when delivering to the basements, and the siting of a hot-water furnace. I want the interior to have a feel of dignified domesticity, while providing the space that befits an academic establishment. All this will happen, I guarantee.

Weeks, months and the best part of a year pass. The student rooms are near completion. Each student will have two rooms consisting of a sitting room and a bedroom, with wide double doors between them. I am determined they will be warm and comfortable. All these young women will be leaving home for the first time and Girton must provide them with a comfortable and safe place to study and spend their leisure time. We will encourage students to bring personal possessions with which they can make their rooms feel familiar and help to assuage homesickness.

I am essentially a home-maker, and in order for Emily to feel comfortable I have earmarked a carpet and some bookcases for her study. She has reluctantly taken on the role of Mistress and, in my experience, people work best in surroundings which do not impose, but provide

Chapter 34

a space where one can relax and let one's mind go free. I'm not at all sure that Emily appreciates this gesture: she would work in a potting shed and not complain.

On another issue, I am irritated by an article published by some doctor in the *Fortnightly Review,* titled '*Sex in Mind and Education.*' It once again raises the spectre that women will be damaged by too much mental work and that it may affect their reproductive functions.

If there is one thing we are going to be aware of at Girton, it is the need to provide a healthy environment in which both physical and mental health will be addressed. This is yet another attempt, in my opinion, to weaken the drive towards women's emancipation. I will contact Elizabeth Garrett since she has the medical qualifications to counteract this ridiculous suggestion. I'll ask her to write an article laying out the comprehensive programme we intend to carry out in relation to students' health.

My dream is for the college to be full of highly intelligent women who will, quite rightly, have strong opinions on how the college should be run. They are calling for a student representative on the committee, and have suggested Louisa Lumsden. Emily is against this and has already caused quite a stir. I know that she thinks that I am too conciliatory towards the students, but I have my way and she has hers. Emily, in my opinion, is too authoritarian. This attitude is not conducive to good relations with students, who are perfectly able to think for themselves and this should be respected. Discussion and compromise is always my default position.

The more I work with Emily, the more complicated it becomes. When in Algiers last, I received a letter in which she was obviously struggling in her role as Mistress and saying how much she missed me. 'I need your advice Barbara,' she wrote plaintively. This is entirely in contrast to her behaviour when we meet, which tends to be overbearing and often dictatorial. What to do? I can only continue to be myself and keep a close eye on smoothing troubled waters.

Chapter 35

Today is 1st October 1873 and the first nine students are due to arrive at Girton. I am discomfited by the fact that this is not, as yet, the beautiful prestigious academic establishment we envisaged. The building is far from finished and they will be climbing over builders' rubble to get through the front door. Despite this rather makeshift start, I am sure that every one of the students is aware that they will be making history and, in order to do so, a little hardship is a small price to pay. I will ensure that they are welcomed with open arms. Our brand new fireplace in the entrance hall is functioning and a cheery fire will be lit to greet them along with a glass of sweet Madeira wine. Emily will need some chivvying to ease back on her need to regulate and see the necessity of treating the students like adults. I am sure that by engaging their pioneer spirit we will all achieve our goals.

Anyone who knows me knows that I love parties and I am using this to provide opportunities for the students to meet interesting people and relax away from their studies. Bart's Hospital is a good source and where I recently met a young man called Norman Moore. I was introduced to his mother, Rebecca, by mutual friends. She runs a school in Manchester which gives us much in common, and we correspond regularly. Norman is a great lover of the outdoors and a graduate in Natural Sciences. He has now moved to Bart's Hospital for his clinical studies in Medicine and Comparative Anatomy. I invite him down to Scalands for the weekend, together with any of the girls from Girton who want a weekend in the countryside.

The party is a terrific success. Norman brought some

of his friends and organises a ramble through the estate with the dogs. He proves to be a highly entertaining guest and his love for Irish music provides a great deal of pleasure and opportunities for dancing. Eugène, who is over from Algiers, takes to him immediately.

I write to Rebecca and mention the party and my hope that Norman will now be a frequent visitor at Scalands. I sense, although it has not been stated, that money is short in the family. On discussing this with Eugène one evening, he suggests that Norman may well be interested in becoming a tutor as a way of supplementing his meagre income. This immediately gives me food for thought.

I am of late concerned for my niece, Amy. She uses me as a sounding board for the trials and tribulations she is having with her parents, Willy and Georgina. They have lost several governesses due to Amy's difficult behaviour. I feel that she needs skilled teaching by someone who can inspire her to develop some curiosity about the world around her. One of the stumbling blocks I see is that my brother and his wife are very involved with the county set and not in any way interested in cultural pursuits or academia. Georgina comes from a well-bred family, some of whom are reformers. Sadly, she has made it quite plain that she finds politics boring and has never, that I was aware of, interested herself in current affairs. She makes little secret of the fact that she finds life at Crowham tedious and, although she has never said this directly, finds her marriage a disappointment. They have produced six children. One, a son, died in infancy.

I have to quell my irritation when Georgina complains about the children. How I long to have just one. From my viewpoint, she's has all the ingredients with which to make a reasonably happy life. True, they are not wealthy, but seem to lack the will or vision to improve their situation. I am quite sure she finds me annoying and makes it quite

Chapter 35

plain that fighting for women's rights is not a subject in which she wishes to engage. Such a pity! In her younger days we had a lively friendship. She joined my Folio Club and there was no doubt that she had a talent for art but, for whatever the reason, her interest waned. I tried to persuade her to visit Algiers, but she is reluctant and so I have given up. Willy claims to be interested in farming but some of Crowham land is marshy and he is defeated by it. In fact, I feel he is defeated by life and now drinks heavily to blunt the melancholy.

Amy is a real beauty, but I see that all they want is for her to be equipped to enter society with the hope of attracting a wealthy suitor. I intend visiting the family in the next fortnight and will gauge their reaction. Norman would make an ideal tutor. He has a lively mind and is more than capable of helping Amy grasp the basics.

Ben is becoming quite a person of interest in the press. He is now in Norway from where he is planning to sail around the North Pole and plant the Union flag in the ice. I am so happy for him. These past few years he has been unable to settle on any one project. The expedition will combine adventure and science, providing him with a challenge that will more than stretch his abilities. I understand that need only too well.

During this past winter I am aware that Bella's health is deteriorating. She has suffered from consumption for many years and the possibility of her visiting Algiers is discussed, to see if a change in weather would help. Sadly, I can see that it is now too late. On my last visit she was unable to leave her bed and is showing all the signs that her time on earth is limited.

I am now visiting daily. Bella loves for us to lie on the large plump settee in the morning room; Glottenham is not a homely, cosy place, but I've had her day bed raised, so that she can see out over the fields. Every now and then the General puts his head around the door and gives her a cheery wave. His eyes look rheumy and sad. I will miss my darling Bella; she has never enjoyed good health and this has curtailed her activities. But we enjoyed painting together, and I am closer to her than any of my other siblings.

Norman Moore is now becoming a fixture in our family. I am delighted that he is helping me with Bella's children, Amabel, Harry and Millicent; thirteen, eleven and five years of age respectively. They adore him and he keeps them amused with music, insect hunts and lots of stories. I am regaled with their adventures when I visit. I write to Norman's mother to tell her how grateful we are for her son's support during this anxious time.

All our care and nursing is to no avail: Bella died this morning. The General is heartbroken. The funeral is to be held in the coming week and Bella is to be buried in Guestling churchyard. I ache to remember her wedding, how radiant she looked, how full of life.

Eugène has now returned to Algiers, and I am enjoying a short time visiting friends in the vicinity before I also leave. I recently met a painter called Hercules Brabazon Brabazon. He is called Brabbie for short, thank goodness, and lives nearby in a village called Sedlescombe. He is very well connected with other artists in the area and, once again, I am struggling with that acute feeling of impending loss, before I leave for Algiers. England offers me so much. My family, culture, friends and projects are all here. I feel that I have exhausted Algiers, and can only rely on winter visitors for distraction. Sad to say, unless I am very lucky, they rarely supply intellectual or artistic stimulation.

When visiting Brabbie, I am introduced to a woman called Gertrude Jekyll. She is a garden designer and I hope will do some work for me at Scalands. We have seen one

Chapter 35

another at various houses over the summer, and I enjoy her company. I ask if she would care to accompany me on a trip and stay for a while in Algiers. I plan to travel down through Switzerland, Italy and southern France, visiting galleries *en route*, before making my way to Marseilles.

I realize that I rely on my English friends increasingly to help me tolerate winters in Campagne du Pavillon. In fact, one of my visitors notes that I need the company of good, clever people. Yes, I do! Eugène is a good and clever person, and a loving husband, but I need more, and I do not see that as a failure in my marriage. It is just a fact. I find it impossible to believe that one person could satisfy all my intellectual needs.

Gertrude needs no encouragement to prolong her visit in Algiers and her company certainly helps me through the winter. She is such a creative person and spends her time copying designs from dresses, embroidery and tiles all purchased in the souk. I talk to her about my plans for landscaping the grounds around Girton. We spend many happy evenings together, sketching possibilities. I doubt Emily will be interested in the slightest.

I write to Willy and Georgina this week suggesting Norman as a tutor for Amy. Before leaving, I discussed it with him and he was taken with the idea. They must be quite desperate, as they reply by return of post. They have already made contact with Norman, and he is to start at the end of his academic year, in just three weeks' time. I shall watch this arrangement with great interest. Amy is sorely in need of someone who will embrace her latent talents and help to channel her unfocused energy.

Chapter 36

I decide to leave Algiers early this year. These past few months have been lightened by Gertrude's presence and another artist friend of mine, Frederick Walker. Frederick paints in the style of William Holman Hunt and we spent hours wandering around the countryside. Despite my frustration with the place, I still see its beauty and it is inspiring to see through another's eyes. Frederick is very taken with the soft pastel shades, which can only be caught as the sun is dipping behind the mountains.

My main reason for leaving is the alarming letters I receive from Emily. She is exhausted. The last few years have been very demanding. The building work tested us both to our limits and, although thrilling, setting up Girton was far from easy. It has been galling for her that I was not there when she needed support, but I made it clear from the outset that this would be the case. Emily no longer wishes to be Mistress and has effectively downgraded the post, so that when her replacement is appointed, she will not be a member of the Executive Committee. By doing this, Emily retains her powerful position as head of the Committee. I am determined to be present when a new Mistress is selected because Emily is becoming more overbearing. This is not how I want the college to be administered. I need to be there and very present, to ensure that the next Mistress is someone who upholds the open and democratic ethos that I envision for Girton.

In one letter she mentions that one of our students has decided to move to Newnham, as Emily will not consent to her postponing her Tripos for a fourth year. Is this more

Chapter 36

evidence of Emily's inflexibility? I feel sure that some compromise can be found. Emily sees Newnham Hall as a rival to Girton. I refuse to engage in any resentment concerning Newnham, a college that was set up by one of our old tutors at Hitchin, Mr Sidgwick. There is room for both colleges. We must strive to provide the best education possible for the young women of this country.

Arriving back in Sussex is more pleasant than I expect. We enjoy a warm spring and the wild flowers are early, making their appearance in the hedgerows. This weekend I invite the most promising candidate for the post of Mistress down to Scalands. Her name is Miss Frances Bernard. She was brought up in diplomatic circles and possesses a willingness to compromise and holds a liberal concept of authority. Oh my, how we need that! All I can hope is that Emily keeps in the background and concentrates on utilising her organisational skills.

We now have twenty-three students. I suggest to Emily that Amy be given a place to study at Girton, but she insists that Amy take Girton's entrance exam, like any other student. This is an ongoing dispute and I don't press it as I have yet to see any evidence that Amy would be able to cope with the curriculum at Girton. She is nearing seventeen years of age and is still being tutored by Norman. Things seem quieter at home, so I assume they are making good progress.

I was recently introduced to a young woman who most certainly would be able to cope with the entrance exam and the curriculum at Girton. Her name is Sarah Phoebe Marks. Her friends call her Hertha, a nickname taken from a heroine in one of Bremer's novels. She is the daughter of Jewish refugees from Poland. Her father, an itinerant watchmaker, died when Hertha was seven years old, leaving her mother with seven children and an eighth on the way.

Alice, Hertha's mother, is a skilled needle-woman and supports the whole family with her talent. At the age of nine, Hertha was offered a place at a small school in Camden where she was taught French and developed a love of music. A cousin tutored her in mathematics and Latin, but at sixteen she had to leave school and work as a governess in order to supplement the family income. Through a friend she was informed of the Hitchin school, where she could study for the Girton College entrance exam. Initially Emily interviewed her but was not impressed. I heard of Hertha's accomplishments and persistence and so arrange a meeting at Blandford Square.

Sometimes things happen in your life which have an impact far beyond expectations. When Hertha is shown into the drawing room, I sense immediately that she and I will become close. Her face is lit with a lively intelligence, beautiful eyes and a bush of curly hair, which she does nothing to control. The very sight of her makes me want to sing with joy. We talk for an hour and from the outset I knew that this young woman will go far. She insists that her family's needs must come first and that she cannot jeopardise their livelihood in any way. I hold back, but want to shout from the rooftops: if we can't help such a woman, then we are not an establishment I want to be part of.

I write inviting Hertha down to Scalands, as I think this will give us some uninterrupted time in which we can plan her future. I suggest she brings some strong boots for walking around the lanes.

The following week I receive a reply bearing sad tidings. Tragically, Hertha's sister Winnie had been taken ill and Hertha has to leave her governess post to care for

Chapter 36

her. I realize that the loss of income is significant and immediately offer her a loan which she refuses. I then put my mind as to how she can work from home in order to augment the family income.

Hertha has excellent sewing skills passed on from her mother, and this gives me the idea of sending her an embroidery frame and the Arab embroidery samples I brought back from Algeria. With this, I think, she can make ready money and I send her an advance payment, with an order for the first piece of work she produces.

I write setting out my suggestions and initially Hertha is reluctant, fearing that her work will not be up to standard. Despite all her misgivings, it is excellent. I then promote her far and wide and commissions roll in. But the strain of caring for her sister and keeping up with the demand for her intricate and exotic embroidery soon takes its toll. Her studies falter.

I do not intend to give up on Hertha. I contact every friend I know who is in a financial position to contribute and set about raising the necessary funds for her to gain a scholarship to Girton. She is working hard on Greek in preparation for the exam, but is troubled by self-doubt. Her letters wring my heart. '*The nearer I get to the exam, the more sure I feel that I shall not get the scholarship. The standard of work demanded in examinations is, I am sure, not the kind I can do. Will you lose all your faith in me if I don't get it?*' Receiving this piteous message I think long and hard. I want to be sure that I am doing the right thing, and not weighing Hertha down with my own expectations. I reply, '*I shall be sorry if you don't get the scholarship my dear, but if you don't, I will continue to support you in any way I possibly can.*'

A year has gone by since Hertha and I first met, and in accordance with my first impressions, she now occupies a central part of my life. There are many things which contribute to this. Firstly, her character which I consider exemplary and which exhibits many of the values I hold dear. Secondly, and this is most important to me, Hertha speaks fluent French and has a lively interest in all things scientific. This aspect of her nature endears her to Eugène, and I believe that she embodies the child we never had. I am now past fifty years of age, so all hope of bearing a child has gone. Hertha does much to assuage that bitter disappointment.

Eugène and I return to Algiers for the winter. We have some interesting guests: Mary Ewart, a long-standing fellow campaigner for girls' education, and Katie Scott, a dear friend from my early youth. Mary is an avid supporter of women's education and joined Henry Sidgwick, the founder of Newnham Hall. As I have said before, I have no truck with the competition, fostered by some, between Newnham and Girton. The more establishments which exist to improve academic standards for women, the happier I will be.

Our guests are enjoying the warm weather and I am enjoying their lively conversation. The pleasure they are experiencing on visiting Algeria for the first time is catching and I am seeing it with new eyes. One day we travel up the coast by steamer to Philippeville, a town new to me. As the boat pulls into the harbour, we look up to see tree-clad hills stretching far above us. A small train stands by the dock to take us to the top of the mountain where Philippeville stands, perched on the edge of limestone cliffs. The town is bustling and colourful, full of markets and beautiful neo-Moorish architecture. Wide boulevards constructed by the French, are lined with palm trees and lead to a crystal-clear lake with small

Chapter 36

cafes lining the banks. Sitting under shady parasols, we drink delicious cups of cardamom-scented Arabic coffee, served with dates on bone-china plates.

Despite having lived in this country for near on a decade, I remain conscious it is occupied by a foreign power. I doubt the residents look kindly on the French invaders. They arrived in 1838 and renamed the city Philippeville, previously known as Rusicade. Such arrogance astounds me. But as we wander through the parks and admire its stunning location, I put these thoughts aside and set out to enjoy our visit. Reaching the edge of town we look down onto a river and are shocked to see that it is used as a receptacle for the town's refuse. The banks teem with flocks of scrabbling vultures, devouring what? I hate to imagine! Storks stand above us like sentinels, guarding their ramshackle nests, perched on the chimney pots.

As the sun sets over the sea we return to Campagne du Pavillon weary, but satisfied with our excursion and full of questions for Eugène. Because of my lack of Arabic, it is difficult for me to gauge just how the French are seen in Algiers. All I can say is that, historically, occupying forces are rarely welcome anywhere. Maybe Eugène will have a point of view on that.

During her visit I have many conversations with Kate in regard to Cornwall. We enjoyed several weeks together in Zennor last year where I spent many happy hours painting on the cliffs. A painting entitled, *The Land's End*, was the result of my efforts. While there, we viewed an empty parish poorhouse for sale and on my return to Scalands I decide to make enquiries as to its purchase price. According to Kate, it is still up for sale and the idea germinates in my mind that on my return to England, I will make an offer.

After three weeks Kate and Mary leave for England

and the familiar gloom descends. The very thought of spending undiluted time with Nannie makes me want to flee.

Chapter 37

In this morning's post I receive a letter from Willy, which leaves me thunderstruck. Apparently, Norman declared his undying love for Amy and has asked for her hand in marriage. This unexpected disclosure has toppled the whole family into taking sides which is disastrous. It seems that while Willy and Georgina are happy to employ him as a tutor, they in no way consider Norman a suitable match for their daughter.

Ben has now, apparently, thrown himself into the fray and makes no secret of his disapproval. He believes that Norman is a fortune hunter. Anything more ridiculous is hard to imagine! With father gone, Ben sees himself as head of the family. I like to point out to him that I am the first-born and so my opinion is equal to his. Letters fly back and forth and people who are not family members, like Bessie, chip in.

A letter also arrives this morning from Amy. She is caught in a state of flux between the family's refusal to accept Norman as her beau and Willy's insistence that the family leave for a tour around the continent of Europe. This diversion, they believe, will separate her from Norman and hopefully 'cure' their wayward daughter of her inappropriate attachment. Amy has never been abroad before and, of course, the idea is exciting but mixed painfully with the forced separation from a man she considers to be the love of her life.

I swiftly drop a letter in the post in which I encourage Amy to put aside her unhappiness for a while and enjoy the delights of Europe. I encourage her to have faith that Norman will still be there, waiting on her return. Ben joins the family in Paris for the weekend and continues to put Amy under enormous pressure. She writes paraphrasing his comments.... '*Norman will never provide you with the life you take for granted. The lack of servants will be intolerable, etc. etc.*' Ben returns to England where he is preparing for his next expedition. I hope his absence will take the pressure off Amy so that she can relax and find ways to enjoy herself with her parents.

From Willy's letters, it appears that this extended tour has awakened their long dormant spirits. I receive an hilarious letter from Switzerland. Willy had enticed Amy out of Montreux and into the mountains. Her love of nature is captured in her letters.... '*There was a fairy land I used to go to – a field made of forget-me-nots, cowslips and blue mountains....*' Her child-like prose amuses me and makes me think that she may be too young to embark on marriage.

My heart goes out to my darling girl but my hopes for her are continually challenged by her actions. She makes little attempt to conceal in her letters to Ben that neither he, nor her parents, will destroy the love she has for Norman. Ben's part in all this is a mystery to me. He is an uncle and should not feel that he has the right to dictate to his niece what course her life should take. As far as I can see, he has scant experience of romantic relationships and really has no understanding of the feelings involved.

I can't help but admit that this upset with Amy has shaken me considerably. I have been in constant communication with her over the past five years and we have a closeness which, I feel, has been trampled on by her unthinking parents. I am sure that Norman is feeling distraught, and I will make sure that he is left in no doubt that I will champion his cause.

Two months passed after Mary and Kate's departure. I really can't stay here for the whole winter. I discuss this

Chapter 37

with Eugène, and he is happy for me to return to England and will join me in May. Once again, I am sure this arrangement will cause tongues to wag. So be it! We both know that our love is strong enough to take the pressure of my absence. I am aware that I'm finding it more and more difficult to stay away from England. My heart is there and so are the projects which are so precious to me.

Arriving in London I spend some weeks catching up on Girton news and meeting friends. I find that the journey from Algiers tires me more than it has done in the past, and I long to get down to Scalands for some peace and quiet. The trains now run to Hastings regularly, making the journey much easier. This year I am there for Christmas and intend to make it a really festive occasion. I have a deep love of Scalands. It feels like my own creation and contains all the things I enjoy most in life. I can sit and look through the window at a scene which never fails to move me. There is something about England which lends itself to every season. Even in winter when the meadows are glittering with frost, I feel the need to be outdoors with the dogs, striding along the paths, my boots caked with mud, and often thinking about Eugène. He also contributes to Scalands and I get pleasure on checking his projects, and ensuring that they survive the winter. The thought of returning to a roaring log fire and a glass of mulled wine is heart-warming.

Amy and her parents are now back in Crowham, but meeting up with Georgina and Willy is difficult. I am still smarting from the harsh treatment they meted out to Norman Moore. Knowing him as I do, a sensitive and intelligent man, I am convinced that he would have thought long and hard before declaring his feelings. I have yet to know what Amy's thoughts are on the matter and I sense a reluctance in her to attend any family gatherings at which I may be present. I believe her parents are manipulating her. Norman is twelve years older than Amy. Some may feel that the age gap is too large, but I am of the opinion that if the relationship is sound, then age is of little importance. At nineteen, surely, she should be allowed at least to become engaged.

Sadly, this morning I hear that Hertha has not won a scholarship to Girton. She writes me a despondent letter, saying that she tried her best but is feeling exhausted. Elizabeth orders her to stop work entirely and rest for several months in the country. I intend inviting her down to Scalands and maybe, if she is strong enough, she would enjoy a trip down to Zennor. My poor little bird, she is so determined but life has put too great a burden upon her. My next project is to make sure that the promised funds are still available to cover her fees. Far from losing faith in her, my dream is to see her in Girton, receiving the education which she deserves.

In the morning's post is a letter from Ben. He makes it quite clear that the matter is settled with Amy and that I should not interfere. Well, I am quite determined that this is not the last of it. I invite him to tea at Scalands next week. Georgina and Willy seem to be keeping a distance, but I will ignore the frost and call on them soon. I will have to be circumspect in voicing my opinion on the matter. They are obviously determined to separate the couple, as Amy is somewhere in France. I receive a short letter from her and it was quite obvious that she remains in love with Norman and is set on becoming his wife. I would like to talk to her. Nineteen is young to marry in my opinion, particularly as Amy is so immature, but if some compromise can be found, such as a long engagement, this could placate them both. Amy needs time to mature and achieve a modicum of education. She is such a goose!

I lay out my thoughts quite clearly to Georgina in a

Chapter 37

letter and point out that Norman is a highly intelligent man who is making impressive headway in his career at St. Bartholomew's Hospital. I describe the wonderful weekends we enjoyed at Scalands when he visited as a student and how he'd slipped so easily into the family and impressed me as an affectionate and sensitive man. His character is flawless in my opinion.

My view on this matter was brusquely dismissed when Ben arrives for tea on Friday afternoon. He leaves me in no doubt that, as head of the family, he has advised Willy to dismiss Norman and keep Amy out of the country. This has been done and is the end of the matter. I can do nothing but hold my tongue, and we part disagreeably. He is insufferable and snobbish. I hate to say that of my brother, but this is how I find him. I have a plan and will not be silenced. With a little subterfuge on my part, I am convinced it will work.

On reflection I understand that we are an unconventional family. Each one of us is staunchly individual and very different from each other. We are all stubborn and I suppose that is a family trait. In my opinion, Ben, along with Nannie, stand out as intolerant of people who do not fall in with their particular view on life. I have lived a little too close to Nannie and often my opinion of her gets skewed. Ben has always been distant and lacked sociability; I sense that he is more at ease in men's company.

As children, I was in charge as the oldest and we all got along well. He'd always had a very adventurous nature and I have fond memories of playing around the harbour in Hastings and exploring the America Ground. After he left for university, we saw each other less. I do recall that he was always rather disparaging of my fight for women's suffrage. This was never stated openl,y but I know that he didn't feel comfortable with the idea of women's emancipation.

This business with Amy is quite a mystery. I know that he adores her and she has always been his favourite, but it is entirely wrong of him to try to manipulate her life in this way. I will wait until he sets off on another expedition, and then I'll have another try to influence Georgina and Willy.

Chapter 38

Thank goodness Hertha will soon be arriving at Scalands. I am heartily sick of my family at present, and need the company of a young friend to distract me. She has now been offered a place at Girton and will be going up in October; all the funds are in place, and she has passed the entrance exam. This gives me ample time to build her up, to make quite sure that she is feeling strong and able to cope when she gets there. It will be daunting, joining a group of highly educated women, who are mostly middle class and from wealthy backgrounds. All I can hope for is that our educational system will improve over time and benefit women from all classes.

I meet Hertha at Hastings railway station on Saturday morning. This remains a novelty to me. I love to see that monster train emerge from the tunnel; steam billowing, the whistle jubilantly announcing its arrival. I want to wrap her in cotton wool and feed her until she is plump as a piglet. I can see that Hertha needs simple exercise and lots of rest. My suggestion that we purchase a selection of fabrics for a new wardrobe is met with great enthusiasm, but some reluctance to accept charity, as she describes it. I manage to persuade her to put this concern aside. Our friendship is precious and it gives me enormous pleasure to indulge her. To watch Hertha sew is a privilege. She is greatly taken with the cut of my gowns, which are simple in style, and usually made from coarse silk. This makes the whole endeavour simple. She trims the patterns which I'd had sent from America, to her size. We spend hours looking through colour swatches and giggling like schoolchildren, whilst she tries to teach me how to sew a straight hem. Several weeks pass and, at the end of it, we had produce a fine selection of day dresses, and one far grander silk gown for parties. Together with a fine wool coat and sturdy shoes, she is set up for the winter at Girton.

Our friendship brings me such joy and the opportunity to talk openly on subjects, often taboo, is appreciated by both of us. She tells me that she lost her faith around the age of sixteen, but still feels strongly Jewish. We agree that problems arise when relinquishing a religious faith and in the search to find an ethical philosophy to replace it. Seeking a guide, is how Hertha describes it, and how I sympathise with this dilemma. I can only say that I find my guide in nature and that good, wise friends provide me with a source of support when I have the need to discuss life's quandaries. The love and support we both experience during our times together need no words. I feel blessed.

Hertha has declined my invitation to Cornwall as she is feeling much stronger and wants to return to London to see her family. This is just the time to put my plan into operation. I recently invited the Bonham Carters down to Scalands for the weekend to meet Norman and his mother. I want to make it quite an event, with the view to introducing Norman to every family of note in the area. This is purely designed to impress Ben and Willy, who are silly enough to be influenced by such social snobbery. I smile to myself as I sit down and compose invitations to the most prestigious friends in my address book and send a note to Norman suggesting he finds sponsors to put him up for membership of the Reform Club.

This week I am in Zennor having purchased the old poorhouse. Not without complications. It has been

Chapter 38

bought in the name of Catherine Scott who will hold it in trust for me. This is to ensure that my husband has no legal claim on it. How ridiculous! I trust Eugène completely and know that he has no designs on my property whatsoever. I doubt that Eugène will ever be welcomed unrestrainedly into our family. Since arriving back in England I have written to him regularly but, strangely, have heard little from him. Nannie declares him impossible and is convinced that his behaviour is becoming even more irrational.

Norman and Brabbie travel with me to Cornwall. They are good company and help me to sort out the house. It is very old but solidly built. I love to bring life into such buildings and will be searching for felt-lined curtains and some thick rush mats to warm up the place. The weather here is wild. Walking on the cliffs and watching the sea crashing onto the rocks below is exhilarating. At long last I relax into painting. Girton is running smoothly and I have done all I possibly can to help Amy and Norman.

My paintings are selling briskly in London which is quite gratifying. I win a silver medal for *The Sea* which cheers me up no end. And, at last, my dear Hertha is ensconced in Girton and loving every minute.

Chapter 39

Lying in my bed I hear a strong north wind whining around the chimneys, but try as I might, I cannot find the strength to move. Norman is sitting beside me, which is odd: he looks concerned. I attempt to speak but my mouth will not obey me and feels numb. He leans over and holds my hand. 'Can you hear me, Barbara?' he asks in a firm voice. I nod and am surprised to hear my reply contort into a slurred garble. 'You must lie still my dear; you have suffered a stroke. I have contacted Dr Thompson to come down and examine you.' Norman's face looms over me, I do as I am told, I feel frightened and helpless.

Days pass in a fog, none of which I can remember clearly. It becomes obvious, even to me, that the stroke has inflicted considerable damage. Dr Thompson arrives from London and in serious tones informs me that the stroke has induced a measure of paralysis which has affected my left side and my ability to speak.

Norman returns to London but, before leaving, he employs a woman from the village to care for me. Bessie will arrive next week and Brabbie will remain with me until she arrives. I wrestle with a feeling of dread which sinks over me like a wraith. I fear that I will never paint again and tears slide down my cheeks unchecked. I have to rest, indeed I have no choice as my body does not respond to my wishes. This enforced weakness is so frustrating. The previous day I felt faint when trying to wash myself and this convinces me that, for a while, I have to comply with doctor's orders. Before leaving he made this quite clear, 'I want you to try just a few assisted

Chapter 39

steps each day, Mrs Bodichon, any more will be too exhausting. You must be patient and give your brain time to recover.' Dr Thompson departs for London, leaving me in the care of a local doctor who is a stranger to me.

Bessie's arrival brings a wave of emotion which is quite overwhelming. Lying in my bed I hear the carriage clatter down the drive, coming to a halt in a flurry of gravel. Tears fill my eyes when I hear her voice at the door and her feet pounding up the stairs. 'My darling girl, I have been so worried,' she cries. My face contorts into a travesty of a smile, and for the first time I find the strength to speak a few words. Bessie ignores my mangled efforts.

'I can see that you are still my dear Barbara,' she declares with authority. 'Well, I'm going to make myself comfortable, I can see that I'll be here for quite a while.' In the coming weeks, with her warmth and energy she nurtures my stubborn determination, always so much part of my nature, to strive and find small goals to achieve each day. She draws amusing diagrams, illustrating gentle foot and hand exercises. Holding a paint brush for a short while is my first success. The second goal is to be taken out for a drive.

Letters stream in from friends but not from all of my family and there is still no news from Eugène. Norman has informed him of my cerebral accident (as he describes it) but it would not be wise for Eugène to visit. I am far too weak and he'd hate the house, so full of people.

A month passes and to my relief there are signs of improvement. I am now able to sit up and walk very slowly around the bedroom. Also, and this is very encouraging, my speech has improved with Bessie's help, and I can make myself understood, albeit with some patience from the listener. Bessie has to leave for London and I am relieved that Gertrude will be arriving to stay for a couple of weeks. I have a project to put to her. For several years now I have dreamt of building a small extension on to the side of Scalands in which I can start a night school. Since suffering this stroke, I've ample time to think and plan; the school is my lifeline, a project I can return to in my imagination when the hours press down. My ideas for expanding educational opportunities have been alive for many years, but I find from experience that it is difficult to make them a reality. The night school I have in mind is to be staffed by volunteers who are interested in teaching local working men from the Hastings area to read and write. Some of these plans are already in place and Aunt Ju is top of the volunteer list, as is William Ranson, now retired editor of the *Hastings and St Leonards News*. I well remember William's enthusiasm for the project when I first mooted the idea, before leaving for Cornwall. I can easily provide books for a small library and will become a nuisance in begging them off my friends and family. The thought makes me smile.

I am constantly reminded that I must take things easy and relax but – people have to realise – planning projects has always been my life's work. I am fighting a constant battle against tiredness and confusion, but the school is a dream I have long held: it gives me a reason to keep using the faculties I have left. Gertrude promises that she will prepare drawings for us to discuss on her next visit.

My doctor is quite firm and restricts visitors, but there are some exceptions. Hertha asks if she can come down in July and it will be helpful if she can take over my correspondence. I remember, counting up, that on average I used to write fifteen letters a day to friends and colleagues before this awful stroke afflicted me. I hate to think that this pleasurable activity is no longer possible. I shall undoubtedly need paid help if I am to keep abreast of things.

One person I long to see is Ben. I have had a great deal

Chapter 39

of time to think over how it is that we became estranged. Surely a reconciliation is not beyond the realms of possibility? Bessie intends asking Dr Thompson to write to Ben and suggest that a visit from him would raise my spirits. It's possible he might relent under such eminent persuasion.

Meanwhile, I have Gertrude's forthcoming visit to look forward to. I have to imagine what dimensions and facilities I want for the school, as even holding a pencil is beyond me.

As I hope, Gertrude comes laden with beautifully crafted drawings which bring the whole project alive. No medicine can compare to the surge of hope and energy this gives me. The new extension will be constructed on the side of the main house with its own entrance. It will be a simple building of brick and will contain a large stove to keep the pupils warm in the winter, with a privy behind the wood shed.

By the end of the first week we make great strides. From Gertrude's sketch I see how she has blended the lines of the building sensitively, giving the impression of a natural addition, rather than an ugly carbuncle sitting on the side of the house. Sadly, Gertrude has to leave after two weeks. She intends visiting Scalands to ensure that our plans will indeed work and to follow up my suggestion of finding a local builder to dig out the foundations.

At last, I feel strong enough to embark on the journey to Sussex. Hertha is to escort me to London. I intend staying at Blandford Square for a while to recover from the journey before continuing down to Scalands.

The journey from Zennor to London is arduous, part by carriage and part by train. By the time we reach

London I feel exhausted. The staff are waiting on our arrival and have prepared the house for my semi-invalid state. Even so, many are shocked at the difficulty I have on negotiating the steps up to the front door. I notice that a new Bath chair has been purchased and is standing in the hall, no doubt on the advice of dear Norman. These difficulties give me indisputable evidence that I will need to give serious consideration as to how to manage my life from now on. I have always taken my natural strength for granted, but the stroke and my resulting disability has changed all that.

It takes weeks of rest for me to recover from the journey and to feel strong enough to continue on to Scalands. I doubt that I would have made it at all without one huge incentive. The night school is now nearing completion. Aunt Ju is eagerly awaiting my return. What a valiant supporter she has been all my life! At the age of eighty-two and with failing hearing, she still has the energy and determination to work for others. She intends teaching the pupils early reading skills which will be a great help.

Christmas this year is a subdued affair. I had great plans to decorate Scalands: bringing in a huge tree from the estate and filling the kitchen with the delicious aromas of roast duck and Christmas pudding, but I can't find the energy for it. My recovery has plateaued. I walk a little, leaning heavily on my stick, even so my left foot drags. How I miss the wind on my face and the arms of the natural world around me, a place of solace which has so long been my salvation. I am glad that my speech is improving and I am able to converse for a longer time, without becoming too tired.

No doubt against his will and feeling awkward, Ben is coming to visit me. I will make sure that we stay away from all contentious discussion. I am feeling fragile and certainly not able to fight my corner. I have made my

Chapter 39

case in regard to Norman and Amy: I must let matters take their course.

On his arrival Ben suggests we go for a short drive around the estate. My nurse wraps me up in woollen blankets and winds a scarf around my head. Even so the brisk January air feels icy. Ben carries me down to the carriage and gently places me on the cushions. The next hour is pure delight as he skilfully guides the horses down the drive and up through the lanes. Everything looks amazing to me. I feel overcome with the sight of the scudding clouds and the stark leafless trees reaching for the sky.

Since Ben's visit, I feel energised and am taken by surprise when Hertha brings to my notice that Emily is disputing my position as one of the founding members of Girton. This confirms a viewpoint, long held by Nannie, that Emily will take my money, but ignore the facts that it was my original idea to build a women's college and also the many hours of work I put in to make this dream a reality. I have no wish to deny Emily full recognition for her achievements and am happy to accept that her energy, organisational skills and her unrelenting determination to get the job done, are major factors in Girton's success. But I wouldn't like to be remembered as just a benefactor.

Maybe this tussle always ensues when more than one person is involved in pursuing a vision. The one with the biggest need to be heard and the driving ambition to push for centre stage will carry the prize.

At this point in my life I don't really care, but others, who are my friends, see it otherwise. I am told that my portrait has been commissioned, and an artist called Emily Mary Osborne chosen. Emily has long been an artist I admire. Her name was included on the petition to the Royal Academy in our drive for them to open its schools to women. The portrait will first be exhibited in the Grosvenor Gallery in London, after which it will be transferred to Girton College. All I wish for is to be acknowledged alongside others as equal. After all, the driving force in my adult life had been to see equality for women and how it can be achieved through education.

I see that Hertha, despite her examination difficulties, is a fighter. She personifies for me how women in the future will be respected and their achievements acknowledged. It is her originality of mind which excites me and, in past eras, may have seen her labelled as unstable or even dangerous. Who, for heaven's sake, could dream up such irrationality? A thought occurs to me after one of our free-ranging discussions that, 'originality of mind is frequently antagonistic to receptivity.' I notice that Hertha does not learn things by being told or even from books: she learns by experiment. I am proud of her achievements and the love I have for her is deeper than a blood tie.

Chapter 40

The news from Algiers is not good. I receive a letter from Louis Le Grand, a relative of Eugène's, to say that Eugène is no longer able to manage his affairs. The bank refused to pay him his dividends and this action has tipped him over the edge of reason. He was found naked in the grounds of Campagne du Pavillon and knocked on Nannie's door at 5 a.m. asking to be taken to Scalands. She says that he terrifies the local people by roaming the area with a loaded shotgun and a fierce dog. This situation is truly heart-breaking. I cannot not help him. It is desperately sad to be apart when we need each other so much. I send funds for him to come to England. As I expect, I am strongly advised against this by the family, but I have to try and, perhaps, if we are together, it will help him regain his sanity.

What a cheering sight! Today Gertrude wheels me outside in my chair to join the opening of Scalands Night School. I invited all the people most involved in its creation, including a representative of Hastings Council. It is a pleasure to see them all together, celebrating this achievement. The school is not a huge project on anything like the scale of Girton, but it has the same objective: education for people who might not otherwise have the opportunity. Aunt Ju is here, twinkling with enthusiasm. I give a very short speech, due to my disability, after which, Gertrude and Hertha take over, playing the role of hosts.

Much as I love these occasions, it is always a shock to be confronted with the devastating effects of the stroke. I am a shadow of my former self. I try to sweep these thoughts from my mind, but it is a fact. I physically cannot stand in front of an audience for any length of time, I cannot articulate the passion I have for education and I struggle to hold on to the positive enthusiasm which was the core of my nature. Once I could laugh without dribbling and run without falling. It takes the love of my friends to help me hold on to what I have left and to believe that it is worth the effort to get up in the morning.

When such dark thoughts assail me, I try a mental slap. Looking around on this memorable occasion I believe that I am still capable of inspiring people. The Night School is solid evidence of this. The brick walls are painted now with limewash, giving the room a fresh and welcoming feel. Hertha brought in bunches of autumn foliage from the estate, scenting the air with myrtle, a bush Eugène planted on his first visit to Scalands. Looking around this simple room I feel a wave of emotion; my feelings, now more labile than ever since the stroke, threaten to overwhelm me.

There are rows of wooden benches and crude desks provided by a local carpenter. Two sides of the room are covered with bookshelves, quickly filling up with donated books and pamphlets. The stove stands waiting for winter with logs from the estate stacked in neat piles either side.

Through this door will walk young men whose lives will be irrevocably changed, just by being given the skills to read and write. This thought warms my heart. We have lists of potential pupils and my only concern is how will they get here? One young man walked many miles to attend the opening. What a thirst for learning exists in the working community! The Borough Council always offers encouraging words, but when it comes to providing funds, they are often, in reality, unforthcoming. I intend

Chapter 40

pressing them to provide a horse-drawn cart to bring in pupils from the more outlying areas.

This country can only benefit from educating its citizens. Although I am amused to hear that one young man's ambition is to leave for America when he has mastered his letters. He wants to buy a farm there. In many respects this ambition confirms my thinking. Aspiration follows the broadening of knowledge.

My dream is that young women will quickly follow in the men's footsteps. Some of my colleagues question why it is only boys who will attend initially. I understand that this does not appear to coincide with my views on equality, and I have thought long and hard on this question. My struggle for women's equality has been relentless for near on three decades and is ongoing. However, we are still met with considerable opposition from men and, to my despair, some women who view it as a threat and a danger to social stability. The only way, as far as I can see, is to provide an example. If I can produce figures showing the number of young men in our area now literate due to Scalands Night School, then I can move on to the inclusion of girls. I believe it will be prudent to start with young girls in service in the area. I am likely to know their employers and try to convince them that, by employing literate staff, everyone will gain.

By the end of the evening I am exhausted, but also elated. The first group of pupils, who have come by invitation, stand to thank me. Despite being unable to express their gratitude freely and are obviously very shy, I am left in no doubt that they possess the drive to succeed and see very clearly the advantages that literacy can provide.

Six months pass, and I am happy to say that the school is proving to be a considerable success. The classes are always full and pupils continue to attend all through the winter. Sadly, I am unable to engage in any active teaching, but I do listen to the pupils read. It distresses me that this is the only thing I can do to help, but it is extremely gratifying to witness their profound pleasure, when demonstrating how much they have improved and in such a short time. This activity also has a therapeutic aspect from which I benefit. It helps to improve my concentration and diverts my thinking from the bad news I continue to receive from Algiers.

The school gives me a very close and personal experience of working with people who are profoundly disadvantaged. The more I see and hear about their lives, the more apparent the difficulties become which prevent them from being able to improve their lot. Earning money is paramount. Feeding large families and keeping a roof over their heads must come before any of the cultural pursuits in which I am able to indulge and which I believe to be central to my existence.

All of my campaigning has been on women's issues, but talking to these young men, it is obvious that their needs are also pressing. The huge gap between rich and poor will never be bridged without the poor first acquiring a basic education. How I wish I still had the youth and energy to fight for these causes. There is so much to do and, when I witness the lively intelligence and determination shining out from behind their ignorance, I ache to help them.

In preparation for Eugène's arrival I have furnished a light and airy room at the corner of the house which gets the most sunlight. He arrives on Sunday, but I am already

Chapter 40

concerned that this is an ill-conceived idea. I am shocked when first seeing him step down from the carriage. He is in such a state of confusion; his hair unkempt and obviously unwashed for a long while. His eyes give no sign of recognition when I call his name and reach out to him. The wild dog Nannie described stands beside him. A sorry specimen, which looks as emaciated and deranged as its owner. But I realize that Eugène needs the animal and calls it Copain. I had arranged for a companion to accompany Eugène on the journey, but he returned to Algiers after reaching London, giving the excuse that the dog is dangerous. It had already attacked him while on the boat from France.

Several weeks pass and Eugène's behaviour shows no sign of improvement. I find that he sits for hours, staring through the window in a comatose state, the dog at his feet, or, and this is more concerning, leaves the house without telling me where he's going and wanders around the estate. The staff are very nervous of him and the dog.

The head groundsman asked to see me last week after finding Eugène wandering miles from the house in a state of complete delusion. He thought he was in France visiting his parents and became agitated when the poor man tried to explain that he is in England. I wonder sometimes if he even knows who I am and try hard to break through this confusion. Last night I had a log fire lit in the sitting-room and gathered around us all our lovely cushions and ornaments. I spoke to him in my poor French, striving to help him recall memories from our time at Campagne du Pavillon. It was all to no avail. In fact, I came to see that my efforts increased his distress.

Norman visits to give his medical opinion. He continues to provide stalwart support, but is coming to the conclusion now, after a month or so, that it would be better for Eugène to be in Algiers. This makes perfect sense as, after all, Algiers is his natural home; he speaks the language, and the weather is more to his liking. I make contact with his housekeeper at Campagne du Pavillon and offer to double her wages if she will provide extra care and makes sure Eugène gets proper medical attention.

Three more months pass with no sign of improvement. After discussing the situation once again with Norman, he agrees to escort Eugène back to Algiers, on the proviso that Copain is administered a sedative and kept in a cage for the duration of the journey.

I am tired beyond belief and suffering great sadness. My health precludes me from providing any practical or emotional support for my dear husband and it is with great regret that I make arrangements for his return home. At the back of my mind I know that this is the end. I am unlikely ever to be strong enough to travel so far again.

It is quite obvious when he walks towards the carriage with Norman, that Eugène's mental state is dire and irredeemable. He shows no emotion when I hold him close and, looking deep into his eyes, I find no reflected affection or fondness. The man I love more than any other has already gone from me.

I know that there will be much tittle-tattle in the family following Eugène's departure. After observing irrefutable evidence that he is and, in their opinion always was, unstable, they will no doubt take pleasure in witnessing the evidence to support their views. Father was right, I imagine them crowing, he was an unsuitable husband. I have never truly understood their attitude. Is it because of his nationality, or that he is odd and different from the conventional suitors I might have chosen? Whatever it is, I no longer give their opinions much credence and most certainly cannot turn to any in my family for comfort at

Chapter 40

this time. As usual, it is my friends who provide me with love and a sympathetic listening ear.

Norman comes down to see me when he returns from Algiers. 'You have done the right thing,' he reassures me. It is a relief to hear these words and read the letters he brought with him from our housekeeper and Doctor Gerenti, who has known Eugène for many years. He assures me that he will keep me fully informed and make sure that Eugène receives all the help and support he needs. Nannie has been worse than useless as expected, but some of our friends in the English community promise to visit and include Eugène in their gatherings.

Chapter 41

I hear today from Norman that he has been elected a Fellow of the Royal College of Physicians. This is a huge honour. How proud Rebecca, his mother, must be of him! Here is a man who represents the pinnacle of what can be achieved through hard work and education. He came from a difficult background, as his father abandoned the family at an early age, leaving his mother to provide for him. I was first introduced to her at eighteen years of age by Aunt Ju, who had taken me, together with Nannie, to the London Bazaar, a gathering set up to support political campaigns of various kinds. I vividly remember the women I met there. They inspired me with a passion I still have to this day. I returned to Sussex convinced that: whether it is for women's rights, the anti-slavery campaign or the provision of education for all, I will fight throughout my life to support such causes. Real change in society only comes about when people are brave enough to stand by their principles and take action.

I receive a draft of a letter in the post today from Norman, he intends sending it on to Willy after hearing my opinion. One year has passed since he first asked for Amy's hand in marriage. In the letter he sets out his earnings and prospects. His qualifications are impressive but, sadly, they are not of the sort which will impress people like Willy and Georgina. He holds three offices at St Bartholomew's Hospital and, as Warden of the College, he is provided with a comfortably furnished house, all of this maintained by the hospital.

In the letter he declares his enduring love for Amy,

Chapter 41

and assures her parents that she would never want for anything. He even promises that, in the event of his death, his mother would financially support Amy and any children they may have. This letter wrings my heart. I encourage him to go ahead and send the letter, but also to send a copy to Amy, via me if necessary. I doubt it will have any impact. I heard from Aunt Ju that Willy and Georgina are looking for an alternative suitor. This is likely to be a landowner, someone who is wealthy, and who likes to make a splash in society.

I hear this week that this attempt to change Willy's mind fell on stony ground and he has not even graced Norman with a reply. If anything, since receiving Norman's letter, they have become even more punitive towards their daughter. She is in a constantly anxious state. I hear from Aunt Ju that Willy allowed her to read the letter, but she was forbidden to answer it. My mind reels under the cruelty of this. Rebecca has now written to them, suggesting that allowing some form of contact might ease the situation. Following Rebecca's intervention, Amy was allowed to write one letter, after which all contact must cease. Her health is now deteriorating to an alarming extent. I am prevented from offering any advice or opinion on the matter. Ben remains centre stage and determined that Amy shall never be allowed to marry a man so below her station in life. His meddling infuriates me. What right does he have to dictate what Amy should or should not do. I am sure his opinions greatly influence Willy.

Another year passes and a fissure appears in the wall. Norman hears by a circuitous route that Amy will be travelling from Hastings to London by train, to visit her Uncle Ben. I wonder who passed this snippet of information on to him?

Norman is given a likely weekend, which cannot be precise due to the covert nature of the information. In an undertaking, which takes considerable determination, he boards every train travelling through London Bridge from Hastings on those two days, until he finds her. I can only imagine the joy they experience when setting eyes on each other after such a long separation. Norman told me later that he was shocked by Amy's appearance. She had lost weight and her skin was pale and wan.

Amy writes to me from Ben's house in London and describes her incredulity at seeing Norman standing on the platform at London Bridge and then actually boarding the train. Her letter sings with happiness. '*Aunt Barbara, we sat side by side for two stops, holding hands, and just staring into each other's eyes. It was unbelievable. There was so much to say, but we hardly said a word. When we parted at Charing Cross he just melted into the crowd.*'

Apparently Amy didn't tell Ben that she had seen Norman during her visit. There is no doubt that he would have realized immediately that it had been set up, and probably by me. But she does eventually tell him by letter after returning to Crowham and after she has also told her parents. Their reaction was muted and the ban on seeing Norman is reinforced.

Amy's health continues to deteriorate; she becomes so weak that she is unable to come to Scalands and stay with me for a while. Norman is keeping in close touch with me and is becoming extremely concerned. His experience with patients gives him reason for alarm and he knows that unless something in Amy's circumstances changes quickly, she could go into a terminal decline. In a letter sent to Georgina, surely written in a state of agonising concern for her daughter, he wrote, '*The most dangerous condition in which to live, as regards to mental*

Chapter 41

health, is that of a continuously distressed mind. Physical hardship and exposure are safe to most people, compared to endless anxiety with no hope of resolution. I would beg of you please Mrs Leigh Smith to speak to your husband and find a way to accept that Amy will never recover unless we are together. Our love has endured now for over four years, and as I explained to you in my earlier letter, to which you have never replied, the position I hold in the medical profession would allow me to give her all the care she needs to recover.'

At last, a tiny lessening of Amy's isolation is achieved, no doubt influenced by her parents realization that Amy is in serious danger. It is agreed that an exchange of letters will be allowed to take place. Amy does not hold back in expressing her relief and joy at hearing from Norman again. *'I take your letter from under my pillow and kiss it. I can only sleep with it in my hand.'* This pathetic line in one of her letters to Norman gives him some measure of the emotional damage inflicted by her parents. Their obdurate refusal to allow any contact between the pair has caused Amy such emotional and mental distress that, I believe, she is perilously near to a complete breakdown.

Through the years of waiting, Norman has been living in the outside world, forging his career, and keeping the hope alive that one day they will be together. He does this by writing, but never posting, a letter to Amy every day, which he calls, *The New Journal to Stella.* Norman is a romantic and no doubt took this title from Jonathan Swift, the eighteenth-century writer he greatly admires.

For Amy, the enforced separation has been a lonely stifling experience, during which she had little chance to mature and engage with the world. I have long given up hope that she might engage in academia, or even find some passion for art or literature. She has a sweet nature and would, if given the choice, enthusiastically engage in amateur theatricals. Her ethereal beauty and sensitivity would lend itself admirably to this form of creativity. This is my opinion, but I doubt if her parents, or even Norman, would agree to her engaging in a profession which has a dubious reputation and is not seen as entirely respectable.

This dreary winter seems endless. I rent a house in Brighton in the hope that a change of scenery will lift my spirits. There is no doubt that the stroke has damaged my ability to keep motivated and I engage in pursuits which will prevent these awful feelings of doom. I ask Willy if Amy can join me for a week or so. She dutifully does so, but I find that I am not able to cope with Brighton or the company of a younger person. Words come out of my mouth which I later regret.

When I think of all the years I battled to break down Willy and Georgina's opposition to her relationship with Norman, why is it, now when a thaw has set in, that I am unable to take pleasure in it? She is such a darling girl, and I notice that she does anything to avoid giving offence. She reads to me for hours in the evening without complaint and makes sure there is a lively fire in my bedroom throughout the night. I must find a way out of this malaise.

Amy returned to Crowham on Friday, and I receive a most amusing letter from her this morning.

Dear Aunt Bar,

February 1st, 1880

Something has happened, which I must tell you about. I was visiting Hastings with mother this week, she was in the grumps as usual, when she suddenly turned to me and said, 'Perhaps we should look at some clothes for you, Amy.' Her face looked as if she'd swallowed alum; I could hardly believe my ears. Into the shop we went, and to my astonishment, I was measured up for two day dresses, one reception dress in

Chapter 41

coral silk, and a riding habit with matching hat. I could hardly believe what was happening when she went on to order a wool cape and two pairs of fine leather boots. It was all most puzzling. There was nothing said as to why, after all these years, she should deign to spend so much money on me. Needless to say, I was delighted, when she added two corsets, two petticoats, six drawers, and two pairs of stockings. She asked for the huge parcel to be sent to Crowham. I can only imagine that this is the start of wedding plans, and I have to be respectably dressed for the coming events. I thought this news might cheer you up. I will come down to see you again soon. Oh! I forgot to mention that the 30th of March is being considered as a suitable wedding date. None of this has been discussed with me of course. I would have preferred it to be later in the Spring when it would be a little warmer, but Norman and I are just thrilled that we can now see the road ahead for us. I would like to thank you again my dear Aunt Bar, for all the support you have given us over the years. The other piece of wonderful news is that your old maid Henrietta sent me a parcel of items for my trousseau. Inside there were lace trimmed handkerchiefs, two pretty nightgowns and some beautiful embroidered chemises all wrapped up in a delightful Merino wool shawl.

I am feeling overwhelmed. Never in my life have I felt so cosseted. Sadly, this is a slightly bittersweet feeling, as mother and father have never made any secret of the fact that they find me irritating and unlovable. They never call me dear, or pet me. Never mind, I will put this all behind me and look forward to being with my darling Norman, at last.

Much love and kisses,

Amy

When I return to Scalands in early March the wedding preparations are well under way. Amy visits and I offer her the loan of my wedding veil and suggest that we contact Eugène's housekeeper and have a box of orange flowers sent over for the wedding. She tells me that her cousin, Alice Bonham Carter, has offered her a dark-green cashmere gown, trimmed with quilted green satin and turned up with dull red. This sounds wonderful to me, but Amy is concerned that Norman will find it too flamboyant and, anyway, Willy and Georgina want her in nothing other than pure white.

At last I feel my low mood lifting. I am invited over to Crowham and, to my amusement, the house is receiving a spring clean, the like of which it had never experienced before. Amy tells me that for months, in preparation for the wedding, workmen have been scouring the dingy walls which are now freshly painted. The shabby furniture has been recovered, given a good polish, and is now looking more than respectable. On my visit, amidst much hilarity, the maids were washing the windows, using a diluted mixture of vinegar and water. Amy pushes me around the gardens in my Bath chair. It is lovely to see that the gardeners have made sure that early spring flowers are showing colour in the beds surrounding the house, giving it a festive air.

This spring clean is not an entirely joyful affair. Georgina and Willy are still far from welcoming Norman into the family, but they intend to make a show of it. Every neighbour of any note in the vicinity has been invited. In the midst of this uproar, I see that Amy is experiencing a mixture of excitement and unease. Norman's mother has not been invited to stay at Crowham, as would be expected under normal circumstances. This slight embarrasses Amy, although she seems somewhat mollified by my suggestion that Rebecca stays at Scalands. I am so looking forward to spending time with her; we have years of news to catch up on.

Chapter 42

At last the wedding day arrives, and I find that I cannot remember a single occasion in the past that has driven Georgina and Willy to such energised activity. I don't doubt that it is motivated by the need to raise their status in the county set. The end of March was carefully chosen as it does not clash with farming commitments and sits with the old saying, 'Marry in May, rue the day.'

I was driven to Westfield Church accompanied by Rebecca, having had my Bath chair loaded onto a trap and delivered in time for my arrival. The early spring air is crisp, but I am warmly dressed in my long grey woollen coat with a fox-fur trim and a green felt hat decorated with feathers. The drive from Scalands takes us a good hour or so, as the lanes are still potted after the winter storms, but Rebecca and I are oblivious to the discomfort. Our spirits are high and to us it is incredible that, after these long years of strife, Norman and Amy are to be married. As we clatter along Westfield Lane, I am amazed to see that arches of greenery, studded with spring daffodils, have been erected over the road.

Arriving at the church, it is a struggle for the coachman to help me down from the carriage and into my chair, but we manage the transition with some huffing and puffing. Rebecca pushes me into the church where we have a perfect view of the proceedings. I feel a lump rise in my throat as the church bells begin to chime, welcoming the bride. Now that all the guests are seated, orange blossom has been spread on the path outside and the sweet smell of Algiers drifts through the air. I am not a religious person, but the ancient Norman church is decorated so beautifully that I cannot help but appreciate its innate spirituality.

A flutter runs through the congregation when Willy and Amy step through the church door and make their way slowly up the aisle. Amy seems to float, one hand lightly placed on her father's arm and her other holding a spray of white lilies. She is wearing a dress of white silk; her head is covered with the Honiton lace veil I wore at my own wedding.

I wonder what is going through Willy's head at this point. Here he is, about to give his beautiful daughter away to a man for whom he has no respect and considers socially inferior. I have long despaired of changing his mind and can only hope that when Amy has extricated herself from her family's narrow pretensions, she will become stronger. Surely, I hope, that under the influence of her eminently suitable husband, she will develop some of the skills she has, thus far, left unexplored. As she passes me, her eyes catch mine and her face lifts into a smile of pure joy. In that moment I couldn't have felt prouder had she been my own child.

Norman stands at the altar, his best man at his side. He looks splendid in a frock coat, silk waistcoat and grey pin-striped trousers. I sense Rebecca's shoulders shaking. I take her hand and it occurs to me how unrepresentative we both are in respect of society's expectations of marriage. My marriage to Eugène has been conducted entirely outside conventional mores. Eugène never expected me to obey him, only that we should honour and love each other in the purest sense of the words. Rebecca was abandoned by a faithless husband and left to care for her child alone.

My one sadness today is that Ben could not, or would not, put aside his dislike of Norman and attend the wedding of his niece. Sometimes I find it hard to believe that he is my brother. His behaviour is unkind and indicates a stubbornness of mind which doesn't allow him to bend in order to allow for the feelings of others. One only has to look at Amy today to see her happiness. Anyone who loves her surely wouldn't want to deny her that.

I can only imagine that there are other factors, of which I am unaware, as to why he is unable to respect Norman and see that he is a good husband for Amy. Is he jealous of Norman's exemplary credentials, and outstanding success in the medical world? Or has he looked upon Amy as his personal possession? I often feel that his attitude towards her is somewhat unhealthy. Now, it seems, that Millicent, his twelve-year-old niece, is the current favourite. I can only speculate. He is now viewed with some standing in the world of Arctic exploration. I read about him in the papers but see little of him in the flesh.

As the bride and groom leave the church they are showered with grains and nuts, all with the hope of encouraging fertility. We make a grand spectacle, as the procession of carriages makes its way back to Crowham. The villagers line the road waving and shouting their good wishes as the bride and groom drive past, resplendent in an open landau.

Back at Crowham, the house comes into its own. A pale March sun appears and filters down through the trees lining the drive. My maid, Henrietta, is waiting for me and pushes me down the path in the Bath chair. The dining hall is decorated with ribbons and sprays of silver birch, brightening up the room. The wedding feast, spread on a sparkling white damask tablecloth, takes my breath away; polished wine glasses, glittering in the candle light, are proffered by a phalanx of immaculate serving maids, togged out in starched white aprons and caps. How on earth Georgina organised such an occasion, I cannot imagine. Having suffered some of her execrable meals in the past, I find it hard not to laugh aloud as I'm handed a plate of lobster salad and asked to take my pick of at least eight other dishes which take my fancy. I am quite spoilt for choice!

As the wine flows and the speeches delivered, the gathering intermingles into a splendid appropriation of a wedding party. I notice Amy cringe when Willy stands before the gathering to give his speech. He sways slightly and his words slur as he proclaims his love for the beautiful bride and gushes his wish that she will enjoy a long and happy marriage. He surely must have pored over such hypocrisies for hours. By this time it barely matters. Georgina looks on, a slightly acidic smile curling her lips as she watches Norman greeting the guests, exuding charm and bonhomie.

At last it is time for the bridal pair to take their leave. It is now early evening and Amy is looking rather tired. This has also been a long day for me and I breathe a sigh of relief when the guests gather on the front lawn to wave them off. They are spending their wedding night in Norman's London house before leaving for Paris in the morning.

As we move into April, I battle against melancholy, and search for a new project. Painting has now become impossible for me as has writing. Two blows have not helped. Henrietta, a woman who has been my help and companion for so many years is retiring. Amy's wedding was the last family occasion we enjoyed together. I will miss her warm familiarity; she alone knows me, as maybe no other does, except perhaps Eugène. She is to live with

Chapter 42

her sister in Hastings but has promised that she will visit me at Scalands.

The other appalling loss has been the death of my dear friend George Eliot. I have always called her Marion but completely understood when she wrote under a pseudonym. Maybe more than any friend, Marion personified the woman I aspired to be. She lived outside conventional society and seemed impervious to the disapproval of many of her peers. She taught me that marital relations was something to enjoy and a natural human drive to celebrate in as free a manner as possible. This was an extraordinary viewpoint on a subject which is rarely spoken of. It set me free and, no doubt, helped to ensure that Eugène and I made good partners in the bedroom. Life goes on, as they say. But there is no doubt that the path gets harder in old age, and is full of potholes.

One pleasure that I do still enjoy is listening to the pupils in the Night School and find that they like to talk to me about their lives. Some listen patiently when I suggest other subjects they could embark upon, or how to improve their job prospects. I imagine they see me as a rambling old woman who has had little experience of their hardships. Some of that is correct of course, but not all of it. As humans, if we attempt to strive, whether rich or poor, we all face obstacles. For instance, I was not always proficient in art, and some of my writing was definitely below standard. But humility is the key, I believe. If you can listen to someone who is expert in these subjects, then you will learn. Persistence brings rewards.

In late April I get a letter from Amy. They have been travelling down through France and Italy and intend staying in Venice for a while.

My Dear Aunt Bar,

April 1880

I do hope you are keeping well and enjoying the spring weather. We were having such a lovely time in Paris that I just couldn't find the time to write, and, as you well know, when you're travelling, it is hard to concentrate. My dear husband is so patient and loving towards me, I can't tell you how glorious these last weeks have been. I am so grateful to you for the delicate instruction you gave me in regard to marital relations. Norman is so sensitive and gentle. I can't imagine any other man taking such trouble to make sure that our love-making is a mutual pleasure. Mother gave me not a hint of what to expect and it did come as a shock, despite your diagrams. In fact I did show them to Norman, he found them most amusing. So I am now properly married, and I know that honeymoons are not real life, but if we can take just some of this magic back to England with us, I know that we will be happy together.

Today we are taking a Gondola along the Grand Canal, and Norman has promised that we will have dinner tonight overlooking the lagoon.

Much love my dear Aunt Bar and thank you for your belief in us.

Your ever-loving niece,

Amy

Chapter 43

Each morning I wake in my comfortable bed at Scalands attempting to soothe my mental unease. I rarely sleep through the night and unless I can find a project for the day, I remain discomfited and restless. I remind myself that many things are going well, not least Amy's letters, which reassure me that she is settling into married life.

The Night School is an undoubted success and my dear Scalands continues to provide me with activities that nourish me, both physically and mentally. The estate is a constant source of interest and the gardener has laid smooth pathways on which I can walk safely. He has created small arbours containing a seat or bench where I can rest. Each one is bursting with colourful plants and flowering bushes which give me pleasure, even in the long winter months. Looking around my bedroom, I see so many objects and paintings which bring back memories of happy times. They remind me that I have not wasted my life but, often, if I am not careful, take me down a path of regret and sadness.

Despite my efforts to remain positive and forward looking, I find anxious thoughts constantly turning towards Ben. He did not attend Amy's wedding; his excuse being that he was too involved in the preparation of his ship, *Eira*, for yet another expedition. According to newspaper reports, his route will take him through the Matotchkin Straits, heading towards Franz Josef's Land. This will be his fifth arctic expedition, the departure date is set for 13th June '81. They are sailing from Peterhead with a crew of twenty-five men, a kitten, a canary and a black retriever named Bob. Aunt Ju remains in close contact with Ben and therefore gleans many of the mundane, but to me fascinating, details of the expedition of which I would remain otherwise unaware.

Following the upset over Amy and Norman's protracted love affair and the ongoing disapproval of my marriage to Eugène, my relationship with Ben has been distant and far from warm over many years. His visit to Scalands before last Christmas was such fun, and one I will cherish, but I can see that we have too many differences to make any reconciliation a possibility. These days I only hear of his adventures and wonderful achievements through the family or newspaper articles. Apparently, he returns from his expeditions with a huge variety of specimens, including plants, fossils, birds' eggs and even live animals. I was much amused by the story of a white bear called Sampson, who managed to escape from his cage and was about to leap overboard when Ben recaptured him with a rugby tackle. There is no doubt he is an extraordinary character, and I can see that he is more suited to this life of derring-do, in the company of men, than he is in general society. So many of his views on women and relationships are out of line with my own, and probably a great many other people, if truth be known. All of this dissent does not preclude me from having deep sisterly feelings for him.

This morning a letter arrives from General Ludlow, my late sister Bella's husband, expressing concern. Ben had intended returning from this expedition by winter, but it is now October with still no news. The Royal Geographical Society and the Government are lobbied by Willy to organise a rescue mission: there is a drive to raise funds. I

Chapter 43

contribute £1,000 and Nannie matches this. I'm afraid it sounds a pitiful sum in relation to the amount needed for such a task, but my funds are somewhat depleted after building the school at Scalands. In fact, I am considering selling Blandford Square. I rarely visit London now and it would certainly enable me to continue supporting my projects. Ben will no doubt disapprove of my selling the house without his say so, but I am within my legal rights; after all, I had owned the house before my marriage to Eugène, left to me by father.

We are now nearing December with no news. There are days when I find it difficult to leave the comfort of my bed and am assailed by dark thoughts. If Ben has perished, I will be left with many regrets. We were so close in the early years when life seemed simple. I can see clearly, looking back in time, that Ben is entirely suited to life at sea and also that his fiercely logical mind lends itself to scientific exploration. Father was quite wrong in his determination that Ben should go into the legal profession. It is a classic example of how parents should encourage their children, but not set out to impose their will upon them. Ben comes into his own outdoors, facing the elements and challenges which, for most people, would be too terrifying to contemplate. I am mystified that my liberal-thinking father became obsessed with forcing his son into a profession for which he was so obviously unsuited. It came near to ruining their relationship. Now, of course, father would be proud of his achievements.

I am relieved to hear that sufficient funds have been raised and a search vessel is being prepared. Nothing has been heard from Ben in all this time. The vessel is called SS *Hope* and that is all we can do at present: wait and hope. Sir Allen Young is commander of the search and Willy is intending to travel with him for part of the journey. They are to set sail in June. After so long, I cannot imagine that Ben has survived the atrocious conditions, but I must stay positive. Much has been done and surely the Government wouldn't have contributed such large sums to a lost cause.

One shaft of light appears in my gloom. Amy has produced a baby boy. They are calling him Alan and, according to Norman, mother and baby are doing well. Another piece of news has circulated reluctantly. Georgina, Amy's mother, is also with child. The baby is expected in March. Needless to say, no missives of joy are sent out from Crowham. Georgina has made no secret of her dislike for motherhood and at the age of forty-seven, no doubt thought it was long behind her. How cruel life is! The stork never arrived for me.

This morning I watch with interest as a horseman turns into the drive and dismounts at the front door. This is unusual and I listen with growing alarm as a sharp rap announces his arrival. Eliza, my new maid, wastes no time in racing up the stairs. I am aware that my heart is pounding. This sort of message rarely brings good news, and with some trepidation I slit open the package. Pages of what I immediately recognise as Aunt Ju's spidery writing, spills onto the bed.

The first words I register proclaim, '*Got back all safe but* Eira *is away.*' This somewhat odd message takes the breath from my lungs. Eliza is standing by the bed and yelps when I drop into a faint. I come around to find her bathing my face and moistening my lips with spoonfuls of tea. It is an indication of my fragile state that I reacted so dramatically, but my anxiety concerning Ben had become unbearable over the past months. I'd prepared myself for the worst. But he is alive!

I spend the rest of my day in bed reading Aunt Ju's handwritten copy of Doctor William Neale's report. He

Chapter 43

is the *Eira's* surgeon. Apparently, Ben does not want to relate any personal details, other than aspects appertaining to science. The doctor's account gives a vivid description of the disaster and offers interesting details concerning the ordeal suffered by the men, while trapped in an icy wilderness....

December 1881

We encountered unexpected weather conditions in the region of Spitsbergen. Thick ice had formed a near impenetrable barrier which was to severely impede our journey. We were already over stretching our time scale by months; the risks were high.

As Mr Smith had feared, the ice proved to be a major hazard. The Eire *was pitched between the ice and land-floes. Due to this state of affairs we sustained catastrophic damage below the water line and were in danger of sinking. Together with the crew Mr Smith and I embarked on saving as much of our stores from the hold as we could. The men were exemplary. They know, that when a ship goes down, the Captain is no longer in command, but after some heated discussion it was agreed that none of us would survive without pulling together.*

Firstly, we took off the lifeboats and placed them well above the water mark, followed by the guns and powder which were to be our salvation. On the ice stood boxes of provisions, together with some small luxuries which would lighten the long weeks ahead; curry powder, rum, sherry, tobacco and a case of champagne. A few packets of dried fruit were saved, enough to make a small Christmas pudding. We were all working as hard as we could, with the darkness closing in around us, when Mr Smith spotted the water rising fast and called out to the men to abandon ship immediately.

Staying calm, as we had been instructed, every man leapt ashore, as the ice floes closed over the poor old Eira. *Now,* with only the tops of her masts showing we set about cutting them down for firewood. While this task was carried out Mr Smith and myself marked out the parameters of the shelter. Every possible piece of useful material had been taken from the Eira in order that we could construct a building, strong enough to protect us from the winter storms. Thirty foot long by twelve wide. Mr Smith named it, Flora Cottage, after his Cousin Flora Smith. With twenty-five men to accommodate it was a tight fit, but we agreed from the outset that, if we were to survive, then cooperation and good humour would be essential.

Bob, the ships' dog, was always a useful distraction. He earned his outstanding reputation for courage and ingenuity by assisting in bear hunts. After a few weeks he had developed a technique in which he would entice a bear from a distance by running near to it, then running away until he brought it within range of the guns. With his help we are never short of meat, which consisted of walrus, polar bear and guillemots. Not one case of scurvy developed, despite losing all our stocks of lime juice.

One member of the crew gave me great cause for concern. He had developed what looked like a cancer on his lower lip. He was often in severe pain. The only comfort I could offer him was a small tot of rum. He is a good man and never complained. I was determined that he should return to his family, but as the weeks and months passed, with temperatures at times sinking to 40 degrees below, it was hard for him to keep his spirits up.

We reached June, ten months had now passed since losing the Eira. For the past three weeks we had watched the temperature slowly rise, our discussions were long and intense on when it would be safe enough to launch the boats. We spent two more weeks checking the three lifeboats and stocking them with provisions. Tinned food had been saved for the journey from the Eira, also damask table clothes to

Chapter 43

use as sails. At last, on June 21^{st,} we set off, leaving our sturdy cabin still intact and clean as a pin. I can say without any exaggeration, that this was the most abominable journey I have ever encountered. The ice continued to present hazards which could up-end us, and we encountered storms which, despite us all being experienced sailors, were terrifying beyond measure. Mountainous waves threatened to swamp our tiny boats, and I am sure that, not one man amongst us, thought we would survive. But, what fighters they were, rowing and sailing for near on five hundred miles, in conditions which were appalling. After forty-three days we espied The Hope, *at a place called Novaya Zemlya. What a sorry sight we were. Burned with wind and salt spray, our clothing in rags. Climbing aboard will be one of the most overwhelming and thankful experiences of my life. I will be eternally grateful to Mr Smith for his strong leadership and unfailing courage.*
Doctor William Neale – Ship's Surgeon

Doctor Neal's report gives me much food for thought. I feel so proud of Ben but have no way to show him this. He is hiding from the wave of public attention that the expedition has attracted in the press. I am told he has received a gold medal from the Royal Geographical Society and asked to give a lecture, which he has refused to do.

Knowing Ben, he will not share his incredible experience in the Arctic or gain any pleasure from the accolades heaped upon him. His contribution to science and understanding of the natural world is fascinating, and many people would love to hear of his adventures. What a frustrating man he is! I see that, by nature, he is withdrawn and shy and any open show of emotion is an anathema to him. It would all be too exposing. Jesus College, Cambridge, where he studied law, has now made him an Honorary Fellow. As the son of a dissenter he was not allowed to obtain a university degree and consequently was given no recognition of his law studies at the time.

We are so different. In contrast, I am a creature of wild passions and affection for my fellow man. Sadly, my advancing age and poor health now prevent me from visiting my vibrant and stimulating friends. I simply must get out of this bed and make an effort. Tomorrow I will contact my solicitor and discuss with him my plans to sell Blandford Square. Also, I will write a letter to Hertha and invite her down to Scalands. That's better! I feel energised already and must ask Eliza to organise a late spring clean.

Chapter 44

The following week I sit by the window in the parlour, watching the drive. The sun glints through the trees, giving a dappled mellow light. I love the spring. Nature is in full force filling the hedgerows with wild flowers and lambs fatten in the fields. I am looking forward to seeing Hertha. She is busy these days with her studies and can rarely find the time for socialising, but she has made space to come down to see me and I do appreciate that. At last the jingle of harness is heard as the horses pull up the lane and there they are, coats gleaming and smartly turned out. Hertha has come down from London by train and I arranged for my carriage to pick her up at Hastings railway station. As she steps down onto the drive, I long to race out and sing my welcome song, but have to be patient until she comes through the door. Her step is light, and she calls out, 'Where are you, Barbara?' My heart melts to see my beautiful surrogate daughter, bright-eyed, and wearing the soft green cotton dress we made together some years ago.

Eliza has done us proud and we sit down in the dining-room to a delicious lunch. I cannot adequately express the pleasure it gives me to look at Hertha and, just as importantly, listen to her endless stream of news. One piece delights me beyond measure. She has decided to attend evening classes at Finsbury Technical College, where she will study electricity. This choice of subject amazes me. Electricity is something of which I have no experience whatsoever. She attempts to explain the experimental work she is undertaking on something called a 'line-divider.' It is her intention to take out foreign patents on it. I'm afraid I don't understand a word she says but it sounds extraordinary and has a touch of alchemy about it.

If Hertha is right in her predictions, the use of electricity will be one of the most important of her generation. She truly is a woman who has an intelligence which lends itself to thinking on a broad and unconventional spectrum. This is really inspiring and, in my opinion, when unconstrained by convention women can achieve much. As I listen to her and soak in her infectious enthusiasm, the evidence of her extraordinary intelligence is blinding.

I silently rejoice that her years at Girton are now long over. Hertha, I am sure, would agree that she didn't shine there academically, ranking third class in her Tripos examinations. Putting that aside, she was socially a star and led the College Choral Society, founded the Girton Fire Brigade, and started a mathematical club with her friend Charlotte Scott. She looks on her years in Girton as a failure; I most certainly do not. But it gives me food for the thought that academia does not suit everyone.

I ask if she remains in contact with any of the friends she made there. And am delighted that she remains close to Charlotte. Remembering Charlotte's time at Girton will always amuse and thrill me. She attained the equivalent of a first-class degree in algebra and trigonometry and when this was announced, her fellow students shouted her name, 'Scott of Girton' and threw their hats in the air. Nothing, in my opinion, influences attitudes more profoundly than success. Charlotte succeeded in a man's field and in an arena which wasn't open to women before Girton. If I need a positive thought to inspire me and help to keep me moving forward, it is the achievement of helping to found Girton.

There is a glow around Hertha and I can see that something else is going on in her life. I wait patiently for

Chapter 44

her to tell me and, after a while, she blushingly confides that she is in love with her tutor William Ayrton. He is, in fact, the founder of the Finsbury Technical College. Hertha proudly informs me that he is a pioneer in electrical engineering. This love affair has not been without it's difficulties, as Mr Ayrton's wife recently died, leaving a daughter, Edith. Hertha explains that due to this delicate situation, the couple are conducting themselves with restrained decorum until next year when they intend to marry. I must say that, in my opinion, Hertha will make an admirable stepmother for the little girl and Mr Ayrton is a very lucky man indeed.

When listening to the young, with all their plans and expectations for the future, it is all too easy to see one's own life narrowing. Often I find myself planning a trip to Algiers or arranging a painting trip with Brabbie, but the complexities of travel make me feel weary and my enthusiasm quickly fades. I am pleased to tell Hertha about my plans for selling Blandford Square. With this injection of capital, I intend giving another grant to Girton and, since hearing of Hertha's invention, will most certainly advance her funds to take out the patent. I have also included her in my will, but didn't mention this, wanting to avoid introducing any gloom into this heavenly day.

After lunch, I suggest a tour of the garden and Hertha expresses interest in viewing the Night School. Eliza brings in my Bath chair from the hall and settles me comfortably. The next hour or so will be imprinted on my memory forever. The late afternoon sun warms my ageing body as Hertha pushes me along the garden paths. She is impressed with the efforts of Sam Benson, my gardener, to provide me with as much natural beauty as is possible to find in an English garden. I am no lightweight and it is a considerable effort for anyone to push me around, but we both agree that this time rates near to the top of the many times we have spent together. Hertha declares stoutly that it is well worth the effort and I am as light as a feather.

The Night School impresses her greatly, and I don't hold back in describing the success it is proving to be. We now have a waiting list and I am constantly searching for more volunteers and books to replenish our stocks. Aunt Ju is a stalwart, but at her great age I try not to burden her.

Hertha is catching the evening train back to London and it is with regret that I wave her off, while extracting a promise that she will return before the end of the summer. I really must make more of an effort to see people and ensure they are full of energy and curiosity for the future. What a treat this visit has been. I will now dictate a letter to Eugène and tell him all of Hertha's news. He will be very interested to hear of her studies in electricity.

A telegram arrives this afternoon, the 28th January, 1885:

> 'DR EUGÈNE BODICHON HAS SADLY PASSED AWAY FOLLOWING A BOUT OF PNEUMONIA. MY SYMPATHIES ARE WITH THE FAMILY.
> DR GERENTI, ALGIERS.'

Part of me dissolves when reading these words. My love has left this earth. I will never again feel the warmth of his body or enjoy the comfort of knowing that I am loved unconditionally. Eugène was that other part of me. The part that sits outside conventional society, but chooses to live alongside the human race in all its complexities. It is of no matter to me that he was, at times, emotionally

Chapter 44

distant, and perhaps behaved in a socially unacceptable manner. He helped me to feel complete within myself. We didn't need to be in each other's sight continually to share this. Love was a fact of our existence together. Surely this was precious beyond price.

Chapter 45

I have taken to my bed. Eliza has created a nest for me. It is a place where I can grieve without prying eyes and hypocritical condolences. Losing Eugène has been a cataclysmic shock to my very being. The hole that is left by his passing cannot, will not, be filled by any other. It would be impossible for anyone else to understand my relationship with him. Women are so often required to express only half of themselves. In our society they are expected to be circumspect and live by a code which denies them the right to be fully developed adult beings. Eugène did not demand this of me. I could be as free and experimental as I chose. I pushed at the barriers, knowing that he was not judging or disapproving. Here, in my safe nest, I can smile at the circumstances which brought us together. An amazing quirk of coincidences. Not in all my years would I have met such a man in England, or even France, the country which banished him. Maybe Algeria gave Eugène a place to live, where it was possible for him to be as odd as he liked. There, he could engage in an intellectual and community life, which encouraged original thinking. Whatever may be said of him, I will always believe him to be unique, a force of nature. What luck to have found him.

Slowly as the days pass, I feel my strength returning. Eliza cossets me like a mother and persuades me that leaving my bed and having lunch by the fire will help to lift my spirits.

I intend writing an obituary for *The Times*. Each word

will proclaim Eugène's impressive achievements. People will be left in no doubt that Dr Eugène Bodichon was an outstanding man. He worked ceaselessly as a physician among the poor and, through his writing, brought about many reforms in Algerian society. It is impossible for me to travel to Algiers to attend his funeral, but Norman has agreed to represent me, an act of kindness for which I will be eternally grateful.

How I long for just one last talk with my dear husband and to apologise for the behaviour of some of my family. I will make sure that his grave is suitably marked. Maybe Nannie, now that Eugène has gone, will behave with some compassion. I don't expect her to have a complete epiphany, but it would help me if she would deign to arrange for a suitable gravestone and ensure that his resting place is cared for.

I see our love as a triumph over the family's disapprobation and, I'll make clear to all who care enough to consider such matters, that there are many ways to achieve a happy and successful marriage. I spend hours in my chair by the fire remembering the early years. Of course, I can see that some of Nannie's accusations are valid. Eugène could be very annoying and outspoken. His attire attracted bemused curiosity in England and many of my relatives did not feel comfortable with this. The fact that his English was poor also laid him open to criticism. But then, why should it have, when my French, and those of most in the family, is no better?

Our extended honeymoon in America often slips into my mind. It was a time when we were both feeling our way and Eugène was very sensitive to my fear that we would not be able to achieve an equal partnership. That did not come to pass. We shared the pain of remaining childless and overcame it by filling our lives with young people. Hertha in particular appreciated his love of science and liberal approach to life.

In the early days, Algiers was a fascinating place to explore. Eugène taught me to recognise the indigenous plants and flowers and explained how certain plants could be used for healing purposes. What an intelligent man he was and how delightfully sensitive to my needs. He was the first and only man to know me sexually and taught me how to enjoy my body. What bliss we found together; what joy in finding another human being who possessed the ability and generosity of spirit to reach out and embrace the differences between us. Sometimes, in the early hours of the morning, Eugène visits me. I dance away with him, back to Louisiana, or go riding out into the desert on a painting expedition, skirts flying. My memories sustain me.

Hertha visited at the weekend and together we wrote his obituary.

Dr Eugène Bodichon, one of the last of the little group known as 'Republicans of 30' and the author of many valuable works on Algeria, died at Algiers on the 28th January, 1885, aged 74.

Born of a noble Breton family at Nantes, Dr Bodichon early showed that adherence to Republican principles shared by his intimate friends, Ledru Rollin, Louis Blanc, Guepin of Nantes and others, and was associated with them in their work of political propaganda. Dissatisfied with the condition of things in France, he settled in Algeria 40 years ago, devoting himself to gratuitous services as a physician among the poor, and amassing materials for his 'Considerations sur L'Algerie,' sited by the late eminent historian M. Henri Martin as second only in interest and importance to the writings of the late General Daumas. In 1848, on being appointed Corresponding Member of the Chamber of Deputies for Algiers, he immediately advised the liberation

Chapter 45

of the slaves throughout the province of Algeria, which was done. On the establishment of the Empire his movements were closely watched and the typeset plates of his work 'De L'Humanité' were broken up by the Imperial Police. The work, which contains a striking study of the first Napoleon, was afterwards published at Brussels.

Dr Bodichon was one of the first to draw attention to the valuable febrifugal qualities of the Eucalyptus Globulus, and of late years entirely devoted himself to its dissemination throughout the colony.

Chapter 46

Eliza tells me that it is now six years since Eugène died. My invalid state has destroyed my memory and, despite my efforts to expand my life and dreams of filling Scalands with visitors, I find that my bed is the only place in which I can feel comfortable and relaxed. Giving up on the struggle to use my damaged and weary body seems to allow my mind to function, albeit in a very limited fashion. Dr Bagshawe rode over from Hastings yesterday and I think he told me that I have suffered another minor stroke, one of many. This would explain the confusion I am struggling with. Eliza has had the bed moved so that I can see down the valley from the window, without placing a foot on the floor. I am not sure if this is good for me, but find it near impossible to do much else.

I have a comfortable armchair placed by the bed and, for the past week, several people have come to see me and sat in it. Eliza brings tea and I enjoy having someone who feels familiar sitting close to me. I like to hear a voice, but I can't always remember once they've gone, just who they might have been. Dr Bagshawe assures me that I will improve with rest.

I can't understand why Norman doesn't come down to see me. I had a dream last night that he has converted to Catholicism. I remember that the last time he visited we had a small disagreement. He seems to have changed in his later years. We had so much fun here at Scalands when he was a student and all his friends came down to stay. I remember dancing: can that be right? I can't imagine him dancing now; he seems so stern and formal with me. I never see Amy and the children. Why has this

Chapter 46

happened? I tried so hard to get Norman accepted into the family. It all seems to have gone wrong.

Eliza often sits by the bed and strokes my hand. She lights a fire and I listen to her stories. She grew up in Hastings, the third daughter in a family of six children. Her father worked as a fisherman. She describes waiting on the shore for him to return and racing home with fish for tea, if the catch was good. Her mother died in childbirth, after which Eliza was sent into service with a local family; she was around twelve years of age, I believe. She never married. 'It wasn't a bad life,' she tells me cheerfully, but we agree that losing a mother early leaves scars. I can't remember how long she has been with me, since Harriet left probably. I know that Aunt Ju taught her to read which Eliza says changed her life. I rarely see her now without a book tucked into her pocket.

Three weeks pass; Eliza keeps a small calendar on the wall and marks it off every day. I have had many visits from Ben, one I do remember. He told me that he intends getting married. This astounding news startled me out of my semi-comatose state. I listened intently as he explained that he has been courting a young lady who is the sister of Hertha's friend, Eugenie. I have a vague memory of Eugenie visiting Scalands with her sister some years ago, but how Ben met her sister I have no idea. I spend hours trying to understand this situation. The young lady is called Charlotte but known as Charlie.

Eliza reads me a letter today which arrives from Nannie. How Nannie knows all of this news at such a distance I cannot imagine, but she says in the letter that she is appalled at Ben's behaviour. The young woman (Charlie) is only twenty-two years of age apparently, and Ben is now fifty-nine. This is so confusing. I just cannot understand what has happened to him. He spent so many years disapproving of Norman and Amy's love for each other and, now at the age when he would normally become a grandfather, he is embarking on marriage to a woman nearly forty years his junior. Nannie is incensed, and what has added to her complete disapproval, is that Charlie is a Catholic. This is a heinous crime in her opinion.

I have many hours to think over this situation and come to the conclusion that we have had too many arguments and fallings-out over the years in relation to who one can marry, or what constitutes a 'good match.' Eugène and I suffered for years because of Ben's and my extended family's belief that they had the right to interfere with the lives of others. I had a happy marriage with Eugène; Norman and Amy are happy together: there is plenty of evidence that they are ill-equipped to make such judgements on other people's relationships. If Ben and Charlie wish to make a life together, then I shall give them my blessing. I will ask Hertha to send Nannie a note and make my intentions clear.

Nannie as usual is infuriated with my decision and is dripping poison in letters to whomever will take notice. She pontificates endlessly in her next letter, laying out the iniquities she believes are perpetrated in Ben's plans to marry such a young woman. 'This should not be allowed under law.' Charlie, of course, is suspected of being after Ben's money. How neatly she ignores the reality of her own unconventional love affair with Isabella Blythe. This thought makes me smile for the first time since receiving the news.

I ask Eliza to contact my solicitor as I want to change my will. Scalands had been willed to Nannie for many years, but I have decided to change that and leave it to Ben. Also I want to leave ten thousand pounds to Girton College. I often return to Girton in my mind and remember with pleasure the hard work and dogged

Chapter 46

determination it took Emily and me to bring our dreams to fruition. How I would like to visit and sit quietly in the library, watching the students go about their studies. The gardens must now be flourishing and providing quiet places for them to sit and enjoy the fresh air.

Since Eugène's death, Ben and I have slowly rebuilt the closeness we enjoyed as children. I think it probable that I am no longer an embarrassment to him, now that my campaigning days are behind me. Tied to this bed, weakened by my disabilities, all passion spent, he can once again become the head of the family. I've no doubt that he always believed he was, as the oldest male, but I made sure he was challenged in that belief and stood my ground. My heart warms when I hear his carriage pull up below the window and his strong voice calling for Jack, the stable lad.

As one concession to Nannie, I agree that she can cut down Eugène's beloved Eucalyptus trees. This decision gives me much pain as he loved them so much, but I have been persuaded that they now block her view of the sea.

When I look back on all the purposefulness of my life, it is strange that I am now left without the energy or zest to even get out of bed. Perhaps changing my will is the last act of defiance I can muster. What does make me glad is the knowledge that I have given women the right to own property and, because of that, I can leave Scalands to whomever I choose.

Chapter 47

As Barbara's funeral cortège rolled slowly through the lanes to Brightling Churchyard, Nature conspired to mark her death with all the glories of the countryside she so loved. A gentle sun dusted the trees and hedgerows providing an abundance of wild flowers. Villagers left their labours, removed their hats and stood, heads bowed, as she passed. A landau filled with women scholars from Girton followed the hearse, resplendent in caps and gowns. They were accompanied by pupils from Scalands Night School, well-scrubbed up for the occasion. How Barbara would have loved the symbolism this tableau represented.

The church was full to overflowing with family and friends. Ben stood to read the eulogy. Known as a man of few words, he said very little, but his bearing and gravitas demanded attention. Nothing was said of Barbara's political achievements or her success in the art world; much was made of her role of benefactor. How she would have hated that.

Following this sombre and somewhat arid speech, Bessie stood at the lectern and gave full voice to the love and affection held for Barbara by her many friends and acquaintances. Her generosity of spirit was applauded, and full acknowledgement of the esteem she had received from pundits in the art world. Bessie left the congregation in no doubt that, in Barbara's passing, the country had lost a guiding light: someone who would be remembered for her humanitarian ideals and in possession of sufficient courage to fight for women's rights and accept the obligation (as she saw it), to help the less privileged.

Chapter 47

Standing down, Bessie looked around the packed church and silently reflected on the woman she had known for fifty-five years. *What a wonderful ambassador she had been for all those who do not fit the strictures laid down in society: those brave souls who stand apart, think laterally and campaign for causes which are not universally popular. Even here, she thought, I cannot give full validation, to the love and admiration that I had for a woman whom I admired above all others.*

Her thoughts brought a smile, as she saw in her mind's eye, Barbara nodding her head, and dashing off yet another letter in support of some cause or another, or leaping naked into a freezing Welsh lake.

Amidst a murmur of surprise, Hertha stood to pay her respects in a voice strong enough to fill the room. She did not hold back, stating passionately that she had loved Barbara as a mother and could never find the words to express the gratitude she felt for the opportunities Barbara had afforded her. Her voice sent a thrill through the rapt mourners as she proclaimed, 'I am aware that I am an outsider. When my family came to this country from Poland, escaping from Russian persecution, we had materially very little. What we did have was a determination to succeed, which we have done against all odds. I am aware that a certain amount of luck was required in achieving this success and that luck, for me, was personified by Barbara Leigh Smith Bodichon. She believed in me, even when I did not achieve the success I aimed for, at her beloved Girton. She was, in my opinion, an outstanding character. A person who was able to listen and communicate with young and old in an intelligent and easy manner. She nurtured my ambition and I am determined that I will use my gifts to benefit mankind. In this respect Barbara gave me an inspiring example upon which to model my life.'

THE END

Author's Note

While researching Barbara's life it quickly became apparent to me that her life changed irreparably in 1877, after suffering her first stroke. At the age of fifty, the many reforming activities in which she had been energetically engaged came to an abrupt halt. However, her stubborn persistence when confronted with the need for reform, had stood her in good stead during her career. Decades of constant petitions and lobbying were required of a largely unresponsive government but, far from falling at the first post, Barbara had refused to back down until she achieved her objectives. She left much 'work in progress.'

For example: Her engagement with the Hastings Suffrage movement began in the 1850s, when Barbara was twenty-three years of age. It was not until July 1928, after many set-backs, that the Equal Franchise Act, finally enabled women over the age of twenty-one to vote. This campaign had taken approximately eighty years. Barbara had long since died, but her efforts are still acknowledged as influential in those early days of protest.

Thankfully she was still alive to see her first serious foray into women's rights come to fruition. The initial petition to parliament was made in 1855 to change the Married Women's Property laws. The Act was finally passed in 1882. This reform had taken approximately twenty-eight years from its conception to reach the statute books.

The founding of Girton College, Cambridge, in 1873, gave Barbara the most rewarding achievement of her life. It had required infinite depths of patience and will-power to cut through the staunch resistance to women's higher education. Together with Emily Davies, she conquered unrelenting opposition, albeit with some compromises. It was not until 1921, a period of forty-eight years, that the Senate granted degrees to the women students of Girton.

In 1976 a vote was taken to accept male students into the college. Today, Girton College embodies Barbara's dream, that of promoting the principles of excellence, inclusion and care.

Norman Moore became Barbara's protégé as a young man. He lived in straitened circumstances with his mother Rachel, his father having left the family before his birth. His obituary in 1922 set out his achievements, which more than confirmed Barbara's faith in his abilities.... Sir Norman Moore, BT., M.D, LL.D; President of the Royal College of Physicians of London; Consulting Physician to St. Bartholomew's Hospital.

How proud she would have been to witness this remarkable evidence that, given the opportunity of a good education and the unstinting support of two strong women, he was able to reach the pinnacle of his aspirations.

I cannot finish this note without mentioning Sarah Phoebe Marks, (known as Hertha). She was, in all senses apart from birth, Barbara's daughter. Barbara's belief in Hertha was well placed, she became a renowned physicist. In 1899, just seven years after Barbara's death, she was elected to the *Institution of Electrical Engineers*, the only woman member. Her innovative achievements were acclaimed in the new field of electricity and culminated in the award of the *Hughes Medal* in 1906. Hertha was the first woman recipient of this medal, presented by the Royal Society. Full Fellowship of the society was denied her, the reason given, '*We are of the opinion that married women are not eligible as Fellows of the Royal Society.*'

Barbara was what is now described as 'a people person.' and it was her relationship with Hertha which gave me a measure of this remarkable woman. Barbara's many gifts included a far reaching intelligence, which brought a broad vision to her politics, without prejudice to sex, race or class.

Mary Upton

Mary Upton was born in the Forest of Dean, Gloucestershire, and educated at Bell's Grammar School, Coleford.

Her career in the mental health field spanned many years and on retirement, she travelled extensively in the United States, India, Nepal, Australia and New Zealand.

She is the author of three other novels:
Rattenbury – the story of a nineteenth century West Country smuggler who lived in the Devon fishing village of Beer and two Sci Fi novels – ***Union of Opposites*** and ***New Tribe***. They explore the development of an AI enhanced robot, bearing the name of Sarah Miles.

She now lives in St. Leonards-on-Sea, East Sussex, with her husband and extended family.

Acknowledgements

I would like to thank my family and friends for their patience and constant encouragement. In addition, my thanks to Charlotte Moore who generously gave me her time and ignited my early interest in Barbara's life. She also granted me permission to use her Family Tree that appears in her book, *Hancox*, first published by Penguin Books Ltd in 2010. I would also like to thank Hastings Museum for allowing me to use Barbara's painting, *Rocklands,* on the cover of the book.

Also, a big thank you to my writing group, 'Writers Connect', who have given me support and feed-back over the many years it has taken me to complete this book.

In addition I would like to thank the Archivist at Girton College, Cambridge, for her interest and willingness to locate for me obscure details in relation to Barbara's life and career. Among the many references and articles I researched, the biography, *Barbara Leigh Smith Bodichon*, written by Dr Pam Hirsch, also provided much inspiration.

Finally I would like to extend my gratitude to Amanda Helm and my expert readers, Vivien Ford, Maryon Eaton and Lynne Jones, for their editing skills which have proved invaluable and, without which, *Bodichon* may not have seen the light of day. Also a big thank you to Kristie Lincoln, my DIL, whose enthusiasism and interest gave me that extra boost to get me past the finish line.

Copyright © 2022 Veronica Eden
All rights reserved.

No parts of this publication may be reproduced, stored in a retrieval system, or transmitted in any form or by any means, electronic, mechanical, photocopying, recording, or otherwise, without the prior written permission of the copyright owner, except in the case of brief quotations embodied in reviews and certain other noncommercial uses permitted by copyright law. For permission requests, write to the author at this website: www.veronicaedenauthor.com

This is a work of fiction. Names, characters, places, businesses, companies, organizations, locales, events and incidents either are the product of the author's imagination or used fictitiously. Any resemblances to actual persons, living or dead, is unintentional and co-incidental. The author does not have any control over and does not assume any responsibility for author or third-party websites or their content.